Re:ZeRo

-Starting Life in Another World-

The silver-haired girl was surrounded by faint lights that looked as though they were fireflies. It was like holy ground, where—by the influence of the supernatural—only what was sanctified was allowed to be.

Characters

Re:ZERO -Starting Life in Another World-

The only ability Subaru Natsuki gets when he's summoned to another world is
time travel via his own death. But to save her, he'll die as many times as it takes.

Subaru Natsuki

A high school student summoned
suddenly to another world. Our
protagonist, Subaru, is not only
ignorant and without special
abilities, but also powerless, acts
without thinking, and is way out of
step with his surroundings.

???

A beautiful, mysterious girl that Subaru meets in the capital city. She appears to be looking for something, but...

Puck

A cat spirit, Puck is like family to the aforementioned mysterious beautiful girl.

Reinhard

A knight among knights, Reinhard is called the "Master Swordsman."

Rom

As the master of the loot cellar and having handled many such items, Rom has a good eye for appraising valuable items.

Elsa

A gorgeous woman with a seductive aura about her, Elsa appears to be doing business with Felt, but...

Kadomon

With a strong build and characteristically stern expression, Kadomon is nothing more than a simple merchant.

Felt

Raised in the slums of the capital, Felt makes her living by pickpocketing and theft in general.

Re:ZERO -Starting Life in Another World-

The only ability Subaru Natsuki gets when he's summoned to another world is time travel via his own death. But to save her, he'll die as many times as it takes.

CONTENTS

Re:ZeRo

-Starting Life in Another World-

VOLUME 1

TAPPEI NAGATSUKI
ILLUSTRATION: SHINICHIROU OTSUKA

YEN ON

NEW YORK

RE:ZERO Vol. 1
TAPPEI NAGATSUKI

Translation by ZephyrRz
Cover art by Shinichirou Otsuka

This book is a work of fiction. Names, characters, places, and incidents are the product of the author's imagination or are used fictitiously. Any resemblance to actual events, locales, or persons, living or dead, is coincidental.

RE:ZERO KARA HAJIMERU ISEKAI SEIKATSU Vol. 1
© Tappei Nagatsuki / Shinichirou Otsuka 2014
First published in Japan in 2014 by KADOKAWA CORPORATION, Tokyo.
English translation rights reserved by YEN PRESS, LLC
under the license from KADOKAWA CORPORATION, Tokyo, through
Tuttle-Mori Agency, Inc., Tokyo.

English translation © 2016 by Yen Press, LLC

Yen Press, LLC supports the right to free expression and the value of copyright.
The purpose of copyright is to encourage writers and artists to produce the creative works that enrich our culture.

The scanning, uploading, and distribution of this book without permission is a theft of the author's intellectual property. If you would like permission to use material from the book (other than for review purposes), please contact the publisher. Thank you for your support of the author's rights.

Yen On
1290 Avenue of the Americas
New York, NY 10104

Visit us at yenpress.com
facebook.com/yenpress
twitter.com/yenpress
yenpress.tumblr.com

First Yen On Edition: July 2016

Yen On is an imprint of Yen Press, LLC.
The Yen On name and logo are trademarks of Yen Press, LLC.

The publisher is not responsible for websites (or their content) that are not owned by the publisher.

Library of Congress Cataloging-in-Publication Data
Names: Nagatsuki, Tappei, 1987– author. | Otsuka, Shinichirou, illustrator. | ZephyrRz, translator.
Title: Re:ZERO starting life in another world / Tappei Nagatsuki ; illustration by Shinichirou Otsuka ; translation by ZephyrRz.
Other titles: Re:ZERO kara hajimeru isekai seikatsu. English
Description: First Yen On edition. | New York, NY : Yen On, 2016– |
Audience: Ages 13 & up.
Identifiers: LCCN 2016031562| ISBN 9780316315302 (v. 1 : pbk.)
Subjects: | CYAC: Science fiction.
Classification: LCC PZ7.1.N34 Re 2016 | DDC [Fic]—dc23
LC record available at https://lccn.loc.gov/2016031562

ISBNs: 978-0-316-31530-2 (paperback)
978-0-316-39839-8 (ebook)

10   9

LSC-C

Printed in the United States of America

PRoLoGUE
THE WASTE HEAT OF THE BEGINNING

—*This is really, really not good.*

Feeling the hard texture of the ground against his face, he realized that he had fallen facedown on the ground. He couldn't move, even when he tried, and he already couldn't feel his fingers. What he did feel was a certain heat, and it overwhelmed his entire body.

—*It's hot, it's hot, it's hot, it's hot, it's hot, it's hot, it's hot.*

He coughed and vomited the blood he felt rising in his throat—the source of his waning life. So much came out that it frothed at the edges of his mouth. With his hazy vision, he could see the ground in front of him stained red.

—*You've...got to be kidding me... All of this is mine?*

Feeling as though all of the blood in his body had spilled out of him, he reached a shaking hand to try to find the source of the heat that was burning through his body. As his fingertips reached the large cut in his stomach, he understood.

No wonder it felt so hot. His brain must have been mistaking pain for heat. The clean gash that ran through his torso was so deep it had almost sliced him in half. Only bits of skin were still holding him together.

In other words, he had run right into a checkmate in the chess game of his life. As soon as he realized that, his consciousness immediately began to fall away from him.

Before his eyes, he saw a black boot descend, making ripples in the red pool of his fresh blood.

Someone was there, and that someone…was probably the one who killed him.

But he didn't even think to look that person in the face. It didn't matter anymore.

—The one thing he did wish was that *she*, at least, would be safe.

"—baru?"

He felt as if he heard a voice that rang like bells. That he heard that voice, that he *could* hear that voice, felt like salvation to him more than anything else, so—

"!"

With a short scream, someone else crumpled upon the carpet of blood.

She landed right beside him. He lay there, weakly attempting to reach her.

Her white hand fell, powerless. He lightly grasped it in his own bloodstained grip.

He felt the fingers of her hand move slightly to accept his own.

"Just you wait…"

He seized his fading consciousness, pulling it desperately back to buy a bit more time.

"I'm going to…"

—*find a way to save you.*

In the next instant, he—Subaru Natsuki—lost his life.

CHAPTER 1

THE END OF THE BEGINNING

1

—*This is really going to be a problem.*

With no money and no idea what to do, he repeated the thought over and over again in his mind.

Well, it wasn't completely accurate to say he had *no* money. The wallet in his pocket was filled with all the cash he owned, enough to go on a little bit of a shopping spree if he had to—under normal circumstances. But in this case, "no money" is really the only way to describe his situation.

"Yeah, but the currency system here is completely different, isn't it…"

The young man flicked his rare notched ten-yen coin in the air and breathed a deep sigh.

He didn't really have any features about him that stood out. He had short black hair and was of average height, being neither short nor tall. He was a bit muscular, though, as if he had been working out, and the cheap gray tracksuit that he was wearing really suited him quite well. He had small irises, so the whites of his eyes stood out, but right now, the way his eyes were downcast, he didn't have a very aggressive or championing look to him.

He looked average enough to be quickly lost in a crowd…but right now, most of those passing by looked at him out of the corners of their eyes as if they were looking at something strange they had never seen before.

But that was to be expected. After all, among all those onlookers, not one of them had black hair, nor were any of them wearing track-suits. They had blond hair, red hair, and brown hair…some even had blue or green hair, among others, and they were wearing armor, or black robes, or the kind of costume a dancer might wear…that sort of thing.

As he stood before the waves of open stares, the young man crossed his arms and had no other option but to accept the truth.

"This has got to be one of *those*…" he said, snapping his fingers and pointing out toward the crowd of onlookers. "One of those so-called 'I've been summoned to another world' deals, right?" he said as an oxcart-like vehicle pulled by a giant lizard-like thing crossed in front of him.

2

Subaru Natsuki was an extremely ordinary boy, born on Earth, the third planet in the solar system, to a middle-class family in the nation of Japan. If you were to sum up his nearly seventeen years of life, the previous sentence would be enough to describe him, and if you felt the need to add anything else, the extra sentence, "He was a third-year public high school student with a tendency to not show up to class," would be sufficient.

Placed at a fork in the road of life, such as "whether to pursue a college degree or jump straight into the workforce," people are generally forced to make a decision one way or the other. That sort of decision-making is something everyone has to deal with and part of what we call life, but in Subaru's case (you might call it his specialty) he was a bit better than your average Joe at running away from things he did not like. In avoiding such a decision, the number of his unexcused absences had piled up, and before he knew it he was a bona fide truant, the kind parents weep over.

"And to top it all off, now I've been summoned to a whole different world. I guess that seals the deal. I'm a high school dropout now. But seriously, what the hell is going on?"

He felt as if he was having a not-so-well-thought-out dream, but even after pinching his cheeks and smacking his head against a wall, he wouldn't wake up.

Subaru sighed. He had drifted away from where he was, getting all sorts of curious looks, and was now sitting against a wall in an alley just off the main road.

"Assuming I really have been summoned to a fantasy world…the state of civilization appears to be the usual, medieval-like setting. So far, I haven't seen anything mechanical, but the roads are pretty well paved…and of course I can't use any of my cash."

As for whether he could communicate with the people here, and regarding the value of goods, those were things that Subaru checked immediately upon realizing he had been summoned to a different world.

Fortunately, he had no problem communicating, and he was able to confirm that commerce was handled in a currency of gold, silver, and copper coins. His first contact, a merchant at a fruit stand, wasn't all that welcoming to him, though.

As for why Subaru was so quick to accept and understand his current situation, the fact that he was a modern Japanese youth poisoned by anime and games had something to do with it, and for that he was very thankful. It wouldn't be an overstatement to say that as an adolescent boy, this sort of otherworldly summoning was the kind of thing you'd dream would happen to you, but on that note…

"Without a little bit more of a welfare safety-net thing going on, a laid-back guy like myself isn't going to be able to deal, you know?" Subaru complained.

Given his current situation, and pitiful starting equipment, he couldn't help it.

His belongings consisted of a cell phone (which looked like it would run out of batteries soon), a wallet (filled with membership cards from various video rental stores), a cup of instant ramen he'd bought from a convenience store (pork bone and soy sauce flavor), a bag of crispy snacks bought from the same store (corn soup flavor), his favorite gray tracksuit (unwashed), and well-worn sneakers (two years old). That was it.

"I don't even get a single Excalibur? I'm done. What am I supposed to do in *this* getup?"

Well, there's only so much you can hope for when you're summoned to a different world on your way back from the convenience store. It had happened in the blink of an eye.

Subaru had already gotten hungry and eaten half of the one thing he had that might have been of any use—his pack of crispy snacks—before realizing that he had just gone through his only source of food. But worrying about it wasn't going to help him now.

Even if he'd wanted to put his hopes on the possibility that this was being staged as part of an elaborate reality TV show, the large lizard carts and look of all the people passing by nipped that in the bud.

"The fact that no one seems to be paying attention to them means that they're probably normal...both those giant lizards and the half-humans."

Subaru grumbled and looked on as people with strange outfits and colorful hair passed by, but out of all of them, the ones who really drove home the fact that he had been summoned to another world were the half-humans.

Without having to look too long Subaru could see people with dog ears and cat ears, and there were even some who looked like they were lizardmen. But of course there were also ordinary humans, the same as Subaru.

"So this is a world with half-humans...and probably wars and adventures, too. As for whether there are any animals I'm used to around... I'm not too sure, but given that lizard cart thing...it looks like they use animals in the same way we do."

After putting all of that together, Subaru let out a long breath, but not a sigh. If things unfolded the way he had fantasized about before about otherworldly summoning, he ought to be able to use his knowledge of modern civilization to hold sway over everyone else...but there were a lot of things that still didn't make any sense.

"The truth is, I have no idea what to do next, and I still have no idea how or why I was summoned. I don't remember stepping into a mirror or falling in a pond, and if I'm to believe this is the otherworldly summoning format I'm used to, where is the beautiful girl who summoned me?"

The lack of a main heroine in this otherworldly summoning setup was a big hole in the plot. If this were taking place in a 2D world, someone in the creative department was seriously slacking off. If Subaru was really summoned for no reason and then abandoned just like that, it put him on the same level as single-use disposable goods.

Now that Subaru had finished establishing the state of his surroundings, he really couldn't think of anything better to do than return to his default state of escaping from reality.

"I guess if I keep this up, it's no different from locking myself up in my room back home."

The thought of his parents crossed his mind, but right now he wasn't in a position where he could just sit around feeling homesick. Thinking he had to do something about his current situation, he stood back up and turned back toward the main road, but...

Just as Subaru was about to walk out onto the main road, he almost bumped into someone who moved out in front of him.

"Oh. Sorry 'bout that." Subaru gave a short apology and tried to continue past, but...

"Hold up!"

...he was grabbed firmly by the shoulder and pulled back into the alley. Nearly falling over himself as he turned around, Subaru looked up to see that the person who had thrown him back was a man with a large build.

Behind that man were two of his buddies, and the three men stood in such a way as to block Subaru from exiting the alley onto the main road.

The way they moved, it didn't appear this was the first time these men had done this, and Subaru had a bad feeling about what was going to come next.

"Umm... May I ask what you three fine fellows plan on doing with me?"

"Oh, it looks like this one here's a smart one! Well, nothing to worry about. Just give us everything you've got on you, and there's no need for anyone to get hurt."

"So that's the deal, huh? Yeah, I guess it would be. Ha-ha... This really sucks."

The men's gazes were filled with scorn and ridicule. They looked like they were in their twenties, with the meanness of their personalities reflected in their faces and dirty appearances. They didn't look like they were half-humans, but they certainly weren't saints, either.

You couldn't call it an unusual plot development. Encountering thugs was a way to show the dangers of everyday life. In other words...

"Damn, I've triggered a compulsory event."

3

As he looked at the men smirking, Subaru tried to hold the status quo with a fake smile and considered his options. He was in quite a pinch, but since the beginning of time, in stories where humans are summoned to other worlds, those humans tended to be able to wield some kind of superpower. If Subaru had been summoned to this world under the same conditions as the stories he was familiar with, it was very likely that he had been given some sort of power. With that thought, Subaru felt that his body was a little lighter than usual.

"I'm starting to get the feeling that this world's gravity is, like, only a tenth of my world's. I can do this. I can do this! I'm going to mow you all down and make this the first chapter of my glorious future! You're only here so I can pull experience points off of you, you scum!"

"What the hell is he going on about?" said one of the men.

"I don't know, but I'm pretty sure he's making fun of us. Let's kill 'im," replied another.

"Took the words right out of my mouth... You're going to regret this!" returned Subaru, before flying forward with a straight jab from his right hand, aiming for the big man in front. Subaru's fist collided with the man's nose, but he also cut his fist on one of the man's front teeth and started bleeding.

—*I hit someone for the first time in my life! Wow! It hurts way more than I expected.*

Subaru was confident in his fighting form, but he had never been in a real fight before. The man who was punched fell to the ground. Without taking a moment to pause, Subaru leapt at another of the men, caught off guard, as his next target. With a clean arc he landed a kick on the side of the next man's head, slamming him into the wall of the alley.

This was going even better than he'd expected, and he started to be sure of the notion that he was invincible in this new world.

"I guess in this world my stats are pretty good! What a rush! Now to finish this!"

Turning back around, Subaru bent forward to beat down the last man standing, when his eyes centered on what that man was holding in his hand: a glinting knife.

Immediately Subaru dropped to his knees, bent over forward, and with a spectacular single motion prostrated himself, pressing his forehead against the ground.

"I'm sorry, that was absolutely terrible of me, I ask that you forgive me and please find it in your generous hearts to spare my life!"

Prostration—it was the most exteme form of showing absolute submission to another and the lowest form of Japanese humility. Just where did all of that fired-up feeling go? Subaru felt as if he could hear the blood drain from his body. Desperately clinging to any hope of mercy, he tried to make himself seem small and continued to apologize.

With a knife involved, fighting was out of the question. No matter how you might train yourself, if you were stabbed, it was all over. All things in life are transient.

Before he knew it, the two that Subaru thought he had defeated were back on their feet. One was holding his bleeding nose and the other was shaking his head back and forth, but other than that both looked as though they were in surprisingly good condition.

"What?! You mean to tell me that my one-hit knockout punch only did that much damage?! What about my superpowers?!"

"I dunno what you're going on about, but shut your trap! You've really done it now!"

It looked as though Subaru had been completely wrong about being summoned into another world coming with the promise of some kind of powers. He wasn't really any stronger than he had been before.

One of the men stepped on the back of Subaru's head, scraping his forehead against the ground and causing him to bleed. Another then kicked him in the face, and Subaru curled into a ball as tightly as he could as he was subjected to further acts of violence.

After all, the one who hit first was Subaru. The men didn't hold back at all.

—Crap, this really, really hurts. Like, I could die. No, seriously.

Unlike in his own world, there was no guarantee that these thugs wouldn't take his life. At this rate, it would be better to try one last-ditch effort to retaliate before he was beaten to death…

"Stop moving, you whelp!"

"Ow! No, don't… Ow! Ow! Ow!!"

The man with the knife stomped on Subaru's hand as he tried to get up, then readjusted his grip on the knife so that the tip was held back toward his arm, ready to strike.

"After we make sure you can't move we're going to take everything you've got. That's what you get for acting tough, you punk…"

"I-if you're looking for money or valuables, I'm sorry but you're out of luck. After all, I don't have a cent on me…!"

"Then those strange-looking clothes and shoes'll do just fine. You can just stay down and be food for the alley rats!"

Oh, so there are rats in this world, too, Subaru thought. *I hope they aren't big, like monster rats or anything.* Subaru looked at the knife about to come down as if it didn't concern him at all, distancing himself from reality as best he could.

Subaru didn't see his life flash before his eyes, and he didn't feel like time was slowing down, either. The end would probably come like the cutting of a thread, he thought.

—But just then…

"Hey! Out of the way! Out of the way! I'm talking to you! Move!" yelled someone in a flustered-sounding voice as they dashed into the alley.

Like the men, who suddenly looked up, Subaru managed to glance up in the direction of the voice, though he couldn't move his body.

What he saw was a small girl with longish blond hair dashing by. From her red eyes, you could sense a strong will, and her one canine tooth sticking out made her look like quite a prankster. She seemed more cheeky than anything else, but Subaru felt that if she smiled she would look pretty cute.

As if it had been staged for a comeback, the fading light of hope Subaru had been holding lit anew.

He was waiting for this kind of development.

The girl, in her well-worn clothes and unclean appearance, had stumbled upon this attempted murder and robbery in the act! What would surely happen next, was that with an overflowing sense of justice this girl would save Subaru's life, right from the clutches of death…

"Whoa! You look like you're in quite a pinch there, but sorry! I've got my hands full right now! Good luck! Live life to the fullest!"

"Wait, what?! Are you serious?!"

Unfortunately, that hope was shattered in an instant.

The girl raised her hand in an apologetic sort of gesture and didn't slow down as she continued racing down the alley. She went right past the men and kept going toward what should have been a dead end, kicked off against a wooden plank set up against the end wall, grabbed the top of the wall, and lightly flung herself up onto the roof of one of the surrounding buildings, where she disappeared.

After the girl was gone, a silence fell upon the alley. It was as if a hurricane had just passed. Both Subaru and the men were dumbstruck.

However, this didn't mean that Subaru's situation had improved at all.

"Doesn't what just happened make your anger just sort of melt away and make you want to change your minds about all of this?!"

"More like it killed the mood and now I'm even angrier. Don't think you'll get to die a pleasant death!"

The men kept their feet planted on Subaru so he couldn't move. As Subaru looked at the glint of the knife in the man's hand, the death that loomed before him seemed ever more real.

—*No, I mean, you've got to be kidding. I can't die this easily, can I?*

A twitching smile formed on Subaru's face as he looked around desperately for someone to deny the death that was coming his way. However, no such convenient development came. The tip of the knife drew ever closer.

A feeling of resignation came over Subaru and he felt tears welling up in his eyes. It wasn't fear that overwhelmed him; it was more the feeling of emptiness that this would all end without him accomplishing anything.

In the midst of this overwhelming despair, feeling as if he had been abandoned by everyone and everything...

"Hold it right there, you evildoers!"

That voice overcame the noise of the crowd, the vulgar insults of the men, Subaru's own heavy breathing, as well as everything else, and shook the very foundations of the world.

4

When people say, "Time stood still," they must surely be talking about times like this.

There was a girl standing at the entrance to the alley.

She was beautiful. She had long silver hair, with braids in it that reached down to her hips. She was looking straight at Subaru with violet eyes that shone with intelligence. In her soft features were both elements of youth but also mature beauty. There was also a noble air about her that gave her a dangerous and bewitching charm.

The girl was about one head shorter than Subaru, which made her around five feet, three inches tall. The clothes she wore used white as a base color, and there was nothing terribly ornate about them, but on the other hand, the simplicity emphasized her presence.

The one thing that stood out was the white cloak the girl was wearing. It was emblazoned with embroidery that depicted a bird of prey, adding to her impression of majesty.

However, it wasn't the clothes she wore that made her shine so.

"I will not stand by and watch any more of your wrongdoing. That is enough."

Her voice, like silver bells, rang beautifully in Subaru's ears, and for a moment he forgot the situation he was in. He was completely undone by the silver-haired girl's presence.

The other men seemed to be just as shaken up as Subaru was.

"Wha… Who do you think you are…?"

"If you stop right now, I'll let you go. In a way, this is my fault for not being cautious. So do the right thing and give back what you stole."

"Hey, what she's wearing looks expensive. You think she's nobility? Wait, huh…? What we stole?"

"Please. It is very precious to me. I'd be willing to give it up if it were anything else, but I absolutely can't in this case. Please. I won't do anything to you, so please just give it back."

The girl looked as if she was pleading with all her heart.

However, there was an inexplicable feeling of pressure that rose within the group. Something was happening that was hard to explain.

"W-wait a minute! We don't know what you're talking about!"

"…What do you mean?"

The men pointed to Subaru, still underfoot.

"You didn't come here to rescue this guy…did you?"

"…Those are some weird clothes that boy is wearing. Did you all have a fight among yourselves? I don't think three against one is really fair, but…if you're asking me if I know this person, I haven't ever seen him before in my life." Perhaps it was because she thought the men were trying to change the subject, but you could hear an amount of irritation in her voice. Because of that, each of the men rushed to explain themselves.

"Wait a second! If you're not after this guy, then we're not involved! I bet it was that girl from before!"

"You said you had something stolen from you, right?! That wall! You see that wall? She jumped off that wall and ran away on the rooftops!"

"She's farther back! Back past that wall! At the rate she was going, she's probably another three streets down!"

As the men continued to plead their innocence, the girl turned her eyes to Subaru, as if asking whether these men were telling the truth. Without thinking, Subaru nodded.

"Hmm… It doesn't look like you're lying. So the one who stole from me is down farther ahead? I've got to hurry…"

The girl turned away from Subaru and the men and toward the main road. The men clearly looked relieved. Subaru, faced with the reality of his abandonment, started to enter a state of shock, when…

"Still, this situation is one I can't just ignore."

As she turned back around the girl put her hand up, palm facing outward, and a series of shining lights began to dance in front of it.

A dull *thud* rang out, like that of a hard object striking flesh, followed by the cries of the men as they were thrown backward. Then, there was a high-pitched sound as a fist-size clump of ice fell to the ground right beside Subaru.

The clump of ice, which seemed to have formed heedless of both the season and the laws of physics, quickly evaporated as if it were being eaten by the surrounding air.

"…Magic."

The best word to describe what just happened immediately tumbled out of Subaru's mouth.

There wasn't any incantation or anything, but that chunk of ice had definitely shot out of that girl's palm.

Magic—having seen it with his very own eyes for the first time, Subaru realized something.

"It isn't quite as fantasy-like as I imagined… To be honest, this is kind of a letdown."

Subaru had imagined there would be more light and energy being bounced around. In reality, all that happened was an unrefined-looking clump of ice suddenly materialized, was used as a blunt object for physical damage, and then suddenly disappeared. There was no feeling or anything put into it at all.

"Now…you've done it."

Subaru's feelings on magic aside, the other men, who had taken a real hit from those clumps of ice, got back to their feet. To be fair, it was only two of them who managed to get back up. The remaining man must have gotten hit in a bad spot, because he was still knocked out. But rather than this fact taking the fight out of them, it seemed to just make the other two men even angrier. Standing next to the man with the knife, the other drew out a blunt, club-like object, and both were ready to fight.

"I don't care if you're a magic user or nobility or whatever! I've had enough. We're gonna kill you! Do you really think you can win a two-on-one fight?!" yelled the man with the knife, holding his face, blood still dripping from his nose.

In response to his threats, the girl closed one of her eyes. "You're right, one against two sounds like it could be a little tough."

"…In that case, would two on two be bit more fair?" As if it were finishing the girl's sentence, a new, higher-pitched, genderless voice entered the fray.

Startled, Subaru looked around. The other men also followed suit, but there wasn't anyone inside or at the entrance to the alley who looked as though they were the owner of that voice.

Then, as if to show both Subaru and the other men the answer to their question, the girl extended her left hand.

Sitting on top of her palm and white fingers, there it was.

"When you all stare at me like that, full of expectation, it's uh… kind of embarrassing."

Using its paw to clean its face was a small, palm-size cat that stood upright on its two hind legs.

It had gray hair and floppy ears. To the best of Subaru's knowledge it was nearest to an American shorthair. That is, if you ignored the fact that its nose was pink and it had a tail about the length of its body.

Seeing the small, palm-size cat, the man with the knife seemed overcome with fear and yelled, "Y-you're a spirit mage?!"

"That's right. If you want to leave right now, I won't chase after you, but make up your minds quick. I'm in a hurry."

With that, the men rushed to pick up their fallen companion and leave the alley, but as they passed the girl on their way out, one of the men clicked his tongue and said, "I'm going to remember your face, you bitch. The next time we see you it won't go this well for you."

"If you do anything to her I'll curse you and all of your offspring, you know? Though, in that case you won't be having any."

For the thug, that must have been his best attempt at intimidation, but in contrast, the cat's response was light in tone but much more severe.

The cat didn't seem to be completely serious, but the men paled more than they ever had before, and ran out into the main road without another word.

Once the thugs were gone, Subaru was left alone in the alley with the girl and her cat. Thinking that he at least needed to say thanks, Subaru forgot his pain and started to get to his feet, but…

"Don't move," said the girl in a cold emotionless voice. You could see in her eyes that she was being cautious. Even though she realized that Subaru was not with the other thugs, she wasn't about to let her guard down, that much was clear.

It was actually Subaru's reaction that was more out of place. Even though the girl was looking at him like that, he was fixed on her beautiful and bewitching violet eyes. Not used to seeing such beauty, Subaru unthinkingly blushed and looked away.

"See? I knew I was on to something. If he had nothing to hide, he wouldn't look away like that," said the girl.

"I'm not so sure about that. That seems like a very natural reaction for a boy like him. I'm sensing zero evil intentions," responded the cat.

"Be quiet, Puck. ...You know the girl who stole my badge, don't you?" Shushing her cat, the girl turned to Subaru. Her expression, full of confidence, was lovely. However...

"I'm sorry to let you down like this, but I totally don't know her, like, completely not at all."

"Wai—What? Seriously!?"

As her confidence was stripped from her face, Subaru was able to get a glimpse of how she naturally expressed herself, as opposed to her ongoing act. With that dignified air of hers out the window, the girl, flustered, turned quickly to the cat still resting on her palm.

"Wh-wh-what are we going to do? Was this really all just a waste of my time...?"

"A waste that's still in progress... I really think you should hurry. She was really fast when she ran away, so there's a good chance the culprit has some kind of strange protection on her side."

"Ugh... How can you be so unconcerned about all of this, Puck?"

"You're the one who told me not to get too involved, you know? Anyway, what are we going to do about him?" the cat said, as if just remembering about Subaru.

As the topic of conversation centered back on him, Subaru put on a weak smile.

"Oh," said the girl as she finally realized the cat was talking about Subaru.

In response, Subaru put on an empty display of confidence and replied, "Don't worry about me. Thanks to your help, I'll be fine. You're in a hurry, right? You should go..."

Subaru had hoped to finish this off with, *If you'd like, I don't even mind helping you out. How about it, m'lady?* while brushing his hair back and flashing a smile, but...

"...Huh?"

Suddenly dizzy, Subaru reached for the wall but missed, and fell face-first back onto the ground.

"Wait. You shouldn't try to stand up just ye—Well…okay," came the cat's warning, just a step too late.

After falling with zero capacity to catch himself, Subaru felt a sharp pain as his consciousness went winging away.

"…So, what should we do?"

"He has…nothing to do with us. That's not enough to kill him. We're going to leave him."

In the far reaches of his consciousness as it left him, Subaru could hear just a little of the pair's conversation.

That's an otherworldly fantasy for you. Everyone has quite the severe view on the concept of empathy.

Am I just going to be abandoned here in this alley? was the negative take.

Well, I suppose I was going to die, and now I'm not, so I should be super grateful, was a more positive thought.

With those two views in mind, Subaru's consciousness drifted further and further…further and further away…

"Are you *sure*?"

"I'm sure!"

Right before the thread of Subaru's consciousness was cut for good, he was able to see that silver-haired girl, red in the face, turn around and shout.

"There's no way! No way that I'm going to save him, okay?! Okay?!"

—*Man, even when she's angry she's really cute.* Go otherworldly fantasies.

With that last thought, really this time, once and for all, Subaru's consciousness fell into darkness.

5

It occurred to Subaru that the feeling of waking up was similar to having your face rise up from out of a body of water. When he opened his eyes, the sun's light was at an angle and shone into them, causing him to squint at the brightness and rub his eyes. He woke up in a rather pleasant way, and Subaru was the type of person to be fully awake once he opened his eyes.

"Oh, you awake?" said a voice from right above Subaru's head, with him still lying down.

As Subaru turned to look in the direction of the voice, he realized that he was still lying on the ground, but had his head on something soft that was being used as a pillow.

"You shouldn't move. You hit your head, so I can't say whether it's safe to just yet."

This concerned voice also sounded very kind, as Subaru remembered what happened just before he lost consciousness, he thought. Given the circumstances, he might just be in one of those blessed situations one hopes to be in as a boy.

To have one's head in a girl's lap... Responding to this divine revelation, Subaru pretended to turn to readjust so he could enjoy himself to the fullest. With a circular motion he rubbed his cheek against it and reached a feeling of absolute bliss, and far more than he expected he felt a fluffiness from the softness of the hair.

"Wow... Beautiful girls are a lot hairier than I imagin—Hey, wait a minute!" sputtered Subaru as he faced up, this time with his vision fully recovered, and took in what was happening.

Right in front of Subaru, in his upside-down vision, was the face of a giant cat. "I thought that at least until you woke up, I'd make you feel comfortable. You can thank me later."

"First of all, I'd like you to stop with that terrible falsetto voice. There's no way I'd mistake a cat for the heroine."

Subaru had certainly never been in a situation before where he got to use a human-size cat's lap for a pillow and, well, it wasn't like you get to experience this every day, so he decided to make the best of it.

"Wow, this is actually really comfortable. Like, this is amazing. Now I understand why people want to love their cats 'til they go bald."

"Well, if you're going to be this happy about it, I guess it was really worth super-sizing... Don't you think so, too?"

The cat scratched at his face as if it were embarrassed and winked as if seeking a confirmation. At the end of that glance was a silver-haired girl, standing at the entrance to the alley looking unfazed.

It was the same girl from before, if Subaru was to believe his memories, eyes, and heart, which were all deeply branded by her image right before he lost consciousness.

"Umm...I'm sorry about all of this. It looks like you ended up staying here with me until I woke up, and—"

"Don't get any ideas about this. The only reason I stayed is because I still have some questions to ask you. If it weren't for that, I would have left you behind. I mean it. So don't get any ideas."

Pressing the point, the girl put strong emphasis on her words. This was a level of girl power that Subaru, who had no resistance against such beautiful girls, simply could not stand against. It was so strong that Subaru could do nothing but nod, ignoring the content of whatever she was saying.

"The reason I healed your wounds, and the reason I had Puck serve as a pillow until you woke up—all of that was for me. So I'm going to have you make it up to me, okay?"

"I know you're trying to build this up and everything, but if you just have something to ask, go right ahead," said Subaru.

It looked like she was one of those people who took the saying "helping others isn't just for their sake" to heart.

The girl looked sternly at Subaru and shook her head.

"I'm not asking, I'm commanding. You know something about my stolen badge, don't you?" asked the girl, dropping the tone of her voice. However, as this wasn't any different from what she had asked before, Subaru had to tilt his head in confusion.

They had gone through this once already, right before Subaru had passed out.

She keeps calling the thing a "badge," Subaru thought. *So is it something like what police and detectives keep on themselves to prove what they are? I haven't seen anything like that.*

"You didn't hit your head real hard or anything while I was passed out, did you?" Subaru asked.

"You were only out for about ten minutes, and no, nothing like that happened. Answer the question."

"Well...if that's the case, I've got to say I really don't know. Ha-ha..."

You can't do anything about what you don't know. Subaru's answer was no different from before. However, the girl didn't look particularly crestfallen, but instead nodded.

"Well, if you don't know, you don't know. But, the fact that you know absolutely nothing itself is information you have provided to me, and enough for me to justify healing you," the girl replied, using twisted enough logic to baffle any swindler to describe her complete loss.

As Subaru looked on, dumbfounded, the girl clapped her hands together as if to finish things.

"Well, I'm in a hurry, so I'm going to get going now. Your wounds should all be healed, and I threatened those other guys so much I doubt they'll go near you again, but it's still dangerous to enter an alley like this all alone. Oh, and I'm not saying this because I'm worried about you; this is a warning: If I see you in a similar situation again, there won't be any merit to me saving you, so you can't expect me to do so again," said the girl with machine-gun rapidity. She took Subaru's silence as affirmation, nodded to herself, and turned around to leave.

The girl's long silver hair swayed as she moved, and sparkled fantastically in the dim light of the alley.

"I'm sorry about that. She's not really honest with herself. Don't think too strangely of her, okay?" said the cat with a laugh as, having returned to its original size, it jumped up onto the girl's shoulder.

The girl patted its back as if to affirm its touch, and the cat disappeared, slipping behind the curtain of her hair.

Without once looking back, the girl continued to walk on. As he watched her go, Subaru thought about what the cat had said, about her not being honest with herself, and her intentions.

She had something stolen from her, and even though she was in a hurry to get it back, she saved Subaru. Then, after Subaru had passed out, she healed him, and when he woke up, she used terrible reasoning to try to show him that she wasn't worse off for doing so. "She's not really honest with herself" was not going far enough. Her efforts were coming up negative in everything, and it was hard to watch.

The girl had every right to blame Subaru for getting in her way, but she hadn't complained even once, and she didn't even look for an apology.

That's because to her, the only reason she saved Subaru was for her own ends.

"If you live like that, you're just going to keep losing until there's nothing left," said Subaru as he got up, patted his dust- and dirt-covered tracksuit and started running.

Sure, his beloved tracksuit was in pretty bad shape, but on the inside, almost all of his pain was gone. That's after being kicked and punched as much as he was. Again Subaru was reminded of the otherworldliness of magic, as well as the generosity of that girl who, despite going on and on about having Subaru pay her back, took nothing from him in return.

"Hey, wait!" Subaru called out to the girl just as she had reached the entrance to the alley and was in front of the main road, looking unsure of where to go next.

The girl touched her silver hair and looked a bit troubled as she turned around. "What is it? I'm going to tell you right now, I only have a bit more time to spend dealing with you."

"So a little's fine, then?! Anyway, what you lost is really important, right? Let me help you look for it."

The girl blinked a few times, surprised. "But you said you don't know anything..."

"It's true that I don't know the name of the girl who stole that badge from you, or where she's from, but at least I know what she looks like! She's got blond hair, is sort of like a kitten, and has this canine tooth that sticks out that's hard to miss. She's shorter than you and her chest is pretty flat so she's maybe two or three years younger than you! How about that?!"

When he got flustered, Subaru had a bad habit of speaking fast and not really even knowing what he was saying.

Right now that bad habit was running at full blast, and even Subaru wanted to distance himself from his own words.

The ensuing silence was painful. A cold sweat drenched Subaru's back, not to mention his hands and armpits, which was followed by heart palpitations, shortness of breath, as well as dizziness, and in addition to feeling faint, his nose stuffed up in an allergic reaction accompanied by a migraine, such that there were problems on every front. However...

"...You're strange," the girl said with a hand up to her mouth, tilting her head to the side as if she were looking at some rare animal.

With a finger still at her lips she stared at Subaru, sizing him up.

"I should say up front that I can't offer you anything in return for your help. I might not look it, but I don't have a copper piece on me."

"Don't worry, that makes two of us," replied Subaru.

"Three of us, if you count me... Pretty terrible for us as a group," added a voice jokingly from the girl's silver hair, but Subaru ignored it and pounded his chest.

"I don't need anything in thanks. I'm the one who should thank *you*. That's why I want to help."

"I haven't done anything deserving of your thanks. I've already gotten something in return from healing you."

She just won't give it up, will she? Subaru looked at the girl and her stubborn attitude with a weak smile.

"If that's the case, then I'll help you for my own sake. The reason is...yeah, that's it. I'll use you for my 'one good deed a day' project!" said Subaru.

"One good deed a day?"

"That's right. Once a day you do one good thing. If you do that, after you die you've got a one-way ticket to heaven! If I can do it, then a wonderful life of just eating and sleeping is waiting for me—so I hear! So that's why I'm going to help you for my own sake."

Subaru felt like turning to himself and asking what the hell he was going on about, but at least he'd managed to make his point.

The girl stood in thought, considering Subaru's words, when her cat poked at her cheek with its paws.

"I don't sense any evil intentions from him, and I don't really think it's a bad idea, you know? With how large the capital is, it's way better than going on no clues at all."

"But if I get him involved..."

"You're cute when you're stubborn, but it's foolish to let your stubbornness get the best of you and make you lose sight of your goals. I'd really rather not think of my own master as a fool."

The cat added its support in favor of Subaru, but the girl was still hesitant. In response, the cat dropped its expression and continued in a serious voice.

"Plus, the sun is starting to set. If night falls, I won't be able to help you. I'm not worried about you handling a thug or two, but... it's better to be safe than sorry."

"Well, it sounds like you're the one to call if there's danger! But, wait—according to what you said, you can't come out at night? Is that one of the deals of your contract or something?" Subaru asked, taking a step closer.

The cat flicked its whiskers with its front paw and said, "It's more like, I may look cute, but I'm a spirit, you know? I use a lot of mana just by materializing. When night falls, I return to the crystal that is my vessel and prepare for when the sun is out again. I suppose you could say it's the perfect nine-to-five job."

"Nine to five? That sounds like a government job... The conditions to hire a spirit sound more severe than I expected...!"

Subaru was able to talk naturally about spirits, but that was only because of the analytical power he had as a modern otaku, poisoned by anime and games. Even traits looked down on by the public come in handy sometimes.

While Subaru and the cat continued their conversation, the girl continued to anguish over her decision. However, that last point seemed to have tipped the scales, so after much moaning with a number of *buts* and *stills* and *ifs* she finally conceded.

"I'm telling you, I really can't give you anything in return, okay?"

6

After Subaru's first friendly interaction in this different world—a pleasant, heartwarming episode—one hour had passed.

"What is the meaning of this?"

Their investigation had stalled.

As Subaru faced the girl's cold stare, he scratched at his face, trying to find a way out.

"Even with all of my experience, I never thought that it would be this difficult..."

"You seem to have a really high opinion of yourself, but I haven't seen anything from you to prove it. No matter how you slice it, things aren't going well!"

"Nobody says, 'no matter how you slice it,' anymore..."

Pointing that out only made things worse, and the girl's stare grew sharper, at which Subaru shrank away.

Even though they had been searching for a little under an hour, for some reason, Subaru and the girl were back in an alley. Of course, there was a really good reason for this. There were several factors Subaru had discovered that made their search difficult.

First, Subaru didn't know his way around town. Given that he had just been summoned from another world, it was hard to blame him for wanting a pass on this one. Additionally, it seemed that the girl was unfamiliar with the area as well, and at least ten minutes were wasted with both having full confidence that the other knew their way around. It was pretty funny, actually, or so Subaru thought. But the way the girl was staring at Subaru, she didn't seem to find it funny at all.

Second, the characters and symbols written here and there...were completely illegible to Subaru. Given that Subaru didn't have any trouble communicating by speech, he hadn't thought all that much about it, but after a second look he saw that all around, here and there were handwritten symbols. Unless they were all some kind of "mystic charms to protect against evil magic" that tended to be popular, those symbols were probably letters for the common language. And because he couldn't understand them, he couldn't even read the road signs.

In other words, while a miracle common in most otherworldly summoning works of fiction is "for some reason our words and writing are mutually understood!", in Subaru's case, only half of that came true. But given that if Subaru hadn't been able to communicate through words he would have been as good as dead, it was hard to call his situation unlucky.

"Still, why do you have to raise the difficulty like that on me...? The world's not kind at all."

Rather than exhausting all options, it was more of a case of finding a series of critical problems before you even get started.

While despairing at making absolutely no progress over the past hour, Subaru noticed that his companion, that girl, was standing up by the wall of the alley with her eyes closed, paying absolutely no mind to him. Seeing her lips move as she muttered something a few times, he tilted his head in confusion.

"Wonder what she's doing..."

"Oh that? She's communicating with lesser spirits."

Subaru raised his eyebrows in surprise as the girl's gray cat suddenly reappeared right in front of his eyes.

"I thought that I hadn't seen you in a while, but you hadn't gone home or anything; you were here the whole time?"

"There's still a bit of time left before I have to go. Unlike those minor spirits she's talking to, I take my job seriously."

"Well that's quite honorable of you. ...But, what are these uh... lesser spirits again?"

Going by the name, I suppose they're a rank down from regular spirits? Subaru thought.

As if agreeing with Subaru's musing, the cat, floating in midair, waved its long tail back and forth. "Lesser spirits are beings that, in a state prior to becoming real spirits, start to develop some knowledge. If, over time, they gain power and self-awareness, they'll become spirits like me."

As he nodded, listening to the cat's explanation, Subaru noticed that the area around the girl began to glow. The silver-haired girl was surrounded by faint lights that looked as though they were fireflies.

It was the kind of scene that most people would subconsciously hesitate to interfere with. It was like holy ground, whereby the influence of the supernatural, only what was sanctified was allowed to be.

In response to the scene, Subaru…

"Wow! That's so cool! Are all of these glowing things spirits?"

"Ah!"

…intruded on it without a second thought, breaking the fantasy of it all as he started talking to the girl.

As the girl cried out in surprise, you could see droplets of tears that formed in reaction, sparkling in her eyes. Then the girl's flustered state spread to the lights around her and…

"Oh, look at that. They're panicking."

The many lights started to flee this way and that before finally scattering and disappearing into the air.

"…Umm…"

Both Subaru and the girl opened their mouths, dumbstruck, searching for where the lesser spirits had gone. Quickly the girl tried to continue what she had been doing, but it didn't appear the lesser spirits were heeding her call anymore.

"Just look at what you did! They're gone! What are you going to do about this?!"

"Ah… Um… I'm sorry! It was my first time seeing spirits like that and I got a little excited. I mean, it didn't look like they were dangerous or anything."

"It was only safe because I had them under control. If you had done that to an inexperienced spirit mage, it would have been awful. In the worst case, the spirits could have gone berserk and…BAM."

"'Bam?'"

The girl was trying to admonish Subaru for not taking his actions seriously, but using the word "bam" wasn't exactly helpful.

"Oh, come on. There's no way those little sparkly things could be dangerous. Do you really expect me to believe that?"

"Well, to put it one way," Puck said, "I may look pretty cute…but it would only take two seconds for me to turn you into a pile of dust."

"Damn, spirits are scary!" A shiver went down Subaru's spine in response to the cat's peaceful-sounding death threat, and he looked back at the girl. "I definitely hope you don't happen to be so upset you set that cat on me or anything…"

"I would never use Puck for something like that. If I were going to be violent with you, I'd handle you myself… Ugh, it really looks like they aren't going to answer me anymore." Failing to establish a second contact with the lesser spirits, the girl, depressed, shook her head powerlessly.

"I suppose it's not helpful to ask this after the spirits have already gone, but what is it exactly that you were trying to do?"

"I was trying to see if I could get any information from them about what I'm looking for. They disappeared before I was able to ask, though."

"What, really?!" Subaru was struck speechless by the gravity of his mistake. Seeing that, the girl jumped in.

"Um, b-but… It did take some time and lesser spirits don't have the kind of clear awareness that regular spirits have, so I wasn't really expecting much, but… Okay, I'm sorry, that's a lie."

The girl's hesitancy to lie was in conflict with her desire for a positive outlook, so while she tried, she was unable to soften the blow. In fact, her struggle with herself only highlighted to Subaru his own stupidity. At this rate, he wasn't going to be able to do anything but slow her down.

This is bad, both considering the debt I owe and the fact that she's my one precious connection in this world… I'm gonna do my best to cling to this relationship and not let go…!

"From the look on your face, it looks like you're up to no good, but…did you think of something? Um…" In front of Subaru, who had found a questionable new sense of determination, the girl hesitated. Subaru tilted his head and stared at her for a while as she furrowed her brow, but it was the cat that came to her rescue.

"Ah, now that I think of it, we haven't told each other our names yet, have we? Should we introduce ourselves?"

"Oh, you're right. Well then, I guess I'll go ahead and go first!"

In an overly energetic fashion, in part to help cover up for his previous mistake, Subaru struck a pose and pointed to the heavens.

"My name is Subaru Natsuki! The ignorant and unintelligent, forever and everlastingly penniless! Nice to meet you!"

"Well, that doesn't inspire a lot of confidence, does it? Anyway, I'm Puck. Nice to meet you, too."

As Subaru put out his hand, Puck leapt into it with his whole body for a handshake. An onlooker would probably think Subaru was trying to squeeze the cat to death.

The girl blinked in surprise at Subaru's bold interaction. "It's rare to see someone who's willing to approach a spirit so easily... and your name is just as unusual. With black hair and dark eyes like that—just where did you come from?"

"Ha, I was waiting for you to ask that question. Given this trope, I'll have to say I come from a small country to the east!"

This is a pattern that has often come up in otherworldly fiction since times long past. A character will state that they come from a hidden country to the east, called something like "Zipang." There tends to not be that much interaction between countries, so if you say you've traveled to where you are from that country, it will make sense to most people. It's a magically convenient cliché.

"If you look at a map of the continent, Lugunica is the country farthest to the east, so...there's no country to the east of here."

"What, are you serious? We're at the ends of the east?! So...does this make this country my long-yearned-for Zipang?!"

"So you don't know where you are, you don't have any money, you can't read, and you have no one you can count on. I'm starting to think you're worse off than I am..."

While Subaru was shocked at this new development, the girl was also starting to look anxious. With every action she took you could see the element of her personality that made her want to help others. She probably couldn't help but be concerned about Subaru, who to her was looking more and more to be not only defenseless, but absolutely helpless.

The girl looked at Subaru again carefully, from the top down.

"Taking another look at you, you actually look like you're in pretty good shape. Um... Uh... Subaru."

"Huh? Oh. Yep, Subaru. That's my name." Having his name called in such a hesitant way for some reason felt like a fresh new experience to Subaru, and he couldn't help but stumble in his response. After clearing his throat to hide the fact that he was shaken up, he showed his biceps. "I do strength training every day. Since I'm almost always cooped up in my room, I've got to do at least that much to stay in shape."

"I don't really get what you mean by 'cooped up in your room,' but you're from a high-ranking family, aren't you? Weren't you taught some sort of martial art?"

"I'm actually from an extremely ordinary middle-class family, but...what makes you think I'm from a high-class family? Do I exude some refined air of nobility?"

"Well, you do have a bit of a curious air to you, at least."

Subaru jokingly raised his hands as if to acknowledge the flattery.

But then the girl suddenly grabbed those hands, and Subaru, taken aback by the suddenness of her touch, had to hold back a squeak from rising out of his throat.

"It's also these fingers of yours, but your skin and hair are part of it as well. These aren't the hands of a commoner, and your muscles don't look like the product of hard labor."

Subaru blushed as the girl continued to poke at his hands, but understood. He was also impressed by her ability to see that he was not just simply a foreigner in a foreign land. As Subaru stood in wonderment, the girl continued.

"Black hair and dark eyes. I hear that is a common trait of the refugees from the south, but the fact that you are here in Lugunica with those traits means that you are able to live a life of luxury. Also, the craftsmanship of these strange clothes of yours is magnificent… So, have I got it right?"

As Subaru grew quiet, the girl put on a proud smile. Feeling admittedly drawn by the bewitching atmosphere she had made fitting of her beautiful smile, Subaru processed the contents of what she just said and made a reluctant face.

"If you're asking me whether you're wrong or you are right… you're absolutely wrong, but is there any way I can say it so you won't get hurt?"

"If I'm wrong, just tell me I'm wrong. If you don't, it's just going to be more embarrassing for me." The girl blushed as her earlier confidence transformed into embarrassment. As Subaru watched her go silent, he thought about how he was going to explain where he came from.

He could just say, "I'm a loser who was summoned from another world!" but given the precedent set by fantasy fiction about other worlds, that would open the gates for him to be labeled as someone who was wrong in the head. Looking back on the results of what he had said so far, he felt there was a significant risk in telling the truth.

"You don't have to think that hard about it, you know? If it's something you can't talk about, I won't question you any further."

Seeing Subaru struggling with what to say, the girl came to her own conclusions and didn't press him. Given that she had come to his rescue yet again in a way, Subaru grimaced, feeling all the more useless.

"But…really, this isn't looking very good," the girl muttered, in a now-weaker tone, a clouded expression on her face.

"…" Seeing that the girl could no longer hide how hopeless she felt, Subaru felt a faint flame light up inside himself. "What am I, an idiot? Well, yeah, I am an idiot. Just what have I been doing all this time…"

Right in front of Subaru stood the girl who saved his life. Hadn't he offered to help her out so that he could repay her? If that was the case, then how was he supposed to explain his total lack of support?

"Subaru?"

Seeing Subaru fall silent and looking troubled all of a sudden, the girl tilted her head and looked at him puzzled. Watching as with that motion her silver hair tumbled down off her shoulder, Subaru thought as hard as he could.

Subaru tried to remember what had happened when the thief ran through that alley as those thugs were stomping on him. Focusing on that instant in time, he needed to find something, anything that he could use…

"I have a few things that I want to check with you, is that okay?"

"Um…okay, yeah. Go right ahead."

"Thanks. I'm pretty sure I heard you mention it a few times, but this is the capital of whatever country we're in…right? So, basically it's the town that has the king's castle in it, and it's a really big place, is that correct?" Subaru asked, remembering bits of the conversation that he had had with the girl before.

While Subaru realized that his question must have sounded strange, the girl didn't interrupt and simply nodded a yes.

"So in this big city, there's a girl who appears to be making her living stealing things. By the look of her clothes, she definitely doesn't seem to be that well off… Now this may be obvious, but there's got to be a place where people like that live."

"…"

"Is there a place where crime is rampant, or something like a slum in the area…? I'm sure it's hard to exchange stolen goods for money without some connections, so I think there's a good chance she would have to go back to a place like that."

With the image of the thief burned in his memory, Subaru analyzed her from head to toe, and used all of the knowledge he had about fantasy settings to help form his hypothesis.

"So, I think rather than searching around aimlessly, we have a better chance if we aim for that, but… What's wrong?"

"I was just surprised. You really do have a good head on your shoulders."

"Well, rather than a logical conclusion, it's more that it's a common theme in medieval fantasy, but…if this is all it takes for you to start thinking better of me I have a feeling that I've got a long way to go…"

Despite Subaru's response, he seemed to be taking the girl's praise rather well.

While Subaru scratched at the side of his head to try to keep from showing how embarrassed he was, the girl nodded several times. "We'll go with your plan. Let's go back out to the main road and ask some people if they know of a place that's like what you described."

"We're already really behind as it is, after all. Let's hurry up and get going."

After Subaru and the girl looked at each other and nodded, they headed out of the alley and toward the main road. However, right before they could start their search for a spot where a lot of people who they could question were passing by, Subaru remembered something.

"I was just thinking… I know your cat's name now, but I don't think you ever told me your name, ha-ha."

While Subaru thought that bringing this up now might have not been the best time, the girl's eyes widened a bit in surprise. She then closed them, and after a few seconds of silence, said…

"…Satella."

"Oh?"

Subaru, who because of her silence had begun to think that he had made a mistake, was a bit late in reacting to her whispered reply.

In response, the girl turned away from Subaru and continued.

"I don't have a last name, so you can just call me Satella."

Her voice had no emotion in it. Because of her attitude, it was as if, though she was giving her name, she was refusing to be called by it. Through her actions, this girl, who gave her name as "Satella," was putting a distance between herself and Subaru more than she had ever done before.

Subaru, who already thought that he would feel more comfortable having a surname to call her by rather than having to use her personal name, felt that he really couldn't use that name at all. For the time being, looking for a way out, Subaru decided to avoid using her name entirely, and instead just use pronouns.

As he observed Subaru and the girl's exchange from the sidelines, Puck had one thing to say before slipping back under the girl's silver hair.

"...That's in really bad taste, you know," it muttered, though its voice did not even reach the girl's ears, let alone Subaru's.

7

Using the sounds of the bustling crowd as a guide, Subaru and Satella walked back through the alley they were in and reached the main road about ten minutes later.

Shifting his gaze this way and that, Subaru looked for who they should question first, when Satella, who stood beside him, pulled on his sleeve.

"Hey, Subaru..."

When Subaru looked back at Satella he saw that she had her gaze fixed on something on the other side of the street. Subaru looked in the same direction and realized what Satella was looking at.

I have a bad feeling about this, he thought.

Adding further weight to his fears, Satella continued, with a serious look on her face.

"...Do you think that kid is lost?"

Out of all the possible things that could go wrong with this plan, the final one had reared its head.

"...Well, uh..."

One of the several things that Subaru had discovered throughout the day was that the silver-haired girl standing next to him was an incorrigibly kind person. But, whether it was due to a curse or some other reason, she would not ever admit it herself.

Subaru sighed a deep sigh. "Let's just calm down a minute."

"What are we going to do if she gets up and goes somewhere while we're dillydallying?! We've got to go talk to her right away..."

"You know, that kindness of yours is a great virtue, and given the fact that I myself was saved by that kindness I really don't want to say this, but do you have any idea what situation you're in right now?"

Where Satella was looking, near the buildings across the street, there stood a young girl. She looked as though she was around ten years old, with shoulder-length brown hair that was very cute. If she smiled, the people around her probably would not be able to resist smiling back, but unfortunately, at the moment her eyes were filled with anxiety, and she looked moments away from tears.

There was probably an 80 or 90 percent chance that Satella's observation was correct. Subaru was sure it was, but...

"There's also that my screw-ups are partially at fault, but the thief who stole from you is just getting farther and farther away from us. If we waste any more time here, by the time we catch her, she might already have sold it and then we'll have no way to get it back."

"You're probably right...but..."

"Then..."

Certainly it would feel bad to just leave the girl like that, but with all of the other people around, the chance that someone else would help her was high. On the other hand, Subaru and Satella were pressed for time, and needed to gather information to continue their search.

No matter how he thought about it, their current plan should have priority over helping that little girl, but...

"But don't you see, Subaru? Look at her, she's crying."

"..."

"If you don't want to stick around with me, that's just fine. Thanks for everything you've done, Subaru. I'll figure this out on my own... after I help that little girl." While Subaru stood at a loss for words, Satella looked like she had already made her decision. The way she said it, it wasn't as though she was saying that Subaru just didn't understand and she was tired of him, but that she felt guilty for forcing Subaru to play along with her unreasonableness.

Her silver hair dancing behind her, Satella trotted off across the street to where the little girl was standing. The girl, who had been looking down with her teary eyes, noticed that someone had suddenly come to her side. There was a glimmer of hope in her eyes as she looked up, probably because she thought the person she was looking for had found her.

"I'm sorry I'm not the one you're looking for," said Satella as she knelt down to talk to the girl, whose eyes opened wide in surprise.

But in those eyes was not a feeling of relief, but a feeling of fear. You could tell, even from far away, that being spoken to by a stranger had caused her heart to shrink away, afraid.

"I'm sorry if I'm bothering you, but where are your father and mother? Aren't they with you?"

It looked as though Satella had noticed the girl was afraid, and her voice was in a tone that was kinder than Subaru had ever heard it before. However, it wasn't enough to convey her concern to the girl, who had lost sight of her parents and was now shivering because she did not know what to do.

"Umm… Uh… Please don't cry. I won't do anything to hurt you, okay?"

Satella tried to keep open the girl's heart before it shut completely on her, but it didn't seem to work, and the little girl only shook her head back and forth. The tears that had welled up in her eyes looked as though they were about to overflow, when…

"Now feast your eyes on this magnificent notched ten-yen coin!"

"Huh?" said Satella, surprised by the sudden voice that had leapt in, and when she looked up, there was Subaru in his gray tracksuit.

Subaru first smiled weakly at Satella's reaction, and then turned his smile from her to the little girl. The sudden intruder had also surprised her. Subaru then put out his right hand in front of her.

"Now, can you see this coin here in my right hand? I bet you can! All right, now I'm going to squeeze it tight. Like this…*squeeze squeeze squeeze*…"

"Wait, Subaru…what are you…?"

"And would you look at that!"

Ignoring Satella's interruption, Subaru took his fist where he had been holding the notched ten-yen coin and opened it wide for the two to see. When he did, the coin that should have been in his hand was gone.

"Wow! The coin I was squeezing is gone! Now where could it have run off to...?"

The little girl blinked a few times and then stared hard at Subaru's right hand, but whether she looked at the back of his hand or his palm, she couldn't find it. Subaru, emboldened by the girl's reaction, nodded, and then reached out with his left hand and gently brushed his fingers through her hair.

"Would you look at that! So this is where the coin was hiding."

When the little girl saw the coin resting between the fingers of Subaru's left hand, she was stunned.

Satella, who couldn't figure out the trick, was just as confused.

Subaru took a magnificent bow before the two and then dropped the notched ten-yen coin in the little girl's hand.

"I'll let you keep it as a present. It's special, so take good care of it, okay?"

Subaru looked on with a smile as the little girl held the coin close and nodded vigorously.

As he was doing so, Satella poked him in the side. "Hey, Subaru..."

"Don't look at me like that. I mean, I'll admit what I said before was a bit harsh but..."

"How did you do that?"

"Oh, you mean that? You're not questioning my motives, but how I did the trick?"

Subaru promised to explain the trick later to Satella, who looked very interested, before turning back to the little girl, who was looking very curiously at the ten-yen coin. It seemed like Subaru's amazing magic had helped calm down her anxiety. When Subaru knelt down and asked her a few questions, she answered them quickly and clearly.

"I see. So you got separated from your mother, huh. Don't worry, don't worry. Just leave it to your big brother and sister. We'll find her right away!"

After giving the girl another pat on the head, Subaru held out his hand to her, and with a little hesitation, she grabbed it. Satella, who was watching, opened her eyes wide.

"You really look like you're used to this... Subaru, is your profession taming children?"

"When you take it out of context like that, that sounds really, really bad! And no. I'm unemployed."

Technically, Subaru had the incredibly convenient status of being a student. However, given that he hadn't been going to school lately, and particularly now that he had been summoned to a different world, he didn't really feel that he was qualified to call himself that anymore.

But, regardless...

"So, big sister, how about you hold this lonely little girl's hand? She looks like she could use another friend," said Subaru with a wink. The little girl had reached her other hand, the one that was not holding on to Subaru's, out to Satella.

Satella looked surprised for a moment and held her breath, but then let it out and took the little girl's hand in her own. "Right. Don't you worry. Just let your big sister handle this. We'll definitely find your mom, okay?" Satella said, smiling at the little girl as she nodded silently.

Subaru and Satella led the girl along, with her between them, and the three continued down the main road through the waves of people together.

"The way we are now, don't you think there are some people out there who look at us and think that we're a young couple with our child? How embarrassing!"

"...Huh? Even with the benefit of the doubt I don't see how anyone would think that you and that girl are anything other than brother and sister..."

"I can't tell if that's just a really dry joke, or that's really what you thought I meant!"

As Satella and Subaru went on talking, the little girl between them let a small smile spread across her face.

8

Fortunately, perhaps because they really stood out as a group, it didn't take long before they found the little girl's mother. In this case, it wasn't only Subaru who stood out, but also Satella, with her silver hair and extraordinary beauty.

"Thank you so much!"

Once the girl's mother was reunited with her child, she thanked Subaru and Satella several times, though they smiled and played it off as if it were nothing.

As the little girl and her mother were leaving, the girl looked back and waved good-bye several times, and Subaru and Satella waved back. Subaru turned to look at Satella, as she stood beside him waving to the girl, and saw that she had a bright and cheerful expression on her face.

"Now, I get the feeling that we've wasted a lot of time doing this, but what does our big sister have to say? I'm sure she'll find some kind of way to describe this as a means to an end!" Subaru said in an orchestrated manner, snapping his fingers and making fun of Satella's all-too-kind nature.

Of course, he wasn't really criticizing her; it was more that he was just poking fun. After all, Satella had given such a roundabout excuse for why her encounter with Subaru was useful, so he was curious to hear what she would say.

"…It's simple." In response to Subaru's teasing, Satella smiled. "Now we can be in a good mood as we continue to search."

" … "

"Even if we got my badge back, I'm sure I would have regretted not helping that girl. Don't you think it is better to both help the girl *and* get my badge back?"

It didn't look like Satella was just saying that to keep her own hopes up. She looked so refreshed she probably believed it.

With that kind of response, Subaru really didn't know what to say. He would have to rethink his opinion of this girl.

Not only was she the type of person who was so kind she always ended up losing everything, she also was the type of person who wanted to have it all.

"I see. You're right. Thanks to your quick decision, we won't have to say, 'Sure, we abandoned that little anxious crying girl all lost and by herself, but we were able to get the badge back, safe and sound, hooray!'"

"Well that's a really negative way to put it," said Satella, frowning, then glaring at him as though she seemed to have remembered something. "But besides that… Why did you help me? I thought you were against helping the girl, Subaru."

"I just wanted to show off my ability to do magic tricks! …Which is, of course, a lie. Didn't I say so before? I'm going to help you find your badge so I can do my good deed for the day and go to heaven."

"But since you helped the girl, doesn't that count for your good deed for the day already?"

"That's a very good argument! But I mean, it's not like I'm limited to one a day or anything. I can do more. So anyway, I'm going to do enough for tomorrow today! I'm actually planning to get this whole week out of the way!"

Subaru had the feeling that he was getting away from the true meaning of this whole "do one good deed a day" concept, but he still tried to make an argument. Satella stood by, shocked.

"Subaru…with a personality like that, you're going to end up losing everything one day."

"You're the last person I want to hear that from!" Subaru shouted, flipping her words back toward her, but Satella just tilted her head in confusion.

Apparently she really just didn't get it. "You really are a nice boy, aren't you?"

"You know, it kind of bothers me that you're treating me like I'm younger than you. I know that a lot of people think East Asians are younger than they are, but we really can't be that different in age, can we?"

Subaru thought that by a rough estimate Satella looked to be about seventeen or eighteen years old. Given that Subaru had a rather early birthday compared to others in his age group, he was seventeen and thought that it was possible she could even be younger than him.

But in response, Satella narrowed her violet eyes slightly and said, "However old you think I am, I don't think that you're very close... After all, I'm a half-elf."

"..."

Subaru was at a loss for words. Seeing his response, a number of complicated emotions flashed across Satella's eyes. Finally, the emotion that settled was an ineffable mixture of resignation and hopelessness.

"I see. No wonder you're so cute. After all, it's like a given in fantasy worlds that elves are always beautiful."

"...Huh?"

Subaru finally nodded, having come to his own conclusions about Satella being a half-elf. Satella blinked her eyes several times. Her expectations had completely missed their mark.

"Hmm? What's wrong?"

"It's not that anything is wrong, it's just...I mean...I'm a half-elf, and..."

"Yeah...I heard you the first time."

Unsure of what Satella had a problem with, that's the only way Subaru could think to answer, but Satella's reaction was dramatic.

"....ah."

Satella made a strange sound in her throat, before suddenly turning away from Subaru, finding the nearest wall, kneeling beside it, and holding her silver-haired head in her hands.

In the face of such an inexplicable reaction, Subaru just didn't know what to say.

"Take that!"

"Ow! What the hell was that for?!"

The gray cat, which as always seemed to come and go as it pleased, had punched him in the face with its paw like it was reenacting a fancy fighting move.

Puck purred, flicking at his whiskers with the same paw he had punched Subaru with. "I don't know, I just felt this overwhelming frustration and couldn't keep it bottled up inside of me."

"If that's the only reason, it's going to be hard to get rid of the feeling that a great injustice has been done to me, but it was a soft and squishy punch, so I forgive you."

"I mean, I'm not really mad at you or anything. If I had to say one way or the other, I'd say it's the opposite."

"The opposite?" said Subaru, confused.

"Yes, the opposite," Puck said with a nod.

But before Subaru could ask what Puck really meant by that, Satella had returned.

Twisting the ends of her silver hair in her fingers, Satella glared at Subaru.

"Subaru, you...nincompoop."

"Nobody uses the word 'nincompoop' anymore, and what have I done to be insulted by you?"

"Hmph. If you don't understand, that's not my problem. More importantly, we've got to continue our search."

With the subject of Satella's unreasonableness cut off without another word, Subaru looked irritated, but that irritation evaporated as Satella began to act more friendly and familiar. Subaru still didn't know why she'd had such a sudden change in attitude, but there were more important things to think about.

"Anyway, that episode with the little lost girl made it painfully clear—isn't this town just too big to be searching around for something in?"

"Well, it's the capital of Lugunica. It's the largest city in the nation. If I remember correctly, there are about...three hundred thousand people who live here, and a lot of others come and go." Satella answered Subaru's question in detail and with a hint of pride in her voice.

"I see, I see. Three hundred thousand people, huh. That's quite a lot... Thanks for the regurgitated information."

"Urr..." Satella muttered. It appeared Subaru's guess had been on the mark.

Subaru tried to use that new information to picture Lugunica's capital city in his mind. If it had a population of 300,000 people, then for a city in a medieval fantasy setting, it was quite large. Of course, that number only reflected the people who lived in the city, so after adding in traveling merchants and adventurers, the number of people at any given time would probably be greater than that.

As Subaru watched all of the people passing by from the side of the street, he was again astonished by the concentration of such variety in a group of people. There were half-humans, half-beasts, and regular humans all mixed together, and it really was like a melting pot of different races.

The fact that they had gotten lost in the alleyways for almost an hour wasn't just something to laugh about, either.

The area was so large and the roads so complicated that they really had gotten lost.

"In other words, we don't have any more room for error. We have already given up a big advantage to the thief, and if we get stuck again it really will be too late. So let's choose our next move carefully."

"What do you mean?"

"If we run around without some sort of plan, we won't get any results. For instance, if we go back to the place where your badge was stolen, we might be able to get more information out of people. Was there anyone who saw what happened?"

"Actually…I think there may have been." Satella put her hand to her mouth as if she had remembered something and then explained herself to Subaru.

According to Satella, her badge had been stolen in broad daylight, right in the middle of a crowd of people. If so, the theft was a bold move, but looking at the commotion on the street in front of him, Subaru thought that it wasn't necessarily a bad decision on the part of the thief. The more people there are, the easier it is to get lost in the crowd.

"Do you remember where it was stolen from you?"

"Yes, I think…it was this way."

Subaru followed Satella down the street. As they made their way through the confusion of the bustling crowd with its many different kinds of people, Subaru felt his sense of distance and direction taken from him just as quickly as when they had made their way through the maze of alleyways before. He felt as if he no longer had any idea of where he was walking. While the place they were in should have been one he had never seen before, Subaru felt a strange feeling that he had seen it before, and that feeling just wouldn't go away.

"Wait. No, I have definitely seen this place before."

Seeing the place that Satella had led him to, he scratched the side of his face and smiled a half smile.

The place where Satella had had her badge stolen from her was the same street corner to which Subaru had been summoned.

"This is where I was so confused I decided to go cool my head down in an empty alley, and then had my encounter with thugs A, B, and C…"

Remembering what had happened about two hours earlier, Subaru now mused to himself that amazing coincidences like this really did happen sometimes.

If so, he was in in luck. He had someone in mind that they could talk to.

"So that's the situation. I told her, 'Leave it to me!' and came over here to see you, Mr. Fruit Salesman."

Subaru spun around and pointed at the owner of a fruit shop on the side of the main road. The fruit that lined his shop was fresh, and just looking at it made his mouth water.

"…What, it's you again? I was hoping for a customer, Mr. Broke," said the shop owner with a cold glare that didn't seem fitting for one who dealt with customers on a daily basis.

The man wore a bandanna and was very muscular. He had a stern looking face and a deep, threatening voice.

To top it all off, he also had a white scar that ran down the left side of his face, probably left by some kind of blade. No matter how you looked at it, there was no way he was a respectable, law-abiding citizen.

That's why it was so surprising for him to be behind the counter of a fruit shop.

"Oh, don't be so cold, Pops. You were acting pretty nice to me not all that long ago."

"That's because I thought you were a customer. If I had known you had no money on you, I would have chased you out earlier, like I'm about to do now."

Subaru was trying to act like they were best friends, but the shop owner was having none of it. He waved his hand as if he was shooing away a bug.

"Oh, come on," Subaru sighed, relaxing his shoulders. "Are you sure you want to treat me like this? Haven't you noticed that I'm different from the last time I came here?"

"What's that?" said the shop owner, unsure of how to react as Subaru made a triumphant expression, nostrils flaring.

Subaru stepped aside and held both his hands out to show Satella standing behind him.

"Look at that! I brought someone with me! You may have chased me off once you learned I was penniless, but what do you think, now that I've brought in someone who just very well may become a new frequent customer of yours?!"

"Um, Subaru…? I hate to say this when you've got your hopes up, but I don't have any money on me."

"Huh, what, really? You're telling me that we were walking around the capital without so much as a single coin between us?!"

The shop owner gave a sigh as he looked at the two paupers in his shop.

"So? What was it that you wanted to say, now that one beggar's become two?"

"Well, actually, we're looking for something, and I wanted to ask if you could at least hear us out?"

"That was just my way of saying I don't have the time to deal with you people! Take a hint!" the shop owner yelled.

Subaru felt himself take some intense eardrum damage.

"Th-this wasn't a good idea after all, was it?" said Satella, shrinking away as she tugged on Subaru's sleeve.

It might be true that asking for help without buying anything was pretty selfish, but that didn't change the fact that they had no money to buy anything with.

Just when Subaru was about to give up on trying to get any information out of the man, he heard a voice.

"Hmm? Are you...the two from before?"

Subaru and Satella turned around. Standing right in front of them was a woman with long brown hair. It was someone they had both seen before; after all, the woman was not alone. Holding her hand was a little girl who looked very happy to see them.

"We are, but...why are *you* here in a place like this? The only other person here is this heartless, scary-faced man."

"Ha-ha... This is my husband's shop, so I thought I'd stop by and say hello."

"Your husband's shop?"

Subaru and Satella looked at each other, and then turned back to look inside the shop, their gazes finally settling on the scar-faced man, who had folded his arms.

"Pops...you didn't kill this woman's husband and take their shop, did you?"

"What are you going on about? This is my shop, and that is my wife!"

Subaru looked back in shock at the woman, who smiled, looking a bit unsure of how to react. She was a beautiful woman, with fine features and a gentle demeanor. *This* woman and *that* stern-faced man? There had to be some mistake.

He couldn't possibly be threatening her, could he? Subaru thought with a worried look. But despite Subaru's rude conjecture, the little girl who was holding her mother's hand darted past Subaru to the shop owner, who hugged her and picked her up.

"Oh, look at you! Aren't you all excited. Now tell me, do you know these two destitute beggars?"

"Beggars? Dear, don't call them that!"

After hearing her husband's sharp words, the girl's mother raised her eyebrows and began berating her husband. She then explained how she, her daughter, Subaru, and Satella had come to meet.

After hearing what happened, the shop owner set his daughter down.

"I'm sorry about that. That was not the way to talk to the people who saved my daughter. Please forgive me."

"Oh, don't worry about it. I mean, it is true that we don't have any money on us, and…"

"That's right, old man! I hope you think long and hard about your action…s… Um…your cute face looks pretty scary right now." A look from Satella shut Subaru up.

Right after that, the little girl reached out her hand to Satella. In her hand was a small ornament in the shape of a red flower. Satella held her breath, and looked from the ornament to the little girl and back several times, with a slightly troubled expression.

"Please, take it," said the mother, placing her hand on Satella's back, urging her on. "My daughter wants to thank you in her own way."

Satella nodded slightly and then took the flower ornament from the little girl's hand, and pinned it on the left breast of her white cloak, before kneeling down so that the little girl could see it.

"Thank you. I like it very much."

As Subaru watched Satella's brilliant smile from the side, he found himself unable to look away. Seeing that smile, the little girl blushed and looked away, and the shop owner, watching all of this, cleared his throat.

"You saved my daughter. I want to thank you. Ask me whatever you want."

With a strong nod, the stern-faced shop owner put on his best smile.

Satella was surprised, but then looked to Subaru and smiled, but it wasn't the same smile as before. This one was a triumphant one.

"See, I told you. It really did come around and help us in the end!" she said, as if this odd twist of fate was entirely her own doing.

9

—Even though the street was just one off the main road, the atmosphere was full of gloom.

It was still and silent, and there was no sign of any kind of life, let alone traces of people around.

The street Subaru and Satella were on wasn't far from the main road, but the hustle and bustle from before now seemed like a far-off dream.

"We heard from that guy that if we were looking for stolen goods, they would be handled and sold in the slums, but..." whispered Subaru as he peered down the street that supposedly would lead them to the slums, "...the air down there and the mood, not to mention the general character of the people down there, are all probably going to be pretty terrible. Are you sure you really want to go?"

"You're the one who suggested that my badge might be there in the first place, and the owner of that shop said it would probably be there, too..."

"You shouldn't forget that right after he said that, he added that we should probably give up," said Subaru, reflecting back with a sour face on what was said at the fruit shop.

Thirty minutes after unexpectedly reuniting with the little girl and her mother at the fruit shop, and using that coincidence to turn the situation around and gain some valuable information, Subaru and Satella were now at the entrance to the rumored slums, where most stolen goods were said to be brought.

After realizing that Subaru and Satella had helped his daughter, the stern-faced shop owner had warmed up to them, and listened to their plight. Because of that, they were able to get information about the slums, but now they were hesitating.

"I probably should have mentioned this earlier, but wouldn't it be better to ask for help? Like, if we asked the police, or...I guess they would be guards in this case...I'm sure if we asked those kind of people to help us search and they sent a team out to find it, this would get resolved a lot more quickly."

"We can't."

Satella immediately rejected Subaru's suggestion. In fact, she so flatly rejected it that it took Subaru by surprise.

"I'm sorry, but...we can't. I also don't think we can get the guards to act over such a small theft, and...I have other reasons that I can't ask the guards for help," said Satella, pausing for a moment with her lips shut tightly, before looking at Subaru with a look of pleading in her eyes. "I'm sorry, but I can't say why."

Realizing that she quite clearly didn't want to be asked, Subaru raised his hands slightly, conceding. "So, what should we do, then? I suppose we can still employ team tactics with just the two of us," said Subaru in a light and joking tone, trying to keep the mood up.

"Don't forget me!" replied Puck, who had reappeared on Satella's shoulder, looking at Subaru and Satella as it wiped its face with its paw. "But we don't really have the time to just sit around and talk anymore. Even if you want to try those team tactics with two humans and a cat, I've only got about an hour before it's time's-up for me."

As Puck looked up at the sky, Subaru followed its gaze and saw that most of the sky that was peaking through the buildings on either side of the street had already shifted from blue to orange. The reason the slums seemed so dark and dreary wasn't only because of the damp and sour smell coming from it. It was getting closer and closer to sunset—which of course meant that Puck would soon reach his limit.

"So whether you decide to go or turn back, it's best to make that decision soon," finished Puck.

"I don't know what you mean by 'team tactics,' but we've got to keep going. There's no way that we can let this chance go and risk having my badge be out of our reach forever," Satella said, answering Puck. She then turned to Subaru. "All right, so I've decided I'm going, but...the people who live here are probably used to getting into fights, so I want you to be careful, even more than before. If you're scared, you can just wait here for me to come back."

"Wait here?! Just how much of a chicken do you think I am?! I'm going! I'm going to stick to you like I'm a spirit who's come back to haunt you!"

"So in other words you don't want to be in front. That would really, really make it easier on me, though." Satella sighed yet again in the face of Subaru's energetic readiness to flee.

Subaru thought about how, ever since he and Satella had met, he had only made her look troubled. The few times she did smile, the reason had nothing to do with Subaru. It was unfortunate. Given how cute she looked even when she was displaying negative emotions, Subaru thought it would be wonderful if she ever did smile at him.

"All right! Let's do this! It's about time I do something to show you what I'm made of!"

"What are you so excited about all of a sudden? I can see up your nostrils."

"Well, that was a great way to ruin my display-of-determination scene! Thanks!"

Even though he had his energy tripped up a notch from the start, Subaru hurried his pace so he wouldn't fall behind Satella, his arms flailing back and forth as he rushed to not be left behind by this girl who kept continuing on toward her goal.

10

Now, Subaru and Satella entered the next stage on the way to completing their task—the slums. And it looked like they were going to have a lot of trouble… That is, until it became clear that an unlikely character would prove themselves very useful; very useful indeed.

"Who, you ask? Me! Yes, me! For some unknown reason, the people here in the slums are really nice to me! Just what unknown variable is responsible for this?! Has my charm stat finally been adjusted?! I haven't felt so loved since I was in preschool!"

Back in preschool, Subaru was quite the cute one. His hair was long and he was often mistaken for a girl. Given the change to his current state only took ten plus a few years. The passage of time really is cruel and unforgiving.

"Has something about me changed from before? Do I, like, have something on my face?"

"Well, you do have your evil-looking eyes, short ears, and flat nose on your face…"

"I could have gone without the evil eyes and flat nose description!" retorted Subaru before hanging his head.

Satella put her finger to her lips and thought. "Hmm... It probably has to do with the way you look and are dressed right now. You're covered in dust and dirt and there are even traces of blood. The people who live here also have it hard, so they must look at you in pity and can't help but be kind to you..."

"Right now you're doing a good job of making me feel as bad as I look! But you're right! It makes perfect sense! Damn it all!"

As they say, people with the same sickness pity each other. While it was great that Subaru seemed to be more likable in the slums in an unexpected way, Satella's likability was at an all-time low. The reason again probably had to do with the way that she was dressed.

"The thugs from before made similar comments, but you really are dressed pretty well, aren't you?"

"I guess I do stand out, don't I...?" replied Satella, looking at Subaru nervously, as she rolled down the sleeves of her white cloak.

However, while she acknowledged the problem with her fine clothes, she seemed to be oblivious to the fact that it wasn't just the clothes, but the person wearing them as well.

"Um, I have something I'd like to ask you, but—"

"What's that? This is no place for you and your fancy clothes to be walking around in, young lady, so go on now, get outta here!"

Again, Satella was brusquely turned away as she tried to ask someone for help. Given that her low rate of success had to do with both her good looks and her fine clothes, rather than twice worse off, it was better to say she was "worse off squared." However, it wasn't as though Subaru could suggest that she get all dirty like he was.

"At least you might be a little better off if you take off your cloak..." Subaru suggested.

"...I know, but..." Satella gripped both shoulders of her cloak with her hands, but would not take it off. Subaru thought that her response was a little bit strange, but he didn't bring it up.

As Satella looked down, she lightly brushed her hand against the red flower decoration pinned on her left breast. Subaru, seeing how

Satella found comfort in that decoration, couldn't help but feel like smiling, and it made him want to try even harder for her sake.

If Satella couldn't do this on her own, he was glad to make use of his dirty appearance to make progress. *I guess this means that good things can come even from getting beat up by a bunch of thugs in an alley,* Subaru thought. "Well, don't worry too much. You can leave this to me. Anyway, with the fruits of my labor, we'll soon have her cornered, so let's keep chasing after that criminal. So yeah, with the fruits of my labor, we'll soon have her cornered! So! Let's…keep…searching!"

"I understand that you're happy to be useful for once, but it's really lame when you put so much emphasis on yourself like that."

Subaru had struck a pose with every pause of his sentence, which he thought was cool, but when Satella put it like that, it just made Subaru seem like he was hopping up and down as if to say, *Look what I can do!*

Satella stared at Subaru with a face that looked like she regretted raising her opinion of him earlier, and Subaru just responded with a weak smile.

It had been little more than two hours since they had met, but with things like this, Subaru already felt as though he had known Satella for a long time. However, this little episode had a different ending than the last few.

"I'm sorry, but I'm already at my limit," said Puck weakly as he leaned up against Satella's neck. His gray coat glowed with a weak light, and his figure blurred as if he were going to disappear at any moment.

"The way you disappear kind of looks like you're dying."

"I tried to stick around longer than usual because I wanted to protect my precious daughter from this evil-eyed guy hanging around her. But when I work myself to the bone, I end up fading away when it's time for me to disappear."

"That's terrible! But leave it to me! I won't let any dangerous guys near her after you disappear!"

"Wait, does that mean it's okay for me to wipe you off the face of the Earth before I disappear?"

"No! Not okay!" shouted Subaru, stepping away and hugging himself.

"I'm joking," said Puck with a small burst of laughter.

After that, Puck looked to Satella, who took from her breast pocket a crystal that was glowing with a green light.

"I'm sorry for pushing you so hard, Puck. I'll do my best from here on out, so you just get some rest."

The green crystal continued to glow with a faint light in Satella's hand as she held it. It looked different from what you might call a jewel. So far as Subaru could tell, "crystal" was the word that fit best.

Puck crawled down Satella's arm and approached the crystal, then reached out and hugged it to its small body. Finally he turned back toward Satella.

"I'm sure you know this already, but be careful, and don't push yourself too hard. If something happens don't hesitate to use your od to call me back out."

"I know, I know. I'm not a child. I can take care of myself."

"I wonder about that... My precious daughter here always makes me worry when it comes to things like this. I'm counting on you, Subaru."

Puck looked at Satella with affection, the way a parent looks at their child. Satella blushed, but also looked annoyed.

With the conversation thrown his way, Subaru beat on his chest. "All right! Just you leave it to me. You can trust my sixth sense. When it sounds the danger alarm, I'll get us out of there in no time!"

"I really don't understand half of what you're saying, but all right. Now with that out of the way, good night. ...Be careful."

With a last glance directed at Satella, Puck finally vanished. His small body became a small ball of light, which gradually melted away into the world around it as he disappeared.

Other than the fact that it was a talking cat, this was the first time Subaru had seen Puck do anything spirit-like. Now, having seen this fantastical display, he felt mixed feelings of excitement and awe welling up inside him.

As Subaru was getting excited all by himself, Satella ran her hands lightly over the crystal and put it carefully back in her breast pocket.

From the conversations that they had before, Subaru thought that crystal must be holding Puck's core right now.

"Now it'll be just the two of us…but don't get any ideas. I can still use magic, you know."

Apparently Satella had taken Puck's last words seriously, and was on her guard.

"Hey, the last time I was alone with a girl was in elementary school. I'm not really capable of doing anything. Haven't you been paying attention to my lack of human skills thus far?"

"You're totally hopeless, but then again, I'm convinced. …All right. Let's keep going. But remember, with Puck gone we need to be even more careful than before."

Perhaps shocked by Subaru's proud proclamation of his cowardice, Satella couldn't seem to keep up her apprehensions of him, and so tied back up the front of her robe and went on ahead.

"I'll be the vanguard, so you just keep your eyes on what's behind us. If anything happens, call me right away. You mustn't think that you can handle everything on your own. I don't want be mean…but you're really weak."

"Well, when you put it that way, it's hard to get angry about it…"

If Satella just wanted to push Subaru away, "You're really weak" would have been enough.

Given that she couldn't hide what she truly felt, Satella was soft at the core…too soft, even.

Subaru nudged Satella along, even though it looked like she wanted to say something, and the two continued their search.

Despite all the talk, their search continued in the same way as before. Their methods were basic. Whenever they found someone, they would describe who they were looking for and asked if the person had any ideas about who it might be.

Subaru, who was now doing all of the asking, had gotten better at it after having talked to so many different people. He was starting to hit his stride.

"You know? It might be that Felt girl. She was blond and really fast, right?"

A little under an hour after they had entered the slums and started asking around, they had finally run into some valuable information.

The guy who gave the information was someone that Subaru had gone straight up to and said, "Hey, my brother, how's life?" like they were already friends.

"If it's Felt you're looking for, whatever she stole is probably sitting in the loot cellar. She usually takes things there, gets them tagged, and then the old man who's the master there'll get them sold at a market somewhere else."

"That sounds like a pretty strange system… Doesn't anyone worry about the master of the cellar taking off with all of the goods?"

"The reason he's the master is because people trust him not to do that. But, well, even if you go up and tell him it's stolen, he'll probably just say 'So what?' right back at you, so you'd better be prepared to negotiate a price to buy it back. After all, it's the original owner's fault for being stupid and getting it stolen in the first place!" the man finished with a laugh.

Subaru was able to get the guy to tell him the location of the loot cellar, so they would probably be able to find it soon, but there was a new problem. Subaru and Satella were both penniless.

"That guy said we should buy it back, but without any leverage, I get the feeling this master guy would wipe the floor with us."

"Why do I have to pay to get back something I already own…?"

As the problem veered back toward their combined lack of funds, Satella looked worried. She had a point, of course, but it wasn't like they could expect the loot cellar's master to agree.

In order to solve the matter peacefully, and with certainty, it would be best to follow that man's advice and try to negotiate. However…

"It seems a little late to be asking this question, but that badge you say was stolen from you…does it happen to look expensive? Even if we walk in expecting to be overcharged, it would be impossible to negotiate without having any idea of what it's worth."

"…It's small, but there is a jewel embedded in its center. I don't know how much money that someone might buy it for, but I am fairly certain it wouldn't be a small amount."

"A jewel, huh… That seems like it's going to be a problem."

Even for people unfamiliar with how much things are worth, a jewel is one of those convenient items that you can tell is expensive at a glance. Subaru doubted that there was the technology to produce imitations in this world, so most things that resembled jewels were probably jewels. In other words, they would all fetch a high price.

While none of this new information sounded like good news, Subaru thought there was something strange about what Satella was saying. Even though the badge was supposedly hers, she said that she did not know its value. While it was possible it was something she might have received from someone else, it stuck in his mind.

"Anyway, let's first just find this loot-cellar place. It is possible that we can negotiate a way to buy it back at a reasonable price…"

In the worst-case scenario, Subaru had one way to secure funds, although he was reluctant to use it. And he didn't want to tell Satella until right before he had to.

As they walked, Subaru and Satella spent the next ten minutes talking about various ways they might be able to take back her badge, but nothing seemed to come together.

Now that they were in front of the place called the "loot cellar," Subaru and Satella looked at each other.

"This place is a lot bigger than I imagined. Just how well can the market for theft be going these days?" Subaru said.

"I understand them calling it a cellar rather than a shed…if this place is filled only with stolen goods… Either way I'm not sure the people here have any hope of salvation," added Satella.

Of course, as the loot cellar existed as a place to hold items until they were sold, it was unlikely it would be filled to the brim. It wasn't a high-storied building, but it was wide enough to the point where it looked as though it could function as living quarters for a large number of people. The building was right up against a tall defensive wall, and was in the deepest part of the slums.

"That tall wall behind the building...is that...?"

"I think it's one of the walls of the city. Which means that we must have come all the way from the city's center to its edge," replied Satella.

Subaru tried to imagine a map of the city in his mind, given what Satella had said. It was likely that the city was built as a square and had walls like this on all four sides. Additionally, either in the center or on the northernmost side there should be a castle, from which these slums would be positioned far away.

Considering that it had been three to four hours since Subaru and Satella had begun their search, the scope of the city seemed to be a little larger than Subaru had originally imagined.

"All right, according to what we've heard, there should be a master in charge of this cellar who handles all of the stolen goods, but...just how exactly do you want to approach this?"

"We're going to be direct and honest. We'll just say, 'We've had something stolen from us, so if you can find it, please return it to us.'"

Subaru tried to explain that that wasn't going to work, but Satella wouldn't listen to him.

At her core, Satella was too direct and honest herself. If something was twisted or bent, she couldn't help but try to set it right. Of course, that was one of the reasons Satella saved Subaru in the first place.

"All right, I got it. But leave this to me."

Because of Satella's personality, Subaru was all too sure things would get complicated if she was the one doing the talking, so Subaru volunteered himself.

His backup plan... Well, it was hard to call it a "backup plan" if he was already considering using it, but if things got complicated before he had the chance to put it into action, that would also be a problem. Subaru had made his decision; he wasn't one to hesitate at times like this.

Satella looked surprised that Subaru wanted to do the talking, and while Subaru was musing on how cute her surprised expression was, he hurried to try to think of a comeback for whatever argument against it Satella would have, but...

"All right. I'll leave it to you."

"Look, I understand that it's hard for you to let me handle something this important, and I'm not stupid enough to think that I've gained your trust, but I've got a plan, so if you'd just trust me this once—Wait. Huh?!"

"W-why are you so surprised?"

"Going by everything that's happened so far, you'd think that this would signal the start of an argument, right? I imagined you'd say something like, 'Do you really expect me to just let a good-for-nothing like you, whose only ability is to convert oxygen into carbon dioxide, handle something this important? Don't make me laugh! I'd expect a dog to do a better job than you!' Then I, while hurt, would use the opportunity to renew my determination!"

"I would never say something that mean!"

As Subaru exposed his exaggerated persecution complex, Satella didn't look all that happy. However, clearing her throat, she fixed her amethyst eyes on Subaru and said, "Of course I would be lying if I said I didn't think that you were holding me back in any way, and just when I think you're finally being serious, to my chagrin you say something completely stupid..."

"'To my chagrin,' huh? I haven't heard that in a while," joked Subaru. He sighed and relaxed his shoulders, unable to argue back.

"Still, even though you act like a jerk sometimes, it was because of you that we were able to keep that little girl from crying, and I don't think you're the kind of person to lie or do anything without thinking about it first," said Satella, looking back over their much-sidetracked journey thus far. "So...I'll trust you. ...If this all works out I might even think that meeting you was all worth it."

"You know, if instead of that last part you had just looked up at me and said, 'Please, do your best for my sake,' I would have been totally pumped up to do this, you know?"

"I can't force myself to say something like that, but... Good luck."

This was a girl who could not bring herself to lie for any reason.

"...All right, I'll give it my best shot," said Subaru, breaking into a smile before heading toward the entrance of the cellar.

The trump card Subaru had, which he wasn't able to tell Satella about, was the one thing out of what he had brought from the previous world that he could really consider worth anything. Because that thing probably didn't otherwise exist in this world, there was a possibility he could use it to barter. Subaru would have liked to avoid doing that, but at the same time he was fairly certain that in this world, Satella's badge couldn't possibly fetch a higher price than his cell phone, and he didn't think he would have another chance in this world to use his cell phone this way.

"Um... Is anybody home? ...Er, wait...the door's open."

A sour, spoiled sort of smell drifted out of the entrance to the loot cellar. Subaru went to knock on the door, but from a gap in it, he saw that it wasn't locked. As he peeked inside, he could only see that it was incredibly dark.

"It's hard when there's not any kind of light... Well, considering the purpose of the place, I suppose it makes sense, and it even serves as a metaphor for the dark feeling of guilt in doing dirty business."

Subaru stuck his head inside and tried to look around, but not even the light from the moon reached this place in the deepest part of the slums. He couldn't see an inch in front of his face.

As Subaru prepared to go inside, he turned around to Satella. "I didn't hear anyone answer me, but I'm going to go ahead and go inside, so can you please keep watch?"

"Are you sure? Wouldn't it be better for me to go instead...?"

"If on the off chance someone ambushes us and you're the one taken out, then it's all over. If I'm the one attacked, you'll be able both to help me, and to strike back. This is the most reasonable way to do this, so please let's just go with my plan, okay?"

Satella considered Subaru's plan. After a few moments of silence, she took out of her breast pocket a white crystal, which suddenly shone with a white light.

"At least take a light. And call me in whether someone's there or not."

"I know, I know. Puck told us to be careful, so I'll be careful. This is really useful, by the way."

"You can find lagmite ore just about anywhere. You really are ignorant, aren't you, Subaru," said Satella, unable to contain her shock, as she handed Subaru the lagmite ore. The crystal gave off a faint warmth along with its light, which was about as much illumination as you could expect from a candle.

"Okay, well then, I'll go take a look. I don't think I'll be gone too long, but you can go ahead and eat without me."

"Oh, stop being so stupid. Be careful, okay?"

"Gotcha. Also, Satella? Don't come in until I call for you—got it?"

The courage that Subaru had been building up to prepare himself to enter the cellar had pushed him just enough to say her name. Up until now, he had felt too embarrassed to say it, and had hesitated. After clenching his fist together, excited he was able to finally say it, he looked back at Satella.

"…What's wrong?"

Satella was looking at Subaru frozen, with her eyes open wide. This reaction was far different from any that Subaru expected, and so he tilted his head in confusion.

"I'm sorry… It's nothing. Once we get my badge back, I'll apologize properly."

"I don't know what you're planning on apologizing for, but I'd rather hear a 'thank you' instead. It would be even better if that thank-you came along with a smile."

"You dummy."

As those two words came out of her mouth, Satella made a little bit of a smile, which Subaru made sure to burn into his memory. Even with his stupid jokes, Subaru was at last able to make her smile.

If all of this turned out well, he would like to see that smile again, in a brighter place.

"All right. Will it be a snake or a demon that pops out this time? Given the fantasy setting, neither option is one I can just laugh off…" Subaru joked to himself, and with lagmite in hand, he carefully made his way into the cellar.

In the dim light, Subaru could make out a counter in front of him, across from the entrance. The building must have originally been something like an inn. It looked as though they were using the first-floor bar area without any major changes. On top of as well as behind the counter—which was probably serving as something like a reception desk—Subaru could see a lot of different items cluttered close together. There were small boxes and pots, swords and cheap metallic objects, and many other varied items. It was clear that all of these were stolen items, based on the wooden tags that were attached to all of them.

"The way the system works, if you rounded up all of these wooden tags and handed them to the guards, it looks like they could arrest everyone at once..."

However, as was usual with this line of business, there were probably some connections between this place and the not-so-upstanding citizens who offered support. Subaru was suspicious of where most of these stolen items ended up.

Subaru ventured farther into the cellar, looking for Satella's badge. But just then...

"Hmm?"

Subaru suddenly stopped, feeling something strange under the soles of his shoes. It didn't feel like he had stepped on something hard; it was actually the opposite. Like the ground he had stepped on was clinging to him; like there was something sticky on his shoes.

He raised his foot, and touched the bottom of his sneakers. He felt some sort of fluid, something strangely sticky that clung to his fingers, stretching as he pulled them away. It was something that instinctually made him feel uneasy.

"What is this...?"

Subaru brought his fingers close to his nose and tried to smell it, but because of the stagnant air inside the building mixing with it, he couldn't quite pin it down. Unsurprisingly, he didn't have the courage to try tasting it.

After wiping the rest of the substance on the nearest wall, Subaru, urged on by a feeling of unpleasant dread, put the lagmite out in front of him and started forward. Then, he found the source of the slime.

"...Wha?"

Subaru unconsciously let out a foolish sound as he looked on. In the small visible range of his light, what he first saw lying limp on the ground was an arm. Its hand's fingers were reaching out as if to grab something, but the other end of the arm, at the elbow, was missing the body it should have been connected to.

Moving his light and following along the axis of the arm, Subaru saw a leg farther on ahead—a leg attached to a body. With the exception of one arm, that body had all of its other parts, though the throat area was cut wide open. It was the corpse of a large old man.

"Eek!" Subaru squealed pointlessly as he realized what he was looking at.

At that moment, Subaru's mind had blanked out. His thought processes had completely left him, and his hands and feet had frozen in place.

There was a pause, and then...

"...Well, you found it. That's just too bad. Now I have no choice, yes, no choice at all."

Subaru thought that it was the voice of a woman. The voice was low and cold, the voice of a woman who seemed somewhat to be having fun.

"Gwah!"

Subaru didn't have the opportunity to turn around. As soon as he turned to face the voice, his body was blown away by an incredible force. He hit his back against the wall, and on impact let go of his lagmite, and darkness closed in as it tumbled into the distance.

But Subaru wasn't thinking about that. What now ruled over his consciousness was...

"Gu...it's...h-hot."

A *heat* assaulted Subaru Natsuki and completely overwhelmed him.

—*This is really, really not good.*

Feeling the hard texture of the ground against his face, he realized that he had fallen facedown on the ground. He couldn't move, even when he tried, and he already couldn't feel his fingers. What he did feel was heat, and it overwhelmed his entire body.

He coughed and vomited the blood he felt rising in his throat—the source of his waning life. So much came out that it frothed at the edges of his mouth. With his hazy vision, he could see the ground in front of him stained red.

—You've…got to be kidding me… All of this is mine?

Feeling as though all of the blood in his body had spilled out of him, he reached a shaking hand to try to find the source of the heat that was burning through his body. As his fingertips reached the large cut in his stomach, he understood.

No wonder it felt so hot. His brain must have been mistaking pain for heat. The clean cut that ran through his torso was so deep it had almost cut him in half. Only bits of skin were still holding him together.

In other words, he had run right into a checkmate in the chess game of his life. As soon as he realized that, his consciousness immediately began to fall away from him.

Now, even the heat that had been ravaging him disappeared, and the unpleasant feeling of touching his own blood and organs vanished as his consciousness continued to fade. The only thing left behind was his body, which refused to follow his soul.

Right before his eyes, he saw a black boot step down and make ripples in the red carpet of his fresh blood.

Someone was there, and that someone…was probably the one who killed him.

But he didn't even think to look that person in the face. It didn't matter anymore.

—The only thing he did wish for was that she, at least, she would be safe.

"—baru?"

He felt as if he heard a voice that rang like bells. That he heard that voice, that he *could* hear that voice, felt like salvation to him more than anything else, so—

"!"

With a short scream, someone else fell upon the carpet of blood.

She fell right beside him. There he was, weakly attempting to reach her.

Her white hand fell, powerless. He lightly grasped it in his own bloodstained grip.

He felt the fingers of her hand move slightly to grasp his own.

"Just you wait..."

He seized his fading consciousness, pulling it desperately back around to buy a bit more time.

"I'm going to..."

—*find a way to save you.*

In the next instant, he—Subaru Natsuki—lost his life.

CHAPTER 2
A STRUGGLE TOO LATE

1

"…What's wrong, my man? You're staring off into space."

"…Huh?"

When a man with a white scar across his stern face spoke to Subaru, that's all he could respond with.

The man with the scar twisted his face.

"Look, I'm asking you what you're going to do! Are you going to buy that abble or not?!"

"…Huh?"

"An abble! You want to eat one, right? You started talking to me, and then you suddenly stopped and stared off into space! I almost freaked out! …So, what'll it be?"

The muscular, scar-faced man, put a round, cute-looking red fruit into the palm of Subaru's hand. Whatever it was, it looked almost exactly like an apple.

After Subaru looked at the fruit and then back at the man's face, he said, "No—I mean, didn't I tell you already? I'm forever and ever-lastingly broke."

"You kidding me?! I've had enough of you wasting my time. Get outta here! I've got a job to do. I don't have time to deal with your nonsense."

The man annoyedly pushed Subaru aside and went across to another part of the shop.

Subaru continued to look around, puzzled. "Huh? What? What's going on?"

He was so flustered, it was a miracle he was even able to get a sentence out as he tossed his questions around.

2

The main road was full of people as always, and apart from the lizard carts that would pass by, the full width of the street was filled with pedestrians.

It was still at a time when the day was bright. It wasn't as though it was really hot outside, but it would be enough to make you think that the wolflike half-humans walking around in their fur coats must be sweating.

"But this is totally not the time to be reflecting on the state of the setting!"

Subaru held his head in his hands and twisted about, and his strange poses of distress were enough to gather curious glances from all around. However, now, Subaru really didn't have the capacity to worry about that.

"After all…it was just night a minute ago, wasn't it?"

The sun was high in the sky. At the very least, according to what Subaru had sensed, it should already be night.

The night flipped immediately from night to noon. The change was so sudden it reminded Subaru of when he was summoned to this world in the first place. However, that and this were under completely different conditions.

"My stomach…isn't cut open, is it?" Subaru lifted up the top of his tracksuit and looked at his stomach.

Earlier, it had been cut open with what must have been a large blade, and he had bled so much that he was sure he was going to die.

However, not only was the wound not there, there were not even any traces of blood. Actually, Subaru's beloved tracksuit wasn't even dirty.

The convenience store bag he held in his hand was also as full as it had ever been, and his cell phone and wallet were where they should be.

In every sense of the phrase, he was back to square one.

—It was enough to make him feel like he was going crazy.

Realizing there were gaps in his memory, Subaru tried to think of what happened right before he had lost consciousness.

His stomach had been cut open and he was moments from being killed. He thought that he had heard a woman's voice. He had found a corpse in the loot cellar, and the person who probably had killed that man attacked Subaru.

In that state of near death...

"...That's right! Satella!"

Satella, who must have been worried about Subaru and entered the building, had also been cut down by the same weapon that took him out.

As soon as Subaru realized that, he felt his innards twisting in pain. The feeling of guilt was even stronger than the feeling of pain he had felt when he himself was attacked.

"Wasn't I told to take care of Satella?!"

Subaru thought back to Puck's words right before he disappeared.

The promise Subaru made with that cat certainly wasn't a joke. Despite the fact that there were at least three times he should have turned back, he had missed every opportunity to do so.

Satella had told him as well. If anything happened he was to call her. He didn't even do that.

"Am I an idiot? Well, of course I am. I don't even have time to just hang my head depressed like this. I've got to go find Satella and Puck..."

Both of them might be dead. When that thought crossed his mind, Subaru shook his head to brush it away.

Subaru didn't have any positive qualities, and he couldn't make himself useful at all. He was something like a mob character, or at best the comic relief character, and yet he was still alive.

If that were the case, there was no way that good-natured Satella, who could use magic and wasn't honest with herself but was true to her ideals, or that aloof weirdo spirit cat could be dead.

At the very least, he didn't want them to be.

"At any rate, I've got to go back to the loot cellar..."

Since that was the last place he was in before his consciousness was cut off, there must be some kind of hint left there.

As soon as he thought of that, Subaru moved to act. This was where his quick decision-making could shine. In the previous world, most of that was used in decisions like "I'm not going to school today," but right now it was important for him to act quickly and cut off all his doubts.

However, as soon as Subaru had made his decision and was ready to go...

"Hey, kiddo. How about let's have some fun."

Subaru unfortunately had his path from the alley cut off by three men. When Subaru looked at who had talked to him, he couldn't help but gape.

"Hey, what's with the stupid look on yer face?"

"I bet he doesn't realize the mess he's gotten himself into. How 'bout we tell 'im?" said another man in the group mocking Subaru, as they smiled with sinister smiles.

After staring at the men for a little longer, Subaru felt as though he was being forced to watch a farce.

There were three men. Even if you were trying to be nice, you couldn't call them well put together. Their bad personalities and bad upbringings just seeped out of them. They were classic thugs.

With all of this, Subaru was feeling an incredible sense of déjà vu.

"Did all of you guys hit your heads on something while I wasn't looking?"

These were the same guys who had served as the reason for Subaru and Satella's meeting just hours before.

Sure, they were nothing more than mob characters, but it was hard to imagine that three other guys with the exact same faces were doing the exact same thing.

"In other words, now that you've found me alone, you want to get revenge…is that it? I understand that you want to kick me when I'm down, but this is really not the time for me to be dealing with you. You guys…"

"What the hell are you babbling about? Have you lost your mind or something?"

Subaru had wanted to just talk his way out of this, peacefully, but given the way these guys were acting, even Subaru was starting to get ticked off. The only reason that he wanted to solve the issue peacefully in the first place was because he was in a hurry. Normally, Subaru had a pretty short fuse.

"Now listen here, kiddo. If you just put down everything you've got and walk away, we'll let you go."

"Ah, is that right? Everything I've got. Gotcha. I'm in a hurry, so that's fine with me, really."

"But you've got to get down on all fours and act like a dog first! Say, 'Save me, save me, please!' too!"

"All right, I've had it with you idiots!" They just had to push it too far, didn't they? Subaru had already lost it.

The men weren't prepared for Subaru's sudden change of attitude, and were shaking. Of the three, as they stood dumbfounded, Subaru picked the skinniest of the group to hit first. It was the one who had the knife, the source of Subaru's defeat before.

"You're first! Guys like you who don't know the preciousness of life can go to hell!"

Subaru landed an uppercut on the man's jaw with all his strength, and then threw a punch into his open abdomen. The man slammed against the wall and was out like a light. Subaru immediately moved to trip the next man beside him.

Unable to react, the kick landed and the man fell over. As soon as he was down, Subaru tackled the remaining man. His tackle aimed low, and with the force of it he was able to carry the man and slam him into the wall.

After the man lost his breath from the impact of his back against the wall, Subaru landed another kick to finish him.

Subaru then turned around to the man he had just tripped and motioned him with his hand.

"Now it's one-on-one! Come at me with all you've got!"

"Who're you to act all fair and square with that surprise attack?! You little punk!"

The man ran at Subaru and grabbed his collar, trying to push him into the wall.

"Not good enough!" Subaru yelled, and took hold of both of the man's wrists and pulled them away. Looking at the startled man's face, Subaru's expression twisted into a fiendish smile. "Don't underestimate the free time of a truant! I spent so much time swinging around a sword because I didn't have anything better to do that my grip strength is over seventy kilograms of force! I can bench eighty kilos, too!"

The man cried out as Subaru crushed his wrists, and as soon as he had broken his stance, Subaru struck him with his elbow, and the thug cried out.

As Subaru spun around behind him and put his arms around his waist he said, "If I accidentally kill you, don't hate me too much for this, but I've always wanted to try doing a suplex on someone without mats!"

Subaru lifted the man up part of the way and then threw him backward. Unable to react, the thug's head collided with the wall behind them and he slumped to the ground, unmoving.

After making sure the other two men were silent, Subaru walked over to the first man he hit, the one with the knife.

Although the man had comparatively taken little damage, you could see that he was sweating. As Subaru came closer he tried to pull out his knife. But as he did, Subaru kicked him relentlessly in the face. He was out.

"Hmph! Well that was easy! In this world, evil never triumphs!" said Subaru Natsuki as he struck a pose to celebrate his victory.

After checking for sure that none of the men had actually died, Subaru immediately left the alley.

"Even with this, it's not like the situation has gotten any better. I've got to hurry to the loot cellar."

Subaru noticed as he was leaving that there were onlookers who were wowing and gasping in surprise that he had left the alley unscathed.

If you realized I was back there, then you should have gone to the guards! Subaru thought as he held back the urge to lecture them. Right now he couldn't let any minute go to waste.

3

After having enacted his revenge back in the alley, Subaru headed toward the deepest part of the slums, and when he arrived at the entrance to the loot cellar, the sun had already moved far across the sky.

"F-finally...finally I've found it. ...It sure took me a long time, damn," said Subaru, wiping the sweat from his brow, and slumping down to rest.

He had spent nearly two hours running around before he finally had reached his destination.

"I was just here, so I thought I would be able to find it again without getting lost, but..."

Probably the biggest problem was that Subaru couldn't read any of the signs. Additionally, it wasn't as if he could mention the name "loot cellar" outside of the slums, so he had to rely completely on his memory.

"Last time we came here I was talking with Satella, and my eyes were on her most of the time, so I guess it's no surprise I don't remember the way very well, damn it," said Subaru as he continued to drip with sweat.

However, the greatest sin Subaru had to face was now right in front of him. While he was doing his best to ignore it by talking to himself, his heart wouldn't be fooled. It started to beat louder and louder as his pulse quickened, and Subaru felt his hands grow heavy. His mouth felt dry and his ears were ringing again and again inside his head as though someone was hitting him.

The answers that Subaru sought were inside that loot cellar.

For an instant, Subaru had a flashback as he closed his eyes: the old man's corpse, his own sliced-open abdomen, and the figure of Satella, whom he had dragged into all of this.

"Don't be scared. Don't be scared. Don't be scared. Are you an idiot? ...Well, of course I am, but do you think I'm really going to come all this way and then go back empty-handed?"

Of course, it wasn't as though Subaru had any place to return to. Right now, this was the only place that he could cling to.

Finding his determination and facing forward, Subaru realized that his knees were shaking as he tried to walk. He slapped his legs to calm himself down and after a deep breath he finally moved forward.

In the orange light of the early evening, the rough door to the loot cellar looked as though it was wordlessly rejecting him.

"Is there anyone home?"

After pushing away these negative feelings, Subaru knocked on the door and raised his voice.

The dull sound rang out, but there was no answer. With uncomfortable silence as his only answer, Subaru became frightened by that very silence and knocked harder on the door.

"Someone... I know there's someone in there! Come on, answer me! ...Please."

Clinging to a fleeting sense of hope, hoping and praying that what was happening right before him was somehow a mistake, he beat harder. Unable to take the force of Subaru's sudden desperation, the door began to creak and its hinges started to bend, and then...

"Cut it out already! What are you doing, trying to break the door down just because you don't know the password?!"

The door was suddenly opened with a great force, and Subaru, who had been leaning up against it, was thrown back.

Subaru was thrown about five meters from the entrance to the cellar, where he rolled a few times and then looked up, completely startled. At the end of Subaru's gaze was a giant, red-faced, bald old man.

The man had ragged clothes that covered his muscular body, and the red light of the setting sun shone on his polished bald head. In other words, it was a giant, very energetic-looking old geezer.

"Who are you, boy?! I've not seen you around here before! How did you know where to find this place? How did you get here? Who told you?!"

With astonishing speed, the old man closed the distance between him and Subaru and lifted Subaru up by the collar.

Feeling his feet leave the ground, Subaru very quickly learned his place. Subaru had thought that in most circumstances he could win in a fight, but these were not ordinary circumstances. As he was held up by this six- or seven-foot-tall old man, Subaru lost all desire to resist.

"My name is Natsuki Subaru, the ever-busy and never-free wandering vagrant...... For now at least, would you be so kind as to put me down? Let's talk with both our feet on the ground," Subaru added, giving it his all just to squeeze out that indirect request.

4

While his violent first encounter in the place had left a terrible first impression, in the end, Subaru was let in to the loot cellar.

Subaru had described the man from whom he'd first gotten information about the loot cellar, and told the giant old man that he was the one who introduced him to the place.

In front of the counter that was facing the front door, Subaru sat on a fixed chair meant for visitors and shifted uncomfortably. There were splinters sticking up out of the seat, and they kept poking him in the rear. If he'd had to go to the bathroom, those splinters could have been the trigger to make him pop.

"Why do you keep moving about like that? Are you that concerned about where your balls are?"

"Of course not. My boys are just fine. But, really? That's the first thing that comes out of your mouth in this situation?"

"Giant" was the best way to describe the old man, since he wasn't just tall, and he looked cramped as he bent down behind the counter. When he came back up, he had a bottle of liquor in his hand, and after pouring himself a glass, brought it to his lips.

"Well, you interrupted my drinking time. I hope you have a good reason for coming here. If not, that's just terrible."

"The sun's just started to set and you're already drinking? You're going to die an early death if you keep that up." With that retort, Subaru, holding his chin up with his hand and elbow on the counter, took a quick look around the inside of the loot cellar.

There was not a single trace of the tragedy that Subaru had witnessed the previous evening he had been here. As he looked at all of the various stolen items strewn about the room, he couldn't tell whether they were organized in some way or not.

The old man noticed Subaru looking about, and narrowed his eyes in a knowing way.

"So, kid, are you interested in some of these goods?" he said, striking right away at the heart of the matter. The giant old man, who had given his name as "Rom," smiled as he poured himself another shot of liquor into his dirty glass. "There are really only two reasons that people come to this place: they're either bringing something in they stole, or they have some business with the stolen items themselves."

"...Well, one of those is one of the reasons I'm here."

"One of the reasons...huh. So that means you've got some other business being here?" Rom raised one of his eyebrows as Subaru gave a conditional agreement.

Subaru nodded, and then, reluctantly, knowing full well that he probably wasn't going to be taken seriously, said, "This may sound a bit odd, but... Old man, have you...uh, died recently?"

Subaru decided not to add in the details about the decapitated arm or sliced throat.

Old Man Rom opened his gray eyes wide for a few moments

before; as if to signal time starting back up again, he broke into a laugh.

"Ga-ha-ha-ha! I was wondering what you were going to say! Now I may be an old man with not much time left to live, but too bad, I haven't died yet! I suppose when you get to this age, I don't imagine it being that far off, though."

Apparently, Rom took Subaru's question as some kind of edgy joke, and took out another glass for Subaru. "Want a drink?"

Subaru refused the alcohol with a hand signal, followed up by a "Sorry, not right now."

Subaru had managed to get his first question out, but the others inside him were multiplying.

The corpse that Subaru had seen in the loot cellar...there was no question about it. It was definitely the corpse of the old man who was sitting in front of him right now.

Sure, it was dark, and it was the first time Subaru had ever seen a corpse, so it wasn't as though he'd been in a perfect state of mind. However, this old man had so many characteristic features about him, Subaru couldn't imagine mistaking him for someone else.

But Subaru could turn the question he just asked on himself. He, too, had been inflicted with mortal wounds as well.

Subaru started to think that it had somehow been all a dream. He wasn't sure he could trust what was inside his own head.

Was all of what happened here really a dream? If it was, then how much of it was a dream, and why am I here in the first place?

The burning pain Subaru had felt, the warmth he felt from that girl's touch, the overwhelming pangs of guilt...if they were all just some leftover traces of a dream, then why was he here right now?

It would make more sense to say that everything since he'd been summoned to this world in the first place was a dream.

"Rom, have you seen a silver-haired girl around here lately?"

"Silver hair...? No, I can't say I have. Silver hair's one of those things that stands out in a bad way, too, so even if my memory's starting to fail me, I don't think I would have forgotten if I saw someone like that," said Rom, following up with a laugh.

But that didn't make Subaru feel any better.

Rom must have noticed the seriousness in Subaru's expression, because he wiped his own smile away and said, "Drink," putting a glass in front of Subaru again.

Rom tilted the glass and filled it up full with an amber-colored liquid. Seeing that Subaru did nothing but stare silently at the glass, once more he said, "Drink."

"I'm sorry, but I don't feel up to it right now. Plus, I'm not so much a little kid that I want to drink to act like I'm cool."

"What are you talking about? Drinking and acting up is exactly what kids like you are supposed to do! So go ahead and take a big gulp and burn up your insides. When you do that you'll be able to cough up a bunch of things you've got stuck inside because they won't be able to take the heat. So drink!" said Rom a third time, pushing the glass on Subaru.

Overpowered by his attitude, Subaru took the glass in his hand and brought the amber liquid to his nose. A strong smell of alcohol struck the inside of his nose and Subaru's face twisted as he almost started coughing.

However, despite all of Subaru's resistance, there was a part of him that wanted to do as Rom said. Subaru had thought that drowning one's troubles in alcohol was the mark of a lame adult, but…

"All right…here goes!"

Subaru tilted the glass and drank all of it in one gulp. Immediately his esophagus began to scream as it was burned. Subaru slammed his glass on the counter.

"Argh! Gah! That's terrible! It's hot! It's so bad! Ugh! Disgusting!"

"You don't have to say it that many times! Come on! You're going to lose out on half of the fun in life if you can't understand how good liquor tastes!"

As Subaru spewed out comments along with the heat from the liquor, Rom yelled at him and drank again. This time he took the whole bottle up and gulped from it.

After drinking about three times as much as Subaru just had, Rom gave a mighty burp and smiled.

"But still, you should be proud of yourself! That was good form there! So how about it? Do you feel like letting any of that stuff inside you out now?"

"...Yeah! Just a little! Old man, it's time for me to take care of that one other reason I'm here!"

Turning the old man's smile back with a wicked smile of his own, Subaru wiped his mouth with his sleeve and pointed into the back of the cellar, where it looked like most of the stolen articles of value were concentrated.

Rom's face took on an air of seriousness, and Subaru told him directly.

"I'm looking for a badge that's got a jewel embedded in it, and I want you to let me have it."

This was Subaru's original goal. Other than confirming Satella's safety, it was the main reason he was here: to retrieve the thing so important to Satella that she would face danger just to get it back.

Even while Subaru still felt insecure about the state of Satella's well-being, he thought that if he could at least get a handle on the state of the badge, he would have a clue toward finding her.

After Subaru had stated his goal with all of his emotions thrown behind his words, Rom made a difficult expression on his face before replying. "A badge with a jewel... I'm sorry, but no one's brought in anything like that."

"...Really? Think long and hard about it—you sure you're not going senile yet?"

"If I can't remember when I'm at my best with liquor running through me, then I really have to say I don't know. However..."

Just as the last thread of Subaru's hope was about to be cut, Rom gave him a sly grin.

"Someone's made plans with me to bring something in later today. I'm told it's something valuable, too, so it might just be the thing you're looking for."

"Is the person bringing it in, by chance...a girl named Felt?"

"That's exactly the case, but...what? You actually know the name of the thief who took it?"

Subaru couldn't help but strike a victory pose.

Just as he'd thought he had lost all of his leads, things had connected once again. Felt's name had just come up. Felt, the name of the girl who had supposedly taken Satella's badge. If that were the case, Felt's existence would prove Satella's existence. At the very least, Subaru would be able to be sure that Satella wasn't some figment of his imagination.

"I was just about to think that my love of silver-haired heroines had made me delusional..."

"I'm sorry to interrupt your strange sense of relief there, but you don't have any guarantee that you'll be able to buy back the item, even if she brings it here. If it's got a jewel embedded in it, it's going to fetch a high price."

"Ha! You can look around at me all you want, but I'm sorry. I've got nothing! I am eternally and peerlessly penniless!"

"Then you're out of luck!" Rom yelled back, taken by surprise.

But just as he did that, Subaru lifted up a finger in front of his face and waved it back and forth. "Tsk-tsk-tsk. It's true, I may not have any money. However! In this world, you do not necessarily need money to obtain things. There's this wonderful system called 'barter'—haven't you heard?"

Rom didn't argue back, he just nodded in silence, egging Subaru on. Subaru dug around in his pants pocket, and in his hand when he took it out was...

"...What's that? It's the first time I've ever seen anything like it."

"This object that I now raise up is fantastic magical item that can be used to freeze any object in time! It is called a 'cell phone'!"

It was a compact-size, white-colored, thin-model cell phone. As Rom looked on amazed at this mysterious item he had never seen before, Subaru quickly moved his fingers and a moment later a white light flashed in the darkness inside the building.

As a loud shutter sound rang out along with the flash, Rom fell back behind the counter. It was such an exaggerated reaction that Subaru couldn't help but laugh, but Rom was obviously mad.

"What are you doing?! Are you trying to kill me?! Don't think you can fool me with your funny moves!"

"Wait, wait, calm down. Take a deep breath, relax, and come over here and take a look."

Rom was still red in the face, and it wasn't because he had been drinking, but nevertheless Subaru held out his cell phone in front of him. After a doubtful look at Subaru, his eyes opened wide as he looked at what was in front of him.

"This is…this is my face. How did you do that?"

"I told you, didn't I? This is a fantastic item that cuts out a piece of time and freezes it. Using this item, I cut out a bit of your time, just before now, and sealed it within this device."

Then, Subaru changed the direction of the camera and pointed it at himself, and took another picture. When he showed the screen to Rom again, it showed Subaru making a peace sign.

"It cuts out little pieces of time, just like that. So how about it? Pretty rare, huh?"

"I can't get terribly excited about that lame pose of yours, but this really is…hmm…"

After insulting Subaru's pose, Rom looked very intensely at the cell phone. Subaru made a fist and squeezed it, emboldened by the fact that Rom seemed more interested than he expected.

"This is my first time seeing one of these, but…basically, this is a metia, isn't it?"

"A metia?" Subaru was about to say, "It's just a flip phone," but caught himself. Rom nodded again.

"It's what you call things you can use to do magic without opening up a gate, like magic users do. That said, they're mostly used as gifts rather than tools…"

So magic items were called "metia." Subaru nodded, thinking the word fit pretty well. Rom, who had continued to look closely at the cell phone, finally put it back on the counter.

"I'm not sure I can put a definite price on this. I've worked here in the loot cellar for a very long time, but this is my first time handling any metia. ...I can say, though, that it certainly would sell at a high price."

It seemed that rare items commanded attention in any business, even for those working the black market. Rom's voice had quickened in excitement, and he rubbed the tip of his chin as he looked down at Subaru.

"To be honest, even if it has a jewel embedded it in, exchanging something like this for a purely decorative item really puts you at a loss. You'd be better off trading it for something more expensive... Well, really, you can't compare it to any of this stolen junk I have here."

For someone involved in illegal activities, it was strange for Rom to give him such a kind warning, and Subaru responded with a weak smile. To anyone else, what Subaru was trying to do must seem stupid.

"No, it's all right. I'll exchange this metia for the badge that Felt brings in."

"Why would you go so far to do that? Is that badge really worth more than this metia? Or are you saying that it's worth more than money can buy?" asked Rom, unable to come to terms with Subaru's decision.

Honestly, if Subaru was in the same position as Rom, he thought he might have said the same thing.

"Well... Actually, I haven't seen the badge myself yet, but I don't think that it could be worth more in money than this cell phone, and I'm sure I'm going to be taking a loss."

"If you understand all of that, why do you want to go through with it?"

"Isn't it obvious? I want to take a loss."

Rom blinked a few times at Subaru, but at the same time Subaru felt a sense of exhilaration, because this...this was his answer.

"I want to pay someone back. I'm someone who always feels like they have to return a favor. I'm one of those modern kids who can't handle the feeling of being indebted to someone. I wouldn't be able to sleep at night. So, even if I have to take a big loss, I'm going to take back that badge."

"Hmm... So, it sounds like this badge isn't actually yours... Is that right?"

"It belongs to a beautiful silver-haired girl who saved my life. I don't understand why, but it's very precious to her."

"But what about that person who saved you? Why isn't she here?"

"I'm currently looking for her! Actually, right now I'm not even sure she's not a figment of my imagination that I created because I was feeling down!"

Subaru gripped his fist and laughed off his previous anxiety by putting it into words.

Subaru was going to get this badge back, and then once again meet that girl. He wanted to see her smile.

"You're quite the idiot, aren't you?" laughed Rom as he looked on at Subaru and his determination.

5

After having gotten through the first round of negotiations, Subaru spent the next while chatting with Old Man Rom. Given how interested Rom seemed to be in the metia, Subaru mused to himself that gadgets were something men were fond of, no matter what world you were in.

"Whether it be your clothes or this, you've really got a lot of strange stuff on you, don't you? I mean, these things here are delicious!"

"I know, right? Hey, wait! I thought you said a bite! Those are my corn chips! That's the last food I had on me!"

"Oh don't be so stingy. If you keep something as tasty as this all to yourself, you're gonna fall straight to hell, I tell ya."

"Oh and you won't, for eating all them yourself?! Blaming others while you're doing the same yourself is a really bad habit of you baby boomers... I said, stop eating those!"

Subaru thought he was just being kind by sharing some of his snacks, but after seeing them all get eaten like this, he sure did regret it. As he put his empty snack bags back in his convenience store bag, he was close to tears.

By the time they both heard a knock on the door, it was already quite close to sunset.

It was just as Subaru was starting to doze off, and when he looked up, he saw Rom move his giant body lightly toward the door.

After quietly putting one ear against it, Rom whispered.

"To the giant rats...?"

"We give poison."

"To the great white whale...?"

"We lend a fishing hook."

"To our most honorable great dragon...?"

"We say, 'Burn in hell!'"

To each of Rom's short questions came a curt answer. Along with the special knock, those had to be passwords. Satisfied with the answers, Rom unlocked the door.

"Sorry I took so long, Old Man Rom. I had someone really persistent on my tail, and it took me a long time to lose 'em." With a friendly tone in her voice, a young girl slipped past Rom, bragging of her exploits.

The girl's blond hair was semi-long, and her eyes were red like a rabbit's. From the side of her mouth peeked a mischievous canine tooth. The clothes she was wearing looked easy to move in, but they were in tatters.

Subaru stood up without thinking, causing a clatter. The girl immediately looked his way and wiped the smile from her face.

"Who's this? Hey, Rom. I told you I was going to bring something big, so I didn't want anyone to be here, didn't I?"

"I understand how you feel, but that uh...kiddo there has some business with you, Felt, and it's not completely unrelated to that 'big thing' you said you were bringing in."

Rom's answer only made Felt more suspicious. By the way she was unconsciously drawing her hand close to her chest, it appeared that that's where she was holding the badge. Felt continued to be on her guard as she looked at Subaru.

"What's with that guy? You didn't sell me out, did you, Rom?"

"Just how long do you think we've been working together? I'd

never do anything like that. The only reason he's here is because I think that he's got an offer for you that ain't too bad." Rom winked at Subaru, "Right?"

While feeling disgusted at being winked at by an old man, Subaru cleared his throat to help dispel his nervousness and, ignoring Rom's continued gaze, turned to face Felt.

"You don't have to be so nervous. Why don't you just sit down and have a glass of milk first?"

"Stop it with that stupid face of yours. I can tell you don't know what you're doing... Look, I don't know what you're scheming, but I'm not interested in anything you have to say, unless I'm sure it means more money for me. So go ahead and get straight to the point."

Felt's reaction was cold. Subaru's shoulders fell at how bad his first impression went by, but...

"I begged this old man here to give me some time to talk to you, but...my business is actually with that jeweled badge you have hidden away in your pocket there."

The girl raised her eyebrows along with the level of her caution. Subaru knew not only about her theft, but exactly what she stole. But Subaru raised both of his hands in front of her, trying to calm her down. "I'm not planning on doing anything. I've only come here to talk. That is, to negotiate."

Subaru then, with his two hands still in the air, pointed down at a small table near the counter.

"Let's aim for a result where both of us come out on top. In other words, a win-win situation."

After a short pause, Felt nodded, and both sat down on either side of the small table.

Rom then poured two glasses of milk and set both in front of them.

"I'll give you the place and this milk, but you're on your own when it comes to negotiating."

"Don't worry, I've come here prepared to have everything taken from me. Just watch me as I lose it all," said Subaru, punching his fist into his other hand as if he was bragging, about to enter a fight, though saying nothing to be proud of.

Rom snorted, but Felt, who had already begun to drink her milk, twisted her face.

"Hey, Rom. You haven't watered this milk down, have you? It tastes terrible!"

"Why does everybody have to insult the drinks?! I'm showing you some kindness here…!" said Rom before taking his giant hand and rustling Felt's hair.

Subaru thought it looked as though Rom was going to tear Felt's head off, but it was clear from Rom's face that he meant no harm and was just patting her head like any old man would his grand-child. Plus, Felt looked used to it.

"You two look closer than I thought you would be. I'm getting lonely over here all by myself."

"Don't say something wimpy like that when you've got a face that looks just as awful as this old man's."

"I've had my face insulted before, but really? As bad as this guy?! Come on!" yelled Subaru, shocked as he looked back up at Rom's bald head and was stricken with horror.

While Subaru didn't have the most handsome features and was often mistaken for some kind of thug, he didn't think they were so bad as to be compared with this six-foot-tall giant of an old man.

"…You're right. Sorry about that, I went too far," replied Felt.

"Here's where I'd want to say that, to make it up to me, I'd like you to call me 'big brother' in a cute voice for the rest of the discussion, but I'll go ahead and forgive you for now. You've got to be careful so you don't say anything too hurtful, or… Rom, what's wrong?"

"I'm really beginning to think you two have teamed up together just to come in here and make me angry…" Rom was smiling, but a vein was popping out of his forehead. Subaru and Felt looked at each other and shrugged their shoulders.

Rom let out a deep sigh. "Just when I thought Felt had made a new acquaintance around her age, you turn out to be just as twisted as the others."

"…Rom, please. I know you think you're helping, but I'm going to ask you to stop saying such embarrassing things," said Felt.

"Plus, 'around her age'…? Although I suppose from your perspective everyone else looks like they're in the same age group."

Subaru took another look at Felt, but even taking into account the fact that she was probably thinner than she should have been, she looked about twelve or thirteen. If you wanted to give her the benefit of the doubt and stretch your imagination, she might have been able to pass for fourteen years old.

It was enough of an age difference for Subaru to feel embarrassed if Felt were referred to as his acquaintance or friend.

But Subaru's analysis aside, Felt and Rom's argument continued on without him.

"What do you think is going to happen to you if you keep up this 'lone wolf' attitude of yours? Sooner or later, I'm going to get too old to be able to take care of you anymore. Do you really think you can make it on your own?"

"Just how many times have you told me this already? Isn't it a mark of senility to say the same thing over and over again? But other than that, it'll be a long time before you're too old for anything, and before that happens I'll…"

"…You'll do what?" Subaru said, jumping in, as Felt's sentence trailed off. Felt suddenly looked up, irritated.

Given that he seemed to have asked a question he shouldn't have and was in danger of wrecking the mood, Subaru cleared his throat. They had gotten very sidetracked, and it was time to return to the main point.

"Anyway, let's go ahead and start our negotiations. So, uh…Felt. You've got that badge, right?"

"…Yeah, I do."

Subaru cut straight to the point, and in response, Felt answered honestly.

Reaching into her breast pocket, Felt took out something and set it silently on the table.

It was the badge that Subaru had been looking for. What first stood out to Subaru was a design on it that was in the shape of a dragon. The badge itself was about the size where it would fit easily in the palm of your hand. While Subaru couldn't exactly tell what material it was made out of, the design of the winged dragon was intricate, and in the dragon's open mouth was a red jewel that made it look very unique.

Subconsciously, Subaru was drawn to the sparkle of the jewel in the badge's center.

"So..."

Felt's voice caught Subaru's attention and brought him back to where he was. She then slid the badge over to the edge of the table, as if to remind him that it still wasn't his yet.

"Now it's your turn to show me what you've got. As you can see, this is no ordinary badge, and I went through a lot of trouble to get it. If you can show me something that will match both the badge and my efforts, we can both be happy, right?"

"While I see you're trying to test me with that evil-looking smile of yours, I'm sorry. I've only got one card to play. After all, you would have to look far and wide to find one as destitute as me!"

Subaru proudly threw out his chest, but Felt didn't look all that happy.

The moment I say "poor," everyone makes that face at me, don't they? thought Subaru.

But Subaru's feelings aside, he went ahead and played his only card.

Subaru slapped his cell phone on the table, and just as he thought, Felt looked confused. However, that reaction was just the kind he was looking for. Subaru started up the cell phone's camera and...

"Take this! Nine-frames-per-second continuous shooting!"

"Wah! Wha—?! What are you—?! Hey, what's with that noise, and why is it so bright?!"

A white light flashed and a mechanical-like shutter sound went off several times at a rapid pace. Felt seemed like she had something to say about Subaru's terrible breach of manners, but before she could open her mouth, Subaru held the cell phone's screen in front of her face.

Upon seeing her own self on the screen, she opened her eyes wide and said, "That's..."

"That's right! I made a copy of you! This metia cuts out a slice of someone's time and stores it away! I want to trade you this metia for that badge you've got."

Having played his best card right away, Subaru was able to push the negotiations in his favor.

It was an established negotiation tactic, and depending on the situation, could be used to force a conclusion to be made right away.

Of course, this also meant telling the person you're negotiating with that you had no stronger cards to play, and Subaru had said that already in the first place, but it seemed to work.

"I see. That's pretty amazing. Rom, how much do you think this metia would go for?"

Felt looked at the screen and nodded a few times, but Subaru thought that her reaction was incredibly indifferent.

Her eyes didn't light up and she didn't even take the cell phone in her hands to look more closely. She wasn't interested in the cell phone's uses or its rarity, but only how much money she could turn it into.

"So this fascination with high-tech stuff is only limited to men in this world, too?! Somehow that makes me feel really sad and lonely!"

"Oh, shut up. What's there to make a big deal about? If this so-called metia can sell for more than this badge, then I couldn't be happier. For that, I trust Rom to give me a proper appraisal."

"Well, I can't say exactly how much I think it would go for. To be honest, I don't think the two objects can be compared. I think that badge could go for a lot of money...but not as much as this metia. In other words, I think you have a lot to gain by making this trade, Felt. That's what I think."

"I see, I see. If that's the case, then why not?"

Felt seemed pleased when the trade got Rom's seal of approval.

While Felt's reaction was a little bit different from what Subaru had expected, it appeared the trade was going to happen as planned, and Subaru couldn't be any happier about that.

However, as soon as he reached across the table toward the badge, Felt interrupted him.

"Wait. Our cards have been played, but that doesn't mean I'm not going to try to sweeten the deal."

"...I'm not sure how I feel about you saying that so plain and clear, but no matter what you say or do, I don't have anything else. Like I said before, I am peerlessly and infinitely broke."

"I'm not that cruel, and after all, Rom said so himself. Your metia is worth more than this badge. However, I doubt that you don't have any more cards to play."

Felt stood up and looked down at Subaru. Her red eyes were lit up, and he could see that she was sizing him up. A cold sweat ran down Subaru's back.

Subaru had already played the strongest card he could in their negotiations so far. However, Subaru still had a few other things on him that he thought might be valuable in this world. At the very worst, he thought he might be able to play a few more cards, but...

"I said not to worry, didn't I? I don't plan on trying to take any more from you. I'll be happy enough if I know I can just turn this thing here into money."

Felt lightly clapped her hands together and smiled, appearing pleased at the look of anxiety on Subaru's face.

Subaru gulped upon seeing Felt's reaction and, taking a few deep breaths, looked away in hopes that he could hide just how shaken he felt.

"So then, if that's the case, what do you mean when you say you still want to 'sweeten the deal'?"

"Hmm? Oh, that? It's simple. It just means that you're not the only person I'm negotiating with."

Subaru looked confused, but Felt stuck out her pointer finger and explained.

"The reason I stole the badge in the first place is because someone asked me to...in exchange for ten blessed gold coins."

"So you've already got a price settled with the person you stole it for?! Ten gold coins, huh... I don't really understand how much that is, but..."

Subaru glanced at Rom, who took the hint and nodded back.

"If it were me, I might be able to sell this badge for four, at best five gold coins. There's also the possibility that I would get talked down to three."

"So that means that they're already paying twice its worth?"

"Didn't you hear her? She said blessed gold coins. They're made of blessed gold, which is much rarer, so ten blessed gold coins is closer to twenty gold coins in worth."

"So they're paying *four* times as much?!"

"Why are you acting so surprised? With that metia of yours, even in the worst case you could easily get twenty blessed gold coins. Besides, there are probably collectors out there who would pay even more. You can't even compare the two."

Subaru really didn't understand the general cost of goods in this world, but he had thought that gold coins were the most valuable currency. The thought that his cell phone's worth was measured in a currency even greater than that, and not just one or two but twenty coins, was enough to take him by surprise.

"If this metia really does fetch a higher price, then I have no intention of honoring a prior agreement with someone else, and I don't have a problem telling them that."

"Then why are you saying you'll 'sweeten the deal'?!"

Felt's mischievous grin twisted into an even more villainous smile. "If I tell them you've made such a ridiculous counteroffer, if they still want the badge, don't you think they'll try to offer me something more?"

"In other words... Is that what you're saying? If the other side turns around and offers more than twenty blessed golden coins... then if you don't show me all the rest of your cards, you won't have a chance."

Felt's villainous smile had become so villainous it had reached a breaking point and become more like something refreshingly triumphant as she said those last words.

On the other hand, with this ominous turn of events, Subaru's expression started to cloud over.

"So when are you planning on meeting with this person who commissioned you to steal the badge? I assume you'll let me sit in on the negotiations, right?"

"Of course, if I put you at too much of a disadvantage, I might end up losing some of the money there is to be made. But don't worry about the location, we're meeting here," Felt said, tapping the edge of the table with her finger, before leaning against the back of her chair and looking up at Rom.

"As long as Old Man Rom's around, most people will forget about using violence as an option. Just the thought of having to fight this scary old man sends shivers down your spine, don't you think?"

Felt looked to Subaru for agreement, and after one quick glance at Rom, Subaru nodded several times.

On the other hand, Rom didn't seem too bothered about their having that kind of opinion of him.

"You really can't do anything without me, can you, Felt? I worry about you. Would you like another glass of milk? I also have some other things that are a little sweeter."

Rom had started to look like the grandfather who spoils his granddaughter like she was a cute kitten. Rom looked thrilled as he poured another glass of milk for Felt. Subaru looked at the two of them, and let out an exasperated sigh.

"Really, if you had already called that person here in the first place, were you planning on trying to negotiate the price with them even if I didn't show up?"

"Of course I was! Just how much do you think I had to go through to steal this thing? What if poor little me had to meet with them all on my own and got talked down on the reward? Wouldn't that be sad?"

" 'Poor little me,' huh…"

Felt was small and thin and though from that outward appearance one might be tempted to describe her as such, given how strong and stubborn a personality she had Subaru had a problem thinking of her as helpless. Thinking back to when Felt had run away after having stolen the badge, she had left Subaru for dead as he was being assaulted by those thugs.

Remembering that episode left Subaru a bit angry, so he couldn't help but bring it up.

"Speaking of which, don't you remember me at all?"

"Huh? Did we meet somewhere before? I mean, unless it was some really sort of shocking encounter, I don't think I'd remember you. I'm quite busy, and to be honest you look pretty plain. Only your hair and clothes stand out." Felt cackled.

As far as he could tell from the way she said it, Subaru didn't think that Felt was lying. There was also the fact that he had just had the plainness of his overall appearance insulted, so it was enough to put him into a minor state of shock.

It was starting to seem like there really was no such thing as common human decency in this world. Not if anyone could so easily forget passing by the scene of an attempted murder and robbery.

But then again, there were people like Satella, who had saved Subaru even though there was nothing in it for her, and this old man who, despite being a bit of a villain, you just couldn't bring yourself to hate. Even in this different world it wasn't as though everyone was the same. It wouldn't be right just to judge everyone based on the actions of a few bad eggs.

"Anyway, that's enough about your terrible memory, Felt. When is that other person supposed to be coming?"

"I'm not sure I like your attitude... But I said I'd finish the job by sunset, so we agreed to meet here after sunset... Since the sun's already set they should be here any minute now—I think?"

That conversation might have triggered an event flag, because just then came a sharp knock on the door. All three people at the table looked at one another.

"Did you tell 'em about the special knock?"

"Ah... No, I didn't. It's probably for me, so I'll go check." Felt stuck her tongue out at Rom and she leapt from her chair and went over to the door. The way she acted, you'd think she owned the place.

"You really okay with letting her get away with that?" Subaru said as he turned to Rom.

"Well, it's not like I just met her. We've known each other for a long time... I suppose I can let her depend on me every now and then."

Subaru thought Rom actually looked very happy to be depended on, as the old man went into the back of the cellar and returned with a large club.

The club was about the length of a bamboo kendo sword, and it seemed to be made of wood. At the tip and sticking out in various places were sharp points, and it looked like a clean hit would easily leave a fatal wound.

The closest thing to compare it to would be a bat with nails in it, but even in this world it looks like clubs are pretty standard equipment...

Wielding a club like that seemed to suit the six-foot-tall, muscle-bound old man. Subaru thought that if his clothes were a bit more torn and he was wearing a loincloth it would be an even more perfect fit.

"Upon seeing your uncivilized figure in all its glory, even I can't help myself but wince and smile at the same time."

"You sure like to run your mouth, don't you? Just who do you think you have to thank for getting this far? Woe is me," Rom added, shaking his head.

Subaru looked back at Rom for a few moments.

"Well, to be honest, I've very thankful for your help. It's not like everything's over yet, but I'm almost there, and the only reason things have been going so well for me is because of your help, so... thanks."

"...If you suddenly start being honest with me like that, I'm not going to know what to do," said Rom in response to Subaru's thanks, scratching at his bald head before letting out a deep sigh.

"You have more to thank yourself for in finding this place and making use of what you had on ya. I haven't done anything deserving of your thanks."

"You know that's not true. After all, Rom, you knew that Felt was planning on discussing the price of what she stole here with someone, right? Then, as soon as you heard what I had to say, you had all the reason to just throw me out."

"..."

"You're the one who gave me a chance to even talk to Felt. Of course, it was my efforts—my efforts!—that took it from there!"

It was important so Subaru had to say it twice.

As Subaru proudly pointed his thumb at himself, Rom's expression grew complicated and he was silent.

Thinking that Rom had finally grown tired of his antics, Subaru started to regret his eagerness to praise himself.

"I wouldn't call the way I feel about it 'thanks,' but...if either of us is to thank the other, it should be me, rather than you," muttered Rom, softly, just as Subaru's feeling of regret was starting to show on his face.

The old man's wrinkles deepened as he put on a smile.

"There's the fact that you have a metia and then there's your clothes and the look about you... You come from a pretty well-off family, don't you?"

"Well, I wouldn't exactly say that..."

"You don't have to hide it. I bet that you can't make public the fact that Felt stole that badge. If for nothing else, I'm very grateful of the fact that you're trying to settle this in a peaceful way."

It seemed that Rom had formed his own conclusions about Subaru's mysterious background, and that inside his head, Subaru was something of a very thoughtful gentleman.

"Felt and I...we've been together about as long as she can remember, since when she was a little girl," Rom said.

"I remember you saying something like that a little while ago... Have you two been here that whole time?" Subaru nodded his head in the direction of the surrounding slum area.

Rom nodded. "In a place like this, everyone's just struggling to survive. In that kind of environment, the young ones tend to gangs from others like them, but...Felt really isn't suited to that."

"If the way she's been acting is the way she acts to everyone, I'm not that surprised."

Felt's attitude so far seemed resolute and bold, but while that sounded good, there was no question that all of that resolution was geared toward her own ends. *If you act like that,* Subaru thought, *anybody who wants a mutually beneficial relationship with you isn't going to be too thrilled.*

"But isn't there also a problem in how she approaches you, Rom? I don't mean to be rude or anything, but I think that part of the reason her selfishness has gotten so bad is because you're always there for her."

"…I don't have anything I can say to that. After all, it's true that I tend to spoil her," Rom said softly as he ran his hand over his bald head.

The way the old man looked when he said that made it clear to Subaru that Rom felt as though Felt was family to him. They probably weren't related by blood, but at least from Rom's side, there was a clear bond between them.

"Well, I hope it's not a one-sided sort of thing," Subaru muttered, without being clear on who the subject was.

But Rom must have heard, because he whispered, "I don't mind, even if that's the way it is. …Actually, it'd be best if it were that way."

But just then it looked as though their time was up.

"What are you two doing, muttering to yourselves? It's creepy, so cut it out," said Felt, annoyed, as she returned. Behind Felt, who was doing a terrible job of putting on a fake smile, was one other person. "I was right, it was for me. We're over here, would you care to take a seat?" Felt motioned, pushing Subaru aside, and turned back to the person behind her while attempting to be courteous.

When Subaru looked up, preparing himself to face the next person he was going to have to negotiate between, he was a little bit surprised.

Felt had invited in an incredibly beautiful woman.

She was very tall for a woman, about the same height as Subaru, and she looked as though she were in her early twenties. The beautiful woman had eyes that angled down toward their edges and she had a certain calmness about her. One thing that stood out about her in the darkness of the loot cellar was the almost sickly whiteness of her skin. She was wearing a black coat, but the front was open and you could see that her clothes underneath were also black and were tightly fit against her skin. While she was fairly thin, she definitely had curves where they should be, and a very nice body overall.

Like Subaru, the woman also had black hair, which seemed to be very rare in this world. Her hair was tied in a braid that reached all the way to her hips, the tip of which she was twirling around in her fingers.

In short, she was a bewitchingly beautiful older woman. For Subaru, who had no real experience being around women even in his own world, seeing a woman like this was so new to him that he could not help but feel extremely nervous.

Having already lost his cool, Subaru followed Felt's directions and gave up his chair without any complaint. Felt took that seat, and Rom took the seat to the left of her. Subaru just stood to Felt's right, unable to hide his nervousness.

With so many people awaiting her arrival, the woman didn't seem upset, but she did look puzzled. "I get the feeling that there are a lot of unrelated people here."

"I can't just let myself be in a position to be talked down on price, you know? It's the wisdom of the weak. Anyway, Subaru, go fetch us some drinks."

Felt motioned to Subaru with her hand, like she was ordering a servant around, but Subaru couldn't bring himself to talk back, and so went behind the counter and picked out some relatively clean glasses, filled them with milk, and came back to the table to set them down.

The woman said, "Thank you," to Subaru before looking him up and down.

"I understand that old man being here, but who is this?"

The woman must have been able to tell by Subaru's demeanor that he was not very used to the place. Rather than being wary of him, she had posed a simple question.

In response, Felt smiled her evil smile. "This guy here is your rival.

He's come to negotiate as well," she declared, and her process of "sweetening the deal" began.

6

"I see. I understand what's going on now," said the woman before taking a sip from her glass and licking off the milk left on her lips.

The woman, who went by the name Elsa, gave off an air of eroticism in every move she made. While Felt was explaining the current situation to Elsa, she turned her glance several times toward Subaru, which made him so flustered he could hardly handle it.

"That's the way it is, so now we'll start the bidding. I don't really care who walks away with this badge, so it'll go to the one who can offer me the best deal."

"That's a nice attitude you have there. I can't say I dislike it. ...So, how much did that boy over there say he would pay for it?"

Elsa originally said that she would pay ten blessed gold coins.

If Subaru was going to compete with her offer, she must have thought that he had offered more money. Thinking that it would be better to not take a "wait and see" approach, he took out his cell phone for the third time and demonstrated its use. A flash lit up the inside of the cellar and Elsa's image was captured by the device.

Elsa raised her eyebrows in response to Subaru's sudden actions, but Subaru immediately showed her the screen.

"What I have to offer is this metia. It's a rare item, and it's probably the only one in the entire world. According to this muscular man, it should sell for over twenty blessed gold coins."

"A metia..." Elsa said, staring at herself on the screen and slowly nodding. With this, Elsa should have realized that Subaru was looking to barter for the badge, not pay outright, and that his offer was not a bluff.

Elsa took a small leather bag out of her pocket and placed it on the table. In the bag was probably the payment she had prepared for the badge—Subaru could hear the sound of heavy metal objects clanging together as she set it down.

Felt fixed on the bag with her eyes like a curious cat, as Rom wordlessly reprimanded her. Elsa placed her white fingers on top of the bag she had placed on the table.

"The truth is, I was given a little extra by my employer, in case you happened to have second thoughts about the price, so I do have a little more to offer."

"Your employer...? So you're just following someone's directions to pick up the badge?" asked Subaru.

"That's correct. The one who wants the badge is not me, but my employer. ...Are you by chance involved in the same sort of work as I am?"

"If that were the case, then that would mean you'd have to be unemployed!"

"So, this unemployed kid over here is saying he'll pay a much higher price than you offered. Just how much is your master willing to pay?" asked Felt, challenging Elsa.

Elsa silently opened the mouth of the bag, and turned it over. What came tumbling out were several shining blessed gold coins. Felt's eyes sparkled as she saw the coins layer on top of one another, and even Rom made a sound in his throat.

Subaru was more concerned with the number than the coins themselves. If he counted correctly...

"Twenty coins, exactly," said Elsa.

"This is all that my employer has given to me. This is what they decided would be enough to pay for the badge, but...am I correct in thinking their estimates may have been a little off?" asked Elsa, directing her question at Rom, rather than Felt.

After counting the coins, Rom gazed down at a nervous-looking Subaru, and then smiled.

"There's no reason for you to act like such a baby. You should be embarrassed. Aren't you a man? ...It's true that twenty blessed gold coins is an outrageous amount. However, I remember saying that in the worst case, your metia should sell for twenty gold coins. In other words, it's worth more than that."

Rom took his giant callused hand and roughly patted Subaru on the head.

"The way I see it, the negotiations lean in favor of the kid. No offense to your employer, but it looks like you're going to have to bring them their money back," Rom said, shoving the coins back toward Elsa.

Subaru let out a cry of excitement. Felt threw her hands up in the air to signal that she didn't have a problem with the decision, and Elsa shrugged but did not look all that displeased herself. Subaru followed up with a triumphant pose, but that exaggerated action just made him stand out from the crowd.

"W-what? I'm happy, all right? Let me be! This is the first time I've actually accomplished something here! What's wrong with a little celebration?!" said Subaru, embarrassed.

"I didn't say anything. If you want to celebrate, then celebrate. As long as I get my money, I'm happy," said Felt.

"My employer doesn't actually need that badge, so I don't have any reason to beg you to reconsider," added Elsa.

Both Felt and Elsa seemed uninterested in Subaru's antics.

However, while Subaru wasn't so mean-spirited that he was hoping for Elsa to beg and plead, he found it strange how disinterested she seemed, despite the negotiations not going her way.

"Well, I'm sorry, Elsa. I imagine your employer's going to be angry at you."

"There's no helping it. It would be different if I failed because I was the one who made a mistake, but in this case, it's my employer's fault for thinking that they would be able to get away with paying so little for the badge."

"But when you plan for as much as twenty blessed gold coins and that turns out to be not enough, that's got to be tough," remarked Rom.

"Well, I guess it just means that my luck is in full swing! Does this mean that my era of greatness has finally come?" Felt laughed, oblivious to the mood, in contrast to the two males who were showing sympathy for Elsa.

Either way, Subaru had managed to complete one of the goals he had in coming here. Without having to fall back on a plan B, it looked as though there was a glimmer of hope that he would be able to pay Satella back.

Normally, it would be best to report to Satella that Felt and Elsa were the ones responsible for the theft, but Subaru didn't have it in him to do anything that might result in either of them getting locked up.

It had been simple opportunism.

"Well, as the negotiations did not go in my favor, I think I'll take my leave now."

Elsa stood up and gulped down the last of her milk. Again, she used her tongue in an erotic way to lick up the last few drops of milk, before looking at Subaru. As she stared at him, it felt as though her eyes were binding him in place. "By the way, what is it that you were planning on doing with that badge?" Elsa asked in a somewhat deep, frozen sort of voice.

The sweet ring of her voice threatened Subaru's eardrums and made him feel, by some delusion, as though he couldn't lie.

"...Oh, I was planning on returning it to its owner." As soon as he said it he knew he had made a terrible mistake.

He had just declared, in front of both the girl who had stolen it and the woman who had ordered the theft, that he was going to return the stolen item to its owner.

"I see. So you're with them." Subaru's words were enough to set Elsa's cold murderous intent into motion.

"Wha—?!" Subaru felt a sudden impact from his side. The impact was enough to force him to the side, and unable to catch himself, he tumbled to the ground. From Subaru's perspective there was first pain and shock, his vision spinning as he hit the ground. When he looked up he saw that Felt was clinging to his side.

"What do you—"

"Are you an idiot? Pay attention and get out of the way! You want to die?!" Felt yelled.

"—think you are doing?!" The last part of Subaru's shout was drowned out by Felt's.

Subaru was in shock. From his low vantage point he saw Elsa facing toward him.

"Oh, it looks like you managed to dodge that one," she said, her head tilted in surprise.

Elsa held in her hand a weapon that glimmered with a dull light. The weapon was, according to Subaru's knowledge, a kukri blade, and it clashed with the rest of Elsa's image. It was easily a foot long, with the body of the blade bent inward as it extended from the handle. Due to the weight of the tip it was a weapon that was often used similarly to an ax to decapitate enemies or prey, and just by looking at it, it was not hard to imagine the weapon's vicious brutality.

Despite wielding the blade, Elsa's serene smile was unchanged. From her stance, it was clear that she had already swung the weapon once. Which meant the only reason Subaru was safe was that Felt had leapt up and tackled him out of the path of the weapon.

Fear, late in coming, made Subaru's hands and feet shake, and he felt nauseated. However, the situation wasn't going to stop just for him.

"Rrrragh!" Old Man Rom let out a roar as he rushed toward Elsa, swinging the club that had never left his grasp since the negotiations had begun. The spiked part of the club came barreling down toward her head. Despite the club weighing at least twenty pounds, Rom swung it as if he were swinging a twig, and it cut through the air before slamming against the floor of the cellar.

As the club sprang off the floor it felt as though the entire building had shook. Several stolen articles flew from the shock of the impacts, which continued as Rom and Elsa traded blows in front of Subaru.

"This is my first time in mortal combat with a giant," said Elsa.

"Go ahead and keep talking, little girl. I'll turn you into mincemeat and feed you to the giant rats!" As Rom threw his insults he swung his club even faster. Before the power of that swing, any untrained attempt to block would be no more effective than a sheet of paper.

Inside the cellar, there was very little room to move around, and allowing the swings of that club to corner you could easily be a fatal mistake.

However, Elsa's skill was of such a high level it could only be called freakish.

While still wielding her kukri, dangling from one hand, Elsa, herself like a black shadow, was able to slip around each of Rom's surely fatal swings. Her movements were precarious, walking a thin line, just barely away from life-threatening danger, and still it was she who was in control of the fight, not Rom.

This can't be good, thought Subaru instinctively. Something in his head was setting off an alarm. "This is bad..." muttered Subaru, his lips shaking.

"Don't worry. There's no way Old Man Rom can lose! Ever since I can remember, I've never seen Rom lose a fight!" Felt yelled back, putting her trust for Rom in words as if to dispel her own doubts.

In Felt's words were experiences built up over long years; experiences that formed her unshakable trust. But even without Felt telling Subaru outright, he could see their trust in how close they were when they interacted with each other.

Despite Felt's confidence, Subaru was preparing for the worst. But he couldn't figure out why.

"Take that!"

Before Subaru could pin down his anxiety, there was a change in the flow of the fight.

Rom yelled and kicked over the table, the same small wooden table they had been negotiating around. The table split and splintered from the force of the kick, and for an instant Elsa, who was up against a wall, was hidden behind its fragments, her line of sight cut off.

Rom swung his club down with all his might. If the hit landed, it was sure to be an instant kill. However...

"Rom!" Felt's distraught scream shook the air inside the loot cellar.

Subaru then saw the result that scream had sought to prevent.

Something was flying, spinning in the air.

It was Rom's right arm, still tightly gripping his club.

The arm, which had been severed at the shoulder, flew through the air, spraying blood everywhere before it landed against the wall.

The whole room had been showered with blood. Subaru and Felt were no exception.

Felt screamed again.

"If I'm going down, I'm taking you with me!" Having lost his right arm, Rom was spraying blood out of his shoulder like a hose. Without even trying to stop the flow of blood, Rom leapt forward toward Elsa, to attack her with his one remaining arm.

As the splintered wooden table fell to the ground, Elsa stood behind it, still holding the position of the follow-through of her swing.

Before Elsa could flip the kukri back around, Rom's giant body would crush her. But in that fleeting moment of Rom's last stand...

"I forgot to tell you before, but thank you for the milk."

...he was cut short. With her other hand Elsa struck with a broken shard from the very glass she had been drinking from. On the sharp tip of the shard were droplets of blood—blood that had come from Rom's slit throat.

His arm severed and his throat cut, blood frothed from the old man's mouth, and as the light from his eyes vanished, he collapsed on the ground. Though his body convulsed there was no strength left in it, as Rom's life was dragged away even as it clung to his body.

Elsa bowed once gracefully toward the body, as if paying her respects.

While Rom's body continued to twitch, Elsa gently placed the remains of the glass down by his feet. "I'll give this back. I don't need it anymore," she said coldly, before twirling her kukri around in her hand and pointing its red-stained tip toward Subaru and Felt. However, Subaru, still collapsed the floor, was unable to say anything.

All of Subaru's thought processes had been arrested by the slaughter that had taken place before his eyes.

Someone that he had been talking to just a few minutes ago was now dead. Dead not by sickness or an accent, but killed by the actions of another, plain and simple.

"Ah, I see that you're the one with the courage," Elsa said, impressed, and Subaru, still unable to move, looked up.

While Subaru was still in a state of shock, Felt had stood up and was slapping her legs to keep her knees from shaking. She then pushed back her blood-soaked hair.

"How... How dare you..."

Subaru was behind Felt, so he could not see her expression. However, it was clear from her voice that she was not choking back tears.

"If you put up too much of a struggle, you will only end up hurting more," said Elsa.

"I bet you'd still plan on killing us even if we didn't fight back, you psycho...!"

"If you move too much I won't be able to make a clean cut. ...I'm not all that skilled with a blade." As Elsa said this, she twirled the kukri around and pretended as if she were practicing the proper cuts to butcher Felt.

But Felt was empty-handed. There was no way that she could win.

In his mind, Subaru had reached the conclusion that he should cry out. He needed to distract Elsa, even if only a little bit, to allow time for Felt to escape.

If he could just give her time to call for help, or even just escape on her own... But even though Subaru had made his decision, he couldn't stop his body from shaking.

"...I'm sorry for getting you wrapped up in all of this," Felt said to Subaru in an apology little above a whisper.

"I-I..." In response, Subaru's face jolted up toward Felt, and forgetting the words he should have said to her, he could only manage a choked mutter as though pleading for her forgiveness.

But Felt left Subaru's sentiments forever behind her as she dashed forward. There was a loud sound as she kicked off from the ground, and it was as though a gale had suddenly blown through the cellar. Just when Subaru thought that Felt had vanished from his sight, he saw Elsa's body twist.

A high-pitched sound rang out, and Felt clicked her tongue from

Elsa's side. In Felt's hand was a small knife, and with Elsa's overwhelmingly fast reaction she was able to dodge Felt's attack.

Felt leapt back, riding the gust of air she made as she flew. With Felt's irregular movements, even the walls of the cellar became like ground to her. Even Elsa seemed to be surprised by Felt's acrobatic feats.

"So you have the protection of the wind. Oh, how wonderful. The world must adore you…I envy that." Elsa's ecstatic smile suddenly turned, and her eyes were filled with hatred as her arm bent back.

"Wha—" Felt was cut down in midair by a slice that extended across from her shoulder, and unable to catch herself, she hit the ground and entered a roll.

The opening of the wound cut across her chest, from the left shoulder to her right underarm, and it was so deep it cut through bone and into her organs.

Ending her roll faceup, with every beat of her heart Felt spewed blood like a fountain, and it was clear that she had already lost consciousness from the pain and shock of the cut. She didn't move an inch. In just a few seconds the flow of her blood lost its pressure, silently signaling the end of her life.

Subaru could not move.

He wanted to go to Felt's side and try to stop the bleeding. If it was too late for that, then he at least wanted to close her eyelids. But Subaru's arms and legs rejected his plea, and he could do nothing but shiver, shamelessly.

"The old man and the girl are both down, but you won't move. Have you already given up?" Elsa said in a tone as though she pitied him, with eyes that looked bored.

All she had to do was walk a little closer and strike a single time with her knife. That much was obvious to her, hence her bored look. In Elsa's movements was not even the slightest hint of hesitation. It even seemed as though she was trying to hold back a yawn.

In response to Elsa's attitude, Subaru felt an uncontrollable anger welling up inside him. The two people fallen in front of him were people he had met just under an hour ago. But they had not only talked, they had bared emotions to one another. To take those two people and kill them, and feel no guilt whatsoever, was to Subaru absolutely unforgivable.

Furthermore, he could not forgive himself. He had just watched as both of them were slaughtered by this vile woman.

"So you've finally gotten to your feet. It certainly took you a while. I doubt you'll entertain me much, but it could be worse."

The anger welling up inside Subaru, though far too late, finally gave him the power to move his arms and legs.

His limbs still shaking, Subaru slowly pushed against the ground and was somehow able to stand up, though his movements were almost animalistic.

Was his shaking due to fear, or anger? Or was it both? Subaru didn't care.

Facing Elsa and her kukri blade held at the ready, Subaru charged forward with all his strength and spirit, teeth bared.

He would fly at her and beat her down, pushing his own strength past its limits. But that mad rush of Subaru's was...

"Pathetic."

...brought to a swift end as Elsa elbowed him directly in the face. As she spun around, using the least amount of movement necessary, she had stuck Subaru with her elbow, and as he was reeling, Elsa, still in her spin, traced an arc with one of her long legs and landed a kick.

Subaru was thrown back into a shelf filled with porcelain and came crashing to the ground. In one single round of attack, Subaru had both his nose and front teeth broken. His side, which took the brunt of Elsa's kick, was in terrible pain, and he could feel that a number of his ribs had broken.

But still, Subaru shoved his fist against the ground and immediately stood back up. Subaru's brain had already started excreting endorphins and was rejecting the pain, which was greater than any Subaru had felt before.

In this aroused state, his breathing abnormal, Subaru launched another mindless attack...but he was again struck back.

Subaru's flailing arms could not reach Elsa, and with her flowing limbs she struck Subaru with the blunt side of her blade, breaking his left shoulder.

Then, as if she was annoyed by having to listen to his screams of pain, she threw in a kick straight up into his jaw, which immediately shut him up. It also succeeded in knocking out the rest of Subaru's broken front teeth.

Elsa looked down at Subaru as he tumbled to the ground.

"You're no good at all. You're just as inexperienced as you look, and your movements are all over the place. You don't have any divine protection, or any special skills. I thought you might use your head and have some trick up your sleeve, but I see you have nothing. Just how did you ever think you could stand a chance against me?"

"Shuddup... It's called being stubborn... You dink I'll just dake dis lying down?" Subaru's nose was broken, so he couldn't even make a proper comeback.

Thanks to the last counterattack, Subaru couldn't use his arm anymore. Everything from his left shoulder down was dangling limply. He couldn't feel any pain, but the ringing in his ears was getting unbearable. He was intensely nauseated, and it felt as though his anger was seeping away out of his mouth.

Subaru was beaten. He could never win. His chances of even landing a hit were minuscule.

"Well, I'll admit that you've got at least an unusually high amount of determination. If you had gotten yourself up a little earlier, there might have been a different outcome for these two." With the tip of her knife, Elsa pointed to the two bodies lying abandoned on the floor. As Subaru followed Elsa's motion and looked at the corpses he suddenly felt a strange feeling come over him.

Why? Why did he feel that he had seen this all before?

The loot cellar, with its floor a sea of blood... The giant corpse with its missing arm... The dull glint of a reddish blade...

In the back of his mind, a thought shot through him like lightning.

"Let's put an end to all of this. I'll send you off to go meet the angels."

Elsa licked her red lips, and with a sensual smile vanished into the darkness. Whether or not it was by some trick, to Subaru it looked as though Elsa had sunk down into the shadows of the cellar.

Subaru looked left and right, unable to find Elsa. "Wh-where are you?!"

Subaru began to panic, looking this way and that, listening as hard as he could for any sound. He looked like the prey of a ferocious predator just waiting to be devoured. From Elsa's perspective, nothing could make her less excited, but that just made her want to get it over with even more quickly, so in a brilliantly direct slice...

"Wha—?!"

As soon as Subaru realized that the attack was coming for his abdomen, he managed to get clear, with not a hairbreadth to spare.

Subaru jumped back, pulling his stomach in, so that the horizontal slash only just grazed him. The skin of his abdomen was sliced open, but Subaru gritted his teeth and bore the sharp pain.

"Ughraaah!!"

Then with all of his might, Subaru was able to strike Elsa's upper body from the side with a spinning kick. As Subaru twisted himself and landed his critical hit, he was able to confirm that he had been able to retaliate at least once.

However...

"Ah... That one was very satisfying," Elsa said as, with a second kukri she had drawn from her waist, she sliced about 70 percent of the way through Subaru's abdomen with her other hand, spilling out his blood and guts.

"Huh...?" Subaru took one step, two steps back, and as his shoulder brushed up against the wall, he slid down against it and fell to the floor.

As Subaru looked down he could see the blood flowing out of his abdomen and staining the floor bright red. With a shaking arm he tried uselessly to return the blood, but the bloody clumps of tissue spilling out of his stomach pushed his hand away.

"Are you surprised? I opened up your stomach as you rushed me. It's my speciality, really," Elsa said with a smile, walking splish-splash across the sea of blood.

Elsa approached Subaru, who was unable to say anything but gurgle out cries of pain, and stared at his bloody, blackish innards with a look of ecstasy on her face.

"Ah...just as I hoped. Your intestines have such a beautiful color to them."

This woman was out of her mind.

At the pain that even his endorphins could not negate, Subaru's consciousness started to fade. He realized that he seemed to have fallen on his side. With shaking fingertips, he weakly touched Elsa's foot.

"Uu...ugh..."

"Are you in pain? Does it hurt? Are you sad? Do you want to die?"

With his hand still grabbing at her ankle, Elsa knelt down beside Subaru and looked him in the eyes. Elsa's eyes were filled with ecstasy. She had absolutely no qualms about taking another human life.

Instead...she seemed to be incredibly happy, filled with bliss.

"Slowly, slowly, slowly, ever so slowly your body will lose its heat and you will go cold."

Subaru could feel Elsa's voice vibrating his eardrums, torturing him, savoring him, pitying him, affectionate for him, loving him.

Before he knew it, Subaru couldn't see anymore. His loss of blood was too great, and bit by bit he was dying. Now, he couldn't hear anything. He couldn't smell anything. He couldn't see anything. He could only feel his body growing colder, his body dying, and the fear that came with it.

In this space, not knowing exactly when the light of his life would be extinguished, Subaru could not separate himself from the fear of death.

When will I die? When will I die? Am I still alive? Am I not already dead? How do you define life? Can you even say that I'm alive in this state, lesser than any insect? What is life? What is death? Why is dying so frightening? Is it really necessary to live? No?

I'm scared. I'm scared. I'm scared. I'm scared. I'm scared. I'm scared.

I'm scared. I'm scared. I'm scared. I'm scared. I'm scared. I'm scared. I'm scared. I'm scared. I'm scared. I'm scared. I'm scared. I'm scared.

As an absolute and unconditional death grew ever closer, Subaru's mind instinctively rejected it. At the end, that rejection filled everything that Subaru was, and as his vision whited out, he thought...

Ah...I'm dead.

And with that very last thought, Subaru Natsuki's life flickered out.

CHAPTER 3

ENDING AND BEGINNING

1

"Hey, man, don't just stare off into space like that. You want an abble?"

As soon as Subaru's consciousness had returned to him, there was a ripe red fruit in front of his face.

It looked just like an apple, and as he stared at it, the phrase "fruit of knowledge" crossed the back of his mind.

It was that forbidden fruit that, when eaten, resulted in expulsion from paradise.

If Subaru ate that fruit now, would it save him from the inexplicable situation he found himself in?

"Hey, kiddo," said a middle-aged man as he furrowed his brow and called out to Subaru, who was being completely unresponsive.

Subaru slowly drifted from the vague edge of his consciousness back toward reality, and when he was back, he suddenly raised his head. He looked this way and that, his heart beating ferociously and his breathing ragged.

He was in front of the fruit store on the main street, just past noon. There were various colorful vegetables and fruits laid out, and the person standing in front of those goods was a stern-looking man, the shop owner with the white scar across his face.

This was the crowded street that Subaru had already seen several times before. He scratched his head.

"I just don't get it..." he muttered, and then overcome with dizziness and nausea, he collapsed on the spot.

2

As he felt a cold rush of water on his face, Subaru was somehow able to bring his muddied consciousness back to reality.

"..."

Subaru looked at the empty water jug the fruit shop owner had brought Subaru. After Subaru had collapsed in front of his shop, the owner had helped him get himself together.

Subaru was glad that the owner had the heart to worry about him, but the fact that he was so kind as not to ask where Satella had gone struck a deep wound in his heart.

As Subaru sat on the earthen floor, he wiped away the water from his bangs and clenched his teeth. The glint of that blade still haunted the back of his mind, along with that terrible smile as it danced through the stench of blood.

"Hhgh..."

The back of Subaru's throat twitched and as he sat hugging his knees, he couldn't keep his entire body from shaking.

He'd lived a completely normal life up until this point. He had never experienced so much fear, so much despair.

He didn't want to think anymore. He didn't want to remember anymore. He wanted to draw back inside his shell and forget everything.

The glimmer of the blade, the arm flying off, the scream, sinking in a sea of blood, that silver hair...

"..."

The less Subaru wanted to think about it, the more clearly his memories came back to him. Overcome by anguish, Subaru raised his face up to scream, but just as he was about to let everything out...

"Huh...?"

The voice that had risen up inside Subaru dribbled out full of doubt, and he just stared, dumbfounded.

In Subaru's range of vision, with his eyes open wide, he could see a tall figure with skin like a reptile…a beast-like humanoid that was only as tall as his waist…a young dancer with pink hair…a swordsman with six swords at his waist…

…and a young girl in a white robe with silver hair that swayed as she walked.

Those violet eyes of hers took one glance at Subaru as she walked by, but she looked away as though uninterested and walked on.

Those amethyst eyes, full of determination, just looked straight forward as she stared down the road.

In that gallant stance, that delicate beauty, in that girl that Subaru had been searching for, there was no change.

Unable to call out immediately, with rasping breath Subaru struggled to his feet and chased after her. "Wai—! W-wait! Wait up! Please, wait…"

For an instant, the girl reacted to his voice and looked back at Subaru with a cold gaze, as if she was looking at a stranger.

Subaru felt his heart gouged by the chill in her sharp gaze. He had not done what she had asked of him. He had hurt her. He hadn't apologized yet. There was no way that he could be forgiven, but even so Subaru chased after her.

He didn't know how she felt. At the very least he had to know what she was thinking.

If he was going to let what he imagined her to be thinking hurt him, he would rather be hurt by the real her, here in this reality where he could feel pain.

"Wait, please! Satella!"

He wasn't sure of what he wanted to say to her if he could catch her, but when the answer to that question became clear in his mind, Subaru called out Satella's name as if he had just remembered it.

Finally it seemed as if his voice had reached her, because just as she was starting to get away from him the girl stopped immediately in her tracks.

Subaru weaved through the crowd to catch up to her, and put his hand on her thin shoulder.

"Don't…ignore me. It's my fault that I went away and it's my fault for not listening to you, but I've been desperate. After what happened I went to the loot cellar, but I wasn't able to meet you there and…"

As Subaru grabbed her shoulder, Satella looked at him in surprise.

As she turned around and Subaru opened his mouth, what came out was a sort of self-defense that sounded full of excuses.

What made him realize that was Satella's clear eyes.

Her stare was emotionless, and as Subaru faced it, he still felt a sense of ease. As far as he could tell, Satella didn't appear to be wounded. Subaru experienced this as salvation.

"I'm sorry for going on about myself… I'm so glad to see you're okay."

The fact that they were able to meet again made Subaru feel simple happiness.

There were so many things they had to talk about, but before all of that Subaru felt as if nothing he had done was in vain. He was finally and profoundly relieved…

"…What do you think you're doing?"

But as Subaru found this sense of ease, Satella was incredibly angry. Her white cheeks had reddened, as she twisted her body to get Subaru's hand off her shoulder. After taking a step back and putting some space between her and Subaru, Satella's eyes were filled with hostility.

After this unexpectedly stern reaction, Subaru unconsciously gulped.

Still, this reaction made sense. From Satella's perspective, she should be shocked that Subaru would even show his face in front of her. There was no insult too great for her to lob at Subaru and—

"I don't know who you are, but what the hell are you thinking, calling someone the same name as that Witch of Jealousy?!"

After hearing that reaction, which was beyond anything that he could have imagined, everything that Subaru had built up to brace himself was smashed to pieces.

Faced with those unexpected words, Subaru felt as if time had stopped.

The sound of the crowd disappeared. All that Subaru could hear was the violent beating of his heart, and the rough breathing of the silver-haired girl in front of him, tense and defensive. He felt as if all of the other sounds had disappeared...but that was no illusion.

"...What?"

As Subaru looked around he realized that everyone, everyone all around this crowded shopping district, all the pedestrians on the road were staring at them. Everyone looked shaken, and no one would move a single muscle, stock-still and quiet.

It was as if the conversation between Satella and Subaru had taken control of the entire area.

With her severe stare, Satella was waiting for Subaru's answer. However, unsure of what he was guilty of, Subaru couldn't think of how to answer. The reason why Subaru thought Satella would be upset and the real reason she was upset were different.

"I'll ask you one more time. Why are you calling me by the Witch of Jealousy's name?"

"What do you mean? That's what I was told to call you..."

"...I don't know who told you that, but whoever it was, that's in incredibly poor taste. Even if you're not the one who thought of it, it's bad enough that you agreed. This is the Witch of Jealousy we're talking about, the embodiment of all things taboo. Most people would hesitate to even utter such a name, and you're using it to name me?"

With her anger displayed for all to see, Satella...the silver-haired girl threw Subaru into a storm of confusion. Everyone else around seemed to be nodding, agreeing with her, and that, more than anything else, proved that she was right. Subaru had absolutely no idea what was going on. He couldn't understand what she was saying. Subaru had only just called her by her name.

But Satella had rebuked him, and everyone around agreed that she was in the right.

"If that's all you wanted to say, then I'll be on my way. I don't have time to deal with you."

The girl looked on as Subaru simply stood where he was, hanging his head. She then turned and walked off, with her hair dancing behind her, having nothing more to do with him.

Subaru thought to call after her, and started to shout her name, but it got caught in his throat as if it had frozen shut.

If Subaru called her name again, he would simply be making the same mistake twice. But then, what should he call her?

He hesitated, unable to decide what to do.

"!"

Subaru gasped. On the canvas top of a cart on the side of the street, from a position just a head taller than Subaru, something leaped. A small body was pulled by gravity toward the ground, and as soon as it landed it took off on the wind. That little gust of wind, with dirty clothes and blond hair trailing behind it, wove through the crowd with a godlike dexterity, and from it an outstretched arm slipped into a certain girl's hawk-embroidered white robe.

The two only touched for an instant, but to that little gust of wind, that moment was enough.

As the wind made the robe fly up and the girl with the robe twisted around, the wind took off flying again.

"It can't be!"

The silver-haired girl raised her voice in shock and stuck her hand into her robe. She couldn't find what she was looking for, and with eyes opened wide, she looked in the direction of the quickly fleeing wind.

Seeing the dragon-adorned badge in that wind's hand as it passed quickly by, Subaru yelled, "Felt?!"

With Subaru's call, the wind waved for a moment in hesitation, but without slowing down it quickly flew down a narrow alley. Everything happened so incredibly fast that Subaru could only see for an instant what happened, but that had to be—

"I've been had! Is that why you stopped me? Are you two working together?!" moaned the girl as she looked at Subaru standing still.

The girl quickly turned her palm toward Subaru, but apparently changing her mind, she ran off in the direction the wind had gone down the alley.

"Hey, wait! This is a misunderstanding! I..."

Subaru took off after them down the alley, hoping to sort things out. As he ran, his mind was filled with questions and doubts. There was too much information to process, and his panicked mind couldn't deal with it. Even without that, he had just gone through death twice, and everything in his mind was muddled.

"There's got to be someone out there who'll be nice to me! Why the hell was I even summoned here?!" Subaru yelled, having had enough with nothing making sense, as he kept running with unsure footing down the dark alley.

Subaru wasn't sure of his stamina, but at a short distance, he didn't think he would lose to those two girls. However...

"Damn! A wall?!" Subaru spat. Right in front of him was a dead end.

Neither of the two girls was there. Felt probably could easily climb over a wall like that, and he thought that Satella would have been able to do something about it with her magic.

I could try to climb over to the other side, but I don't think I'd be able to catch up to them.

Subaru couldn't afford to waste time here. He had no idea how to get around the capital, so if he lost them here, it would be impossible for him to catch up to them.

"Then should I head to the loot cellar? If Satella and Felt are alive, then Rom must be..."

Even as Subaru said this, he felt that several things were wrong and contradicting themselves. Felt had been cut down. Rom's neck was slit. Satella fell in a pool of blood. Subaru had his abdomen cut open—twice. How was it that everyone was alive...?

"No. Now's not the time. I can't waste time thinking. Right now I've got to..."

Subaru would go on ahead and quickly meet up with Rom. That was what Subaru had to do. He could think later. The best thing for him to do right now was to leave this alley and head to the slums.

Subaru turned around.

"...You've got to be kidding me!"

Right in front of him, blocking the entrance to the alley, were three shadows, three people, with dirty clothes and a rough and barbaric appearance. Three thugs who used these alleys as their hunting grounds. It was Subaru's third time encountering them that day.

3

"Give it a rest already! Just what is it going to take for you punks to learn?!"

Tired of seeing those three thugs again, Subaru furiously stomped on the ground.

This was the third time they had met. Every time was in a back alley, three against one. Given how their first and second efforts were fruitless, Subaru was stunned that they were so determined to catch him that they'd try a third time.

"I don't have the time or the patience to deal with you fools. Out of my way, now!"

The current situation had really put Subaru out of sorts, but there was also the fact that, given what happened last time, he thought he should be able to scare them if he shouted. At least that's what he thought.

"'Get out of my way,' he says. Ha! I don't like your attitude. You don't get it, do you? You're not in a position to be ordering us around."

"It was three-on-one last time and you guys *still* lost like you were nothing! You think you can talk big like that? Even sore losers would show more shame when they wail!"

However, the thugs didn't seem to fear Subaru at all, and kept up their taunting. Subaru bit his lip at their unexpected reactions. Even small-time villains like this had a sense of pride, he thought.

He wanted to avoid wasting any more time and risk losing Felt and Satella. Also, given the risk that a fight would entail, Subaru decided that he should deal with this peacefully.

"Fine. Have it your way. I'll give you everything I've got. That's what you want from me, right?"

Subaru held back his irritation and raised both of his hands in the air, showing that he was giving up.

The thugs all looked at one another after Subaru changed his attitude, and then all burst into laughter.

"What's that?! If you were that scared, you should have just said so!"

"Ha! Look at this guy! Don't talk all big if you're just gonna bend over!"

"Whatever. If he's going to do as we say, that just makes it easier on us, right? But what a coward, huh?"

Subaru was irritated, but he just laughed it off. He decided to name the group of thugs "dumb, dumber, and dumbest" to make himself feel better, and muttered under his breath, so they wouldn't hear. "Once I meet back up with Satella, I'm going to borrow Puck and make them...pay?"

Just as Subaru was about to lay out all that he owned in front of him, he froze.

"Huh...?"

Out of everything that had happened since Subaru had arrived in this new world, this was the most unsettling.

"Why...?"

At Subaru's fingertips, inside his plastic convenience store bag, was a bag of crispy snacks. Corn-soup flavored, they were one of his favorites, and he had grabbed them on a whim at the store to eat in place of his dinner.

When Subaru was with Rom at the loot cellar, he had shown them off to him as a great late-night snack, an act that he had later regretted.

However, that bag was still there, as full and sealed as when he had bought it at the store.

"I shouldn't have these anymore... Rom ate them all, and I complained and...there weren't any left. I'm sure of it."

Why were the snacks back in the bag? There was no trace that it had been opened. It wasn't possible.

Subaru felt his thoughts blocked on all sides. However, in that locked state, Subaru still came to a conclusion about what was happening. Even though he had come to a conclusion, it wasn't doing him any good. As soon as it occurred to him, he rejected it as impossible. His sense of reason denied the possibility.

"Hey, what are you doing?!"

"…What?" Subaru suddenly heard a voice right next to him. Cut from his train of thought, that was the only way he could react.

It was one of the thugs. The smallest one. The one Subaru had just named "Dumbest." While Subaru was lost in thought, Dumbest had walked over and put his hand on Subaru's shoulder.

Subaru twisted and pushed his hand away. "Out of my way…"

"What'd you say?!"

"In every sense of the word, I've run out of time to deal with you guys. I've got to…check something."

"Are you kidding me?" As Subaru pushed Dumbest aside and moved to exit the alley, the other two stood angrily in his way.

"Get out of my way! I've got somewhere to be!" He had to rule out this unbelievably stupid, unthinkable theory…

Faced with Subaru's yell, the men hesitated a bit. If he could break through and get out onto the main street, he would probably be out of harm's way. After deciding that, Subaru stepped down to kick firmly off the ground.

However…

"…Wha?"

Just as Subaru put his foot down it twisted. The strength drained from his legs, and he fell to his knees. He put out his hands to catch his fall, and cursed his idiocy for stumbling at such a critical moment.

"Huh… That's strange…" Just as Subaru tried to push against the ground so he could stand back up again, his arms started shaking. He didn't think he could stand back up again. He didn't think he could even lift his body.

"Well, I've done it now, haven't I…?"

Subaru looked back as he heard that voice tinged with anxiety, and then he realized what had happened. A knife was sticking out of his back.

"Gah... Ah..." As soon as Subaru was conscious of it, an unbearable pain swept through him. He choked. It was a natural reaction to the searing agony.

...I've been stabbed! I've been stabbed! I've been stabbed! I've been stabbed! I've been stabbed! I've been stabbed! I've been stabbed!

Dumber, the one with the knife, had struck first. Subaru didn't notice as he drew his weapon, and just as Subaru was trying to push past him, he was stabbed in the back.

This pain was the same kind of torture that he had experienced in the past few hours, but no matter how many times he experienced it, he didn't think it was possible to ever get used to it.

"What? You really stabbed him?!"

"I didn't have no choice! What do you think would have happened if he had escaped out into the street? Just think of what we'd have to deal with if he did."

"Wait! Don't do that, you idiot! ....Ugh. Yeah, this is bad. His guts are damaged. He's gonna die."

The giant, Dumb, turned Subaru's body over, and as he did, the knife was pushed deeper into his back.

"Ughh...." Still greater suffering was piled on top of Subaru's existing pain and even Subaru's death throes were kept from leaving his throat.

Subaru couldn't call for help or scream out in anger. There was nothing left for him to do. He just repeated his irregular breaths, feeling as though he was going to drown in his own blood as it filled his throat.

The feeling in Subaru's hands and feet started to leave him, and his consciousness was flickering weakly like a light about to go out.

Again, his vision went dark. This was the end, just like last time.

What do you mean, "last time"...? Subaru thought to himself. The fact that he was now clinging to an idea that he had disregarded as stupid before just made him feel even more pitiful.

But if he was going to cling to it, he might as well go all the way.

Turn your thoughts away from dying. Before you die, figure out what's happening around you.

Your eyes are dead. Your arms and legs are gone, too. What you have left is your nose and your ears. Then you'd better use them both to death. It doesn't matter what lingering scent I smell. It doesn't matter if all I hear are insults. I smell the mud of the road. I smell the iron-like smell from the blood pouring from me. Now my nose is dead. It's dead. I doubt my ears will last much longer, either.

"…at…take the…valuables…"

"…ere! The guards! They…"

"…un! No! If we…caught, I'll…"

All I was able to pick up were those bits of conversation. That's great and all, but the part of my brain I need to figure out what that means is already dead. I'm dying so I just listened. I don't know if I'll remember. …What does it mean to remember? Why do I want to remember? What does it mean to want? Why…what?

As Subaru's brain died, his other functions followed soon after. At the very end, with a faint sound of something being pulled from him, something scraping…Subaru lost his life a third time.

4

When Subaru's consciousness awakened, he was in darkness. But realizing that it was a darkness of his own creation, he opened his closed eyelids. The bright sunlight burned his eyes. Subaru groaned a bit and put his hand over his eyes.

"So, kiddo. How's about that abble?"

It was a question that Subaru had grown used to hearing, in a voice he had grown familiar with, that was lobbed at him.

His ears were in perfect working order.

The hustle and bustle of the main street was loud, and completely different from the silence that was around him just before the end.

That was the way things were, despite the fact that, distance-wise, the silence was in an alley just one turn off the main street.

Pretty pathetic that I couldn't even get more than one street away.

The shop owner frowned at not getting an answer to his question. As Subaru saw the white scar being stretched across his face, he thought it made him look even more villainous.

But Subaru knew that he was actually a really kind and thoughtful person who was obsessed with his kid.

Of course, he probably didn't remember what Subaru did.

Thinking of that, he turned once more to the scarred shop owner.

"How many times have you seen my face so far?"

"What do you mean, 'how many times'? I haven't seen you before in my life. The way you stand out, I don't think I'd forget you and that awful expression you've got if I'd seen you before."

"I didn't need to hear that last part about my expression, you know? Anyway, what's the date today?"

"It's Tammuz the 14th. At this point, according to the calendar it's halfway through the year."

"Huh. I see. Tammuz, huh." Subaru had no idea what that date was supposed to mean. To begin with, he had no idea how they fixed the calendar in this world. It was probably too much to expect that they went by a solar calendar, but he couldn't be sure.

"So anyway, kiddo. How's about that abble?"

The shop owner was patient as Subaru went silent, but for him to have to deal with someone this long to just buy a single apple... He seemed to be reaching his limit. His face was starting to twitch.

Now this was a guy who didn't look all that great wearing a smile in the first place. When he was trying his best to smile, it probably had more of an effect of scaring customers away, and Subaru felt that whatever god put this man in this occupation was a cruel god indeed.

As for Subaru's answer to the shop owner's question, he put his hand on his hip and proudly put out his chest.

"I'm sorry, but I'm as broke as the sky is blue!"

"Then get the hell out of here!" The shop owner's yell was enough to throw Subaru back, and he scrambled out of there in a hurry.

I really can't go back to that shop for a while, Subaru thought, with both meanings in mind.

CHAPTER 4

FOURTH TIME'S THE CHARM

1

"Wallet...check. Cell phone...check. My corn soup chips and cup ramen are also here. My tracksuit and sneakers are at zero damage, and of course..."

Subaru lifted up the hem of his tracksuit top and twisted around this way and that to look at his back. There were no scars or any other traces of a wound on his back, around by his hips, or around the front of his abdomen. There wasn't a knife sticking out of him, or anything else unusual.

"Phew. Good. There's no greater embarrassment for a swordsman than getting stabbed in the back. As someone who did kendo in middle school, even if I take a wrong turn off the road when it comes to life, I can't let myself lose the way of the swordsman."

The sun was high in the sky and a gentle breeze brushed up against Subaru's skin. People bustled about, back and forth on the main street, and yet again that same lizard cart passed by.

"Well, with this much circumstantial evidence, I've got no choice but to accept this, do I? It's a little bit hard to believe, but..."

All of the wounds on Subaru's body had disappeared; the rips and bloodstains on his tracksuit were gone as well. In Subaru's hands, inside that plastic convenience store back were his unopened chips, waiting for Subaru to eat them.

"So, it's one of those things, huh…"

He put his hand that had been up against his jaw out in front of him, and then snapped his fingers so that everyone on the street could see him.

"Whenever I die, I start back at square one in my initial state. At least, that's the way it seems."

Subaru had thought that his theory was stupid before, but he finally decided to accept it.

2

"I guess I'll call it 'Return by Death'… The fact that it's a power that assumes you're going to lose really makes it fitting for me, doesn't it?"

It was a power that activated once the user had lost their life. If the heroic thing was to come back from the brink of death and win the day, then getting a chance to do things over after you've lost felt more like something a cheat would do.

"More seriously, though…would you call this sort of thing time travel?"

A loop phenomenon that only activated under certain conditions. If you were to think of it as a game, you could say it was like Subaru was being brought back to an auto-save point, one he had no control over, whenever he died.

"So a loop or a time slip, huh… I mean, I'm used to this sort of thing happening in manga, but I saw somewhere that realistically it was really hard to explain time travel to the past…like, that it would be easier to remake the world from scratch rather than slip back in time."

With what Subaru knew from the Internet, where knowledge was vast but shallow, going back in time was about as unrealistic as you could get. However, given that he had already been summoned to another world, he wasn't really in a position to be debating degrees of unrealism.

"But if you consider that this Return by Death thing is really happening, then everything so far starts to make sense."

Looking back, Subaru had already died three times in this world.

The first time was when he and Satella had visited the loot cellar together. The second time was when he, Rom, and Felt had all been cut down by Elsa's blade. Then the third time, which to Subaru just felt like it happened a few minutes ago, he'd died a dog's death.

Unlike the first and second times, the third death was the worst, and he couldn't make any excuses about it. He didn't think that he could mess up so badly as to be killed by weak mob characters while he was still in the prologue.

"Still, dying three times in only half a day is just way too high of a rate."

Given that normally people only had one life to live, dying three times in half a day was just absurd.

Sure, Subaru had lived the previous seventeen years of his life peacefully, but depending on how you looked at it, if you multiplied 17 years by 365 days, and three resets, Subaru had lived through quite a few days on which he could have died.

"Or...if you looked at it another way, I just suck at living."

The difference between the difficulties of staying alive in his previous world and this one was far too great. There were tons of places here that threatened Subaru's life. There were dangerous places wherever he turned.

"Given the similarities between the first and second time...Elsa was probably the culprit the first time as well."

The first time, the one who was hiding in the shadows of the loot cellar was probably Elsa. The giant corpse was Rom, and he and Satella had arrived after Felt and Elsa had had their negotiations.

"I can't be sure, but Felt probably asked for too much, and after negotiations broke down...that's what happened."

After Elsa had finished making sure no one was left alive to tell what happened, Subaru and Satella had been unlucky enough to walk right in.

"The second time is simple. I was already with Rom and Felt when negotiations broke down... To be killed twice by the same person... Is Elsa the kind of character that when you run into them it means certain death?"

Subaru tried to pass the idea off as a joke so that he could lie to himself about how scared he was of her.

It was obviously foolish to even think of any options he might have if he ran into her.

The only place where Subaru had a chance of encountering Elsa was the loot cellar, and the only reason that Subaru needed to go to the loot cellar was to take back Satella's stolen badge, and the reason he wanted to take back Satella's stolen badge was because he wanted to return the favor to Satella for saving him.

However, because Return by Death had sent him back in time, his duty to return the favor to Satella was left behind in the world of his first run-through.

When Subaru met Satella on his third run-through, her cold reaction to him was proof of that.

Satella didn't know Subaru anymore. The favor that he was supposed to return got lost along the way as he was reset.

If so, it would be best for Subaru to forget about Satella and focus on avoiding the threat of Elsa.

Subaru didn't know why had been thrown into this Return by Death scenario, but because of it, he was fortunate enough to know the future. He knew what mines to avoid. Avoiding them was the right thing to do.

"Well, it's about time I got moving. Fortunately, I know that I can turn my cell phone into cash, so I'll just amass some funds, and live a good life using my modern knowledge. It'll be full of dreams! Don't you think, old man?"

"Just when I thought you were muttering some nonsense to yourself, you're asking my opinion? I don't know what you're talking about, and I don't care."

As Subaru looked back to the man in the shop from before, seeking affirmation, the man gave his retort with an annoyed look on his face.

With that cold response of his Subaru felt a little hurt inside. No matter what world you're in, the way people interact with strangers isn't all that different.

"But you see, there are some people out there who, even if it puts them in a tight spot, can't help but help other people out."

Even after something precious had been stolen from her, and even as she was in the middle of chasing after the person who'd stolen it, Satella had helped a completely and utterly useless stranger, took the time to heal his wounds, and tried to walk off without accepting any thanks.

She accepted that useless person's selfishness and for her trouble met a horrible end.

"When you do the same thing three times, there are a couple of things that you begin to understand. Well, more like after three times you'd have to be incredibly stupid *not* to understand those things. I may be a little stupid, but not *that* stupid."

"Just what nonsense are you talking about?"

"There's probably a pattern here. Some kind of inevitability. No matter how many times you do something over, at least a few things will never change. Or at least there's some sort of strong force that tries to keep things that way. For example..."

All three times, Satella had her badge stolen by Felt. The first and second times, Elsa caused a bloodbath. Even the third time around, it had probably happened as well, unrelated to Subaru's death.

"I don't know if I can win against Elsa. I still don't know. But there is one thing I do know."

If on the fourth time around Subaru didn't do something, Felt and Rom would be killed by Elsa. It was also unavoidable for Elsa and Satella to fight as well.

So what *if those two died?* Subaru thought. *One's a bit of a villain who deals in stolen goods, and the other one is a bold girl who tries to overcharge for those stolen goods without any sense of shame or regret.*

Both of them were criminals, so wouldn't it be better off if they were gone? But still...

"Well…I guess I really am a product of the modern age. Even though I always used to make fun of people like this when I sat in front of a computer screen…"

Subaru used to act as if he thought pity and compassion were stupid. It wasn't that he thought of it as an act, however. He just thought of himself as someone who didn't really care all that much. That way, no matter what situation he found himself in, he was able to keep himself from getting too emotional about it. It didn't matter to him if a few people he knew died. At least, that's how he used to think.

"But you know, I hate it. It feels terrible. I know those two are far from being saints, but knowing that someone you know is going to be killed…that's just impossible to ignore."

In the past, when he acted uncaring, it really must have been nothing more than an act. It was the product of his interactions happening in a virtual world. Now that he had to deal with these heavy issues in real life, there was a whole different level of weight to them. But at the same time, Subaru thought he was shallow for changing one of his core beliefs about life, just as soon as things got hard.

"And of course there's also Satella—I mean, that girl. I just can't just abandon her like that."

After calling her by that name and seeing her reaction, Subaru realized that "Satella" was a fake name. When he thought back to the first time around, she didn't seem to be too fond of being called by that name. Then with the third time, it was painfully clear.

In other words, that meant that she didn't trust him enough when she'd told him that name. Subaru hadn't built up enough relationship points with her, so at one of the scenario forks he failed the test for getting her real name.

"In that case, I guess I'll just have to work hard enough for her to actually give me her real name this time."

Subaru stretched and twisted his body around, popping several joints as he got himself pumped up. The storeowner looked on at Subaru's strange actions with a surprised look on his face.

Subaru, in response, suddenly lifted up his hand and said, "There's just some times where a man's gotta do what a man's gotta do! Right, old man?"

"Yeah, yeah. That's exactly the way it is. Totally agree. So go on and get outta here."

Subaru thought that he had struck a good pose and said that line pretty well, but given the storeowner's terribly monotonic reaction, he could feel his face starting to twitch.

Once the annoyed storeowner finally pushed him out of the store, he hurried along. After running about two hundred meters down the crowded street, he stopped and stood for a moment.

"Now, then…" Subaru lifted up his short bangs with his hand and then in exaggerated motions looked this way and that. Then he put his hand out to a nearby wall and leaned against it.

"Where do I need to go if I want to meet Not-Satella…?" he said. It wasn't a phrase that inspired confidence about his actions, but he wasn't going to just sit around and wait.

3

Now that Subaru thought of it, most of the circumstances surrounding his and Satella's meeting were coincidence.

Both the first time and the third time Subaru had run into Satella in a place not far from this main street, but that was about the only thing in common. At the very least, it would help if Subaru knew when the theft would be taking place…

"Just how long was I sitting glumly there in front of that fruit shop?"

Subaru felt like it could have been a few minutes, but at the same time it could easily have been almost an hour.

"Should I just wander about and leave everything to chance? Hope that the red string of fate between me and her will bring us together?"

Subaru had lifted both of his pinkie fingers in front of his face, twisting them around as if they were dowsing rods while spectators watched on with curious glances.

As Subaru continued searching he realized that he was in a place that he remembered seeing before.

"I guess my ties to fate are working pretty well after all!" Subaru said, full of himself, before realizing just where he was. Before he knew it, he had wandered into an alley.

"Isn't this the place where I first met Satella…?"

He felt that it was similar, but he couldn't be sure. Even if this was the exactly same alley as before, there was no guarantee that she would come running down it.

"After all, the dead end I was at when I was killed the third time was in a completely different place…"

Even if it was certain that Not-Satella would get her badge stolen by Felt every time, the route that they took after that would differ depending on the circumstances. It was possible that the first and second times the route they took was the same, but the third time, because of Subaru's interference, fate must have shifted slightly.

After thinking that far, Subaru realized just how shallow his thinking was. If he entered this familiar alley, it was possible he would run into Felt and Not-Satella. However, that also meant meeting another set of people as well. In other words…

"I really am tired of looking at your faces, Dumb, Dumber, and Dumbest," said Subaru wearily as he turned around, and saw the same three thugs blocking his path out of the alley.

Their looks, their clothes, their faces—everything was the same. Both their goals and their equipment must be the same as well. Subaru was making absolutely no progress at all. Subaru supposed that made sense, though; after all, he was just walking around the same places as before.

"Why these guys when I have so much trouble finding Not-Satella and Puck…"

The reason Subaru was having trouble meeting up with Satella was that her actions were probably affected by several other random factors besides Subaru. However, the reason that Subaru kept encountering Dumb, Dumber, and Dumbest was probably because they had picked him out for a target early on.

That's why, even if he picked a different alley, he would always run into these guys. Their event was unavoidable.

"Even if I've come up with a splendid theory as to why all of this is happening, it doesn't make me any happier. So what do you want with me, guys?"

"Just what is this fool mumbling about?"

"He's probably just too clueless to understand what's going on. How about we show him."

Dumb and Dumber's conversation was the same as ever, and that made Subaru feel even lousier about the whole thing. However, this didn't mean that he could let his guard down.

The bar set for the conditions necessary to clear the Dumb, Dumber, and Dumbest event wasn't very high, but there wasn't a 100 percent chance that Subaru would be able to make it out of this alley. After all, they were the ones who had caused his death the third time around.

As he was thinking about that, Subaru's thoughts drifted to what happened the last time, just as he was dying. As he lay dying, he was able to pick up some of the sounds of what was happening.

Subaru tried to remember the final conversation that Dumb, Dumber, and Dumbest were having. What were they afraid of? There was a word that they said. Subaru thought he should be able to remember it...and it was...

"Guards!!"

Hearing Subaru's sudden and unexpected SOS, Dumb, Dumber, and Dumbest jumped. The silence of the alley was broken and the volume of Subaru's yell was sure to have reached the main street.

With all of Subaru's training in kendo, his sense of shame about suddenly yelling out was long gone.

Additionally, Subaru, who realized at this point in his life what a loser he was, wasn't one to let his pride be hurt by suddenly calling for help.

"Someone! Someone please call some men over here!"

"Wha... What, are you kidding me?! You're really going to start calling for help?! Who does that?!"

"In this sort of situation you're supposed to listen to us if you want to avoid getting hurt! You're just going to ignore us and call for help?! That's not normal!"

"What?! Don't give me 'That's not normal'! In what world is this not normal?! Oh! It can't be! You're not saying that you're trying to do something where it'd be trouble if I called out, are you? Oh my God!"

"Shut up! You know what we mean!"

"I'm not listening! I can't hear you through that thick wall of insincerity! Police!!"

Subaru continued to yell and keep the thugs on their toes, but on the inside he was breaking out into a cold sweat.

As Subaru had been breathing his last during his third time around, just as his consciousness was leaving him, Dumb, Dumber, and Dumbest had said the words "guards" and "run." In other words, in this world, there was an organization that functioned like a police force.

That information led Subaru to the new option, "Call for Help." Even he thought it was a pretty lame tactic.

But unfortunately, Subaru didn't seem to get a very encouraging reaction from the crowd out on the main street.

"Well, looks like that didn't work..."

"Threatening us like that...I almost got a little bit scared there, man."

"Just a little bit!"

"Not even a little bit! Only a tiny bit!"

In unison, Dumb, Dumber, and Dumbest proceeded to deny how pathetic they were, in about the most pathetic way possible.

As the men tried to regain control of the situation, after looking at each other and nodding, each of them took out their weapons. One took out a knife, one took out a rusty hand ax, and finally the last one...

"Why are you the only one without a weapon? What? Didn't you have the money to buy something?" Subaru taunted.

"Shut up! I'm stronger without a weapon! I'll beat you to death, you little punk!"

"Man, I would have loved to show you all what happened to you guys the second time around."

Remembering how he had landed that perfect suplex, Subaru wanted to give himself another pat on the back, but at the same time, he realized that he was in a pretty bad spot right now. It was looking more and more like Subaru wasn't going to make it out of this.

"Can't you guys let me off easy? ...I'm not a big fan of pain."

After going through the experience three times already, Subaru knew that he was never going to get used to dying. To top it all off, the cause of death in all three instances was because of wounds inflicted by a blade. The sharp pain that went along with those wounds always felt fresh and was always a shock, as if his nerves were being whittled away.

Subaru didn't want to experience that kind of death again, and that was not all.

"Just because I've been Returned by Death a few times already, there's no guarantee that it will happen this time as well..."

Subaru had no reason to think his Return by Death had a limitless number of uses. Subaru didn't notice a number on his body or anything, but as the saying goes, Buddha only has the patience to save you three times.

If what was happening to Subaru was a gift of the Buddha's good graces, Subaru had already used up all of his continues.

"If I die here, my life in this new world may really come to an end. ...I guess my best bet is to try to run away, even if I get injured in the process."

The weapon that looked the most able to inflict a mortal wound was, of course, the tried and true knife. The hand ax really did have a lot of rust, so if Subaru blocked himself with his convenience store bag, he'd get away with a blunt hit rather than being cut. Of course, the weaponless guy was a safe bet. So Subaru focused all of his attention on Dumber, the one with the knife, and played through his escape in his head.

Three... Two...

"That's enough."

That voice suddenly and clearly cut right through the dry tension of the alley. In the voice's gallant tone there was no sense of hesitation, and no ounce of mercy. Just listening to the voice was enough to be overpowered by its existence, and it was a perfect match for carrying the voice's owner's intentions.

Subaru lifted up his head, and Dumb, Dumber, and Dumbest turned around. In front of them was a young man.

What stood out about his appearance, more than anything else, was his flaming red hair. Underneath it were sparkling blue eyes that could only be described as "daring." His extraordinary good looks helped magnify his sense of gallantry, and with one glance you could tell that this young man was a cut above the rest.

He was slender and tall and wore well-made black clothes, and while it did not have elaborate decor, around his waist he also wore a knight's sword, which endued him with an inordinately intimidating air.

"No matter what the circumstances are, I will not allow you to perpetrate any more violence against that young man. That is enough."

As the young man said this, he walked straight past Dumb, Dumber, and Dumbest, and got between them and Subaru.

Subaru was at a loss for words at the young man's bold attitude, but Dumb's, Dumber's, and Dumbest's reactions were different.

All of the thugs' faces went pale, and with quivering lips they pointed at the young man.

"That burning red hair and sky-blue eyes...plus that knight's sword sheath engraved with the image of dragon's claws... It can't be..."

The thugs stared on in disbelief.

"Reinhard... Are you the Master Swordsman Reinhard?!"

"Well, I suppose I don't have to waste time introducing myself. ...Although I am not fond of that title everyone gives me. It's still too heavy for me," the man called Reinhard muttered with a tinge of self-deprecation in his voice. But the light in his eyes was unwavering.

The thugs, overpowered by the young man's stare, took one step back. They looked at each other as if trying to determine the best time to escape.

"If you're planning on running away, I'll let you off this time. Just head back out toward the main street. However, if you plan on being stubborn, you will have to deal with me."

Reinhard put his hand on the hilt of his sword and motioned to Subaru behind him with his chin.

"We're down three against two. They have the advantage on us in numbers. I'm not sure if the little help I can give will be enough to make a difference, but I will do the best I can, on my honor as a knight."

"Wha-what?! Are you kidding me? This isn't even a contest!"

After hearing what Reinhard had said, Dumb, Dumber, and Dumbest were completely out of sorts. They scattered like baby spiders, forgetting to even hide their weapons as they ran out onto the main street. Unlike the first time around, none of them threw any insults as they ran. That was a testament to the difference in scale between them and this young man.

As soon as the thugs left the alley, the heightened tension that had permeated it immediately faded away. Realizing that this was something the young man did purposefully, Subaru was again at a loss for words.

More than anything else...

"For you to do all of that and still keep so cool...it's like you and I aren't of the same species."

The level of human purity in his face, his voice, his stance and actions, were all way too high. If his personality and upbringing were also the same way, if he wasn't doing something corrupt on the side, there was no way it all could balance out.

Putting his jealousy aside, Subaru let out a flat-sounding laugh, and then prostrated himself on the ground.

"You have saved my life, and I, Subaru Natsuki, am forever grateful. I must say that I am impressed with both your honorable intentions and bravery..."

"You're giving me too much credit. It was because their advantage of three against one fell to three against two that they became unsure of themselves. It would have been different if it was only me against them."

"No… Given how scared they were of you, even if it were ten against one…or even a hundred against one, I still think they would have run away. But what's with your gallantry stats?! You're like a saint both in body and mind. You're so brilliant I think I'm going to go blind!"

To be honest, there was such a difference in their looks, Subaru really didn't want to be standing next to him. Subaru examined Reinhard again, but the more he looked at him the more he thought that this beautiful young man had to have been chosen by God.

However, he did not look like he was a guard.

"Umm…I can just call you by your name, Mister, uh…Reinhard… right?"

"I don't need the 'Mister.' You don't have to be so formal, Subaru."

"Well, we're pretty close all of sudden, huh? Anyway, thanks again, Reinhard. You're the only one who came running when I called. I have to say, it makes me feel a bit lonely that no one else seemed to care."

Given how many people were out walking on the main street, it wasn't possible that Reinhard was the only person who heard Subaru call out. But as Subaru complained, Reinhard lowered his eyes slightly.

"I don't really want to say this, but I think I can understand them. For the majority of people, the risk of interfering when thugs like those are involved is too great. You were right to call for guards."

"The way you're saying that…are you a guard, Reinhard? You don't look like one at all."

"I get that a lot. I am off duty today so I'm not wearing my uniform, and even I know that the way I look, I'm lacking the sternness of an authority figure," Reinhard said, spreading both his arms, but Subaru thought differently.

The biggest reason that Reinhard didn't look like a guard was that he appeared to be far from the lowly, rough sort of idea Subaru had of what a guard should look like.

"Now that I think of it, didn't they call you something like 'master swordsman'...?"

"My family's position is rather special, you see. So I've got a lot of heavy expectations placed on me. Every day's a battle." Reinhard smiled, shrugging his shoulders. Apparently Reinhard had a sense of humor as well.

Subaru was now completely sure that this guy was the perfect human being. Forget about lamenting to God about the unfairness of it all, at this point, Subaru was just impressed.

"By the way, I thought that your hair and clothes, and also your name are pretty unusual, but... Where are you from? Why did you come to the capital of Lugunica?" Reinhard asked, looking down at Subaru and his appearance.

Given that Subaru's background was unclear, it seemed to be a pretty natural response for someone who was a guard.

"It's a little hard to answer that first question. Last time when I said, 'a small country to the east,' it didn't work, so let me rephrase that. I've come from a place even farther east than here, a place no one has ever seen before—from the ends of the Earth," finished Subaru with a glint in his smile. Subaru thought that it was a pretty safe answer, but Reinhard looked surprised.

"Farther east than Lugunica...? You can't mean beyond the Grand Cascade. Is that supposed to be a joke?"

"Grand Cascade?" Subaru tilted his head with the unfamiliar term.

Cascade...like, a waterfall? Subaru, who wasn't familiar with the geography of the surrounding area, had no idea what Reinhard was talking about. The only places Subaru really knew in this world were the main street, alleys, the slums, and the loot cellar.

"It doesn't seem like you're trying to fool me or anything, but... Well, that's fine. Anyway, it looks certain that you're not from the capital, but you have a reason for being here, right? Right now,

Lugunica is not as peaceful as it usually is. It's falling into a state of unrest. Whatever you're here for, I'd be glad to help."

"Come on, it's your day off, right? There's no need for you to waste a day off just to help me out, you've really done more than enough already. ...But, I would like to ask you a question, if I could."

Subaru shook his head in response to Reinhard's offer, but then he raised up a finger as if he suddenly remembered something.

"I'm all ears. I'm not a very informed individual, so I'm not sure I can help all that much, though."

"Well, it's less of a question and more me asking about a person, so no worries. So anyway, have you seen a silver-haired girl with a white robe walking around in this area?"

Not-Satella's appearance was one that stood out. Of all of the things about her, the color of her hair and that hawk-embroidered white robe in particular stood out the most. If someone like that was walking around in the capital, there was a good chance that Reinhard, a guard, had noticed.

"A white robe and silver hair..."

"If I were to add anything, she's extremely beautiful. Also, there's this cat... Well, it's not like she's carrying it around in front of her, but she has one, if that's helpful."

If there was someone who was wearing a white robe, had silver hair, and had that cat spirit, then it had to be her. However, the cat was usually hidden away inside her hair, so expecting a sighting that included the cat was hoping for a little too much.

"...What do you plan on doing when you find her?"

"Something she lost...er...I guess something she's looking for? Anyway, I want to give what she's looking for back to her."

Of course, Subaru didn't have it on him right now, and it was even possible that she hadn't had it stolen from her yet, but there was no need to complicate things.

Reinhard narrowed his eyes at Subaru's response, and then silently thought for a few moments before answering.

"Unfortunately, I can't say I've seen anyone like that. If you'd like, though, I don't mind helping you find her."

"I can't ask that much of you. It's all right, I'll figure things out on my own." Subaru lifted up his hand to refuse Reinhard's request, and then turned to exit the alley and walk along the main street. It was possible that he would run into Not-Satella again, like he did the third time around.

If possible, it might be better to catch Felt and keep her from stealing the badge in the first place. Considering what would happen otherwise, Subaru thought that might be the best approach to take.

"The problem is, considering how fast Felt is, whether I could really catch her or not. In the worst case, I could get some guards to come to the loot cellar, but..."

"Loot cellar?"

"Oh, don't worry about that. Forget I said anything. It's just the name of a place an old man I know likes to hang out."

As Reinhard reacted to his statement Subaru tried to divert his attention and at the same time rejected the idea of getting guards involved. Even if Subaru brought guards with him, with Elsa as an opponent there was a good chance that it would only result in more casualties. That's just how superhuman that assassin's skills were.

"Well, if all of the guards here were superhuman as well, it might be a different story... Anyway, I guess I should head back to the main street."

"Are you going?"

"Yeah, I am. Thanks again, Reinhard. I'll have to return the favor one day. ...Can I meet you again if I go to a guard station or something?"

"I think so. If you just give my name, they'll know where to find me. I'd love to see you again, so stop by for any reason at all."

"Have I really done anything, or said anything to raise our relationship score that much? ...Anyway, if I ever get stuck or lost again I'll be sure to stop by," said Subaru jokingly, waving his hand good-bye.

"Be careful," said Reinhard, as cool and gallant as ever.

Pushed on by those words, Subaru was able to exit the alley with absolutely zero damage, all the while not noticing just how much the young man with the blue eyes was sizing him up as he watched him leave.

4

Now that Subaru had made it safely back to the main street, he did his best to look for Not-Satella. However, all that he could really do was open his eyes wide and stare at the passing crowd. Using his memories from the third time around, Subaru positioned himself near the fruit store he had become familiar with.

The face of the scarred store owner that Subaru could see out of the corner of his eye was very stern.

"This time our meeting wasn't exactly the best, was it... But, I know that you really are a kindhearted guy!" Subaru said, giving the villainous-looking shop owner a thumbs-up, to which the shop owner turned his face away from, annoyed.

Subaru drew his thumbs back feeling unloved, and then returned his gaze to the street. As always there were tons of people passing by, of all shapes, sizes, and kinds.

It had been over ten minutes since Subaru had started his lookout, and it had already been nearly an hour since he had started his fourth run.

"I'm not sure I can trust my sense of time, but it would be strange if the theft hasn't happened yet..." said Subaru to himself, when an anxious thought crossed his mind.

"Hey, old man."

"What is it, Mr. Penniless?"

When the shop owner came out in front of his store and looked at Subaru, he had already given up trying to hide how annoyed he was.

"Well, it's true that I am penniless, so I won't deny that, but... Old man, I've got something I'd like to ask you. Have you seen any sort of commotion happen around here lately?"

"You've got guts asking me a question without buying anything."

"Well I know that, but last time... Wait..."

As Subaru was talking he realized why the shop owner was in such a bad mood. The first time around, when Subaru and Not-Satella had visited the fruit shop together they had met again with...the shop owner's daughter. She hadn't been saved yet this time around.

"How could I have forgotten about that?! Don't tell me that I have to go find her first?"

"What are you talking about? Oh, fine. Whatever. Look, kiddo. Those sort of 'commotions' you're talking about aren't exactly unusual around here."

"I'm glad you answered my question, but are you serious?!"

Now that Subaru thought about it, the loot cellar was filled with things stolen from all over the capital. If there were that many thefts occurring, it spoke volumes about the level of security in the capital.

"Does this mean I've completely run out of options...?"

"However, the most recent commotion wasn't the usual fare. Someone was using magic and shot off two or three blasts of it. Just look."

The shop owner leaned forward and pointed to a stall about four spaces to the left. When Subaru followed with his gaze, he saw that right beside that stall was an alleyway, and there were a few holes gouged out of the wall leading into it.

"Oh, wow."

"There were some icicle-shaped things that were used like arrows, and one of them stuck inside that wall. It disappeared immediately afterward, though."

Each of the four holes was a little bigger than a quarter. Since they were able to make a hole like that in a stone wall, Subaru shivered to think what would happen if they hit a person.

"This magic looks like it's on a different scale from the first time I saw it... I wonder if Not-Satella's a little more upset than usual this time..."

If Subaru approached her without thinking, he might be the one on the receiving end of that magic. Subaru felt a cold sweat form on his brow.

"But if that's the case then I was too late this time as well."

If the theft had already taken place, it was going to be difficult for Subaru to meet up with Not-Satella on his own. In other words, what he should shoot for now was...

"I need to try to meet up with Felt. If possible, I need to try to catch her before she enters the loot cellar, and then exchange my cell phone for the badge, but..."

Given that was a place at which he had already been killed twice, Subaru wanted to avoid the loot cellar as much as he could.

"If I go too late, then it'll be what happened the first time all over again. However, if I go and meet up with Rom and wait for Felt, then I'll end up repeating what happened the second time around..."

What was most important was Felt's location. Right now, Felt was probably being chased around the capital by Not-Satella. If he could, Subaru wanted to meet up with her before she arrived at the loot cellar.

"Maybe I could just rely on my Return by Death and use this time just to gather information...?"

While that seemed like a viable option, Subaru shook his head and quickly rejected that plan. This was something he realized after experiencing death three times, but every time it was incredibly painful. He didn't want to experience something like that ever again.

Subaru was anxious about relying on his Return by Death power when he didn't know how or why it worked. Say Subaru decided to throw away this fourth time around by watching things unfold with the intention of dying afterward so he could reset everything. What if when he did that, his Return by Death didn't activate because he had run out of the number of times he could use it? No one would be laughing at that end.

"In the end, I've really got to cling to life as long as I can. Well, I suppose that goes without saying, though."

After making his decision, Subaru twisted around to stretch his body. The shop owner didn't seem too pleased as Subaru did his radio exercises in front of his store, but as Subaru finished and was jogging in place he waved back at him.

"I don't know why you suddenly decided to help me, but thanks, old man."

"It's no big deal. Just a little while ago, another penniless person like yourself helped my little girl out, you see."

As he listened to the shop owner's reply, Subaru first was surprised and then burst out laughing. Oh, the power of fate. No matter how troubled this shop owner's little girl was, someone was going to save her. Just knowing that made Subaru feel that it was worth coming here.

"All right! I'm really going to get going now. Next time I'll buy one of your abbles for sure!"

"Well, if you do you'll be a customer, and I'll welcome ya. Work hard, Mr. Penniless," the shop owner said in a monotone.

"Gotcha. I really am praying that the next time I come back here will be with money in my hands, I tell you," said Subaru as he left running.

Subaru's destination was the slums, but this time, in a different direction from the loot cellar. If he headed toward the loot cellar, he was sure to raise a couple of bad flags, so this time he was going to try a different route.

5

"You're looking for where Felt lives? If you just take that road over there until it turns into another street, you should be able to find it."

"Thanks, you really helped me out, brother."

"No problem, brother. You uh…live strong and take care of yourself out there, okay?"

The middle-aged man Subaru was talking to smiled at him weakly as he disappeared behind a creaking door. Throughout their entire conversation, the look of pity on the man's face never once disappeared from his awkward smile.

Subaru tightened his fist, happy that his plan was working.

"It was a strategy I formed after my experiences from the first and second times in the slums, but…I never imagined it would work this well," Subaru said, shaking the sleeve of his tracksuit, which was caked in dried mud.

In order to help him track down Felt, the brilliant plan he'd thought of after arriving at the slums was to make himself look as down and out and destitute as possible.

The first time around, when Subaru visited the slums with Not-Satella, Subaru had not long before been beaten up by Dumb, Dumber, and Dumbest. Because of that, most of the slum's inhabitants had pitied him and been fairly cooperative. The second time, however, when Subaru hadn't taken much damage, the people gave him a comparatively cold reception. The difference was like night and day. So remembering that, Subaru made himself look so bad he had risked overdoing it.

"Well, I did step in the poop of who knows what kind of animal, after all. Anyway, I think I've pinned down where Felt sleeps, but... the problem is whether she'll come back here or not before she goes to the loot cellar."

Fortunately, of the four people he was able to get information from, all of their answers about the location of Felt's living place matched up. However, Subaru thought the chances of her coming back to it were about fifty-fifty. There was also the possibility that she did not want to risk having her place found out by returning there while she was being chased.

"Well, sitting around and worrying about it won't help me at all, so let's stop worrying. Okay!"

No sense in worrying about things that can't be helped. This is where Subaru's decisiveness shone.

As he continued to scrape off more caked mud from his clothes, Subaru dashed off deeper into the slums. It was dark as ever and there were puddles of who knows what here and there that Subaru had to jump over to avoid. But just as he was doing so, he almost ran right into someone who suddenly appeared.

Subaru was able to turn just in time and hit his back against the wall of the alley, giving off a grunt as he lost his breath.

"Oh, I'm sorry about that. Are you all right?"

"Don't worry. Don't worry. I'm actually a pretty sturdy fell...
ow...?!"

As he was trying to play himself off as tough, Subaru looked up
and when he realized who he was looking at his sentence trailed off
and ended in a high-pitched squeal.

After hearing Subaru's voice like that, the black-haired woman
laughed softly.

"What a funny guy. Are you sure you're all right?" she said, lifting
her hair back behind her ear.

Even that simple motion was somehow sexy, and Subaru reaffirmed the belief inside himself that every move this woman made
was extremely erotic.

She was definitely someone Subaru did not want to meet again.

It was the woman who had cut open his abdomen and spilled his
guts—twice. It was Elsa.

"You don't have to act so scared. I won't do anything to you."

"I-I'm not sc-scared, okay? W-why would you think that....?"

"You smell..." replied Elsa, seeing past Subaru's empty attempts
to seem tough as she slowly narrowed her eyes as part of a beautiful
smile.

"Smell?" thought Subaru, confused. But Elsa just breathed in
through her beautifully formed nose.

"When people are afraid, they smell afraid. Right now you are
afraid...and also angry, it seems...at me."

Elsa seemed to be having fun revealing what Subaru was thinking, as she looked up at him. Subaru answered with silence and a
false smile, taking deep breaths and doing his best to control the
quickening pace of his heart.

As Subaru went silent, Elsa narrowed her eyes like a snake. While
Subaru felt pinned down by her stare, at the very least he would not
be so weak as to look away.

Elsa licked her lips in response to Subaru's empty display of
strength.

"...I can't say I'm not curious, but fine. I can't risk causing a fuss
right now."

"Th-that doesn't sound very nice. If you scare people too much your beauty's going to be put to waste, you know?"

"Well, don't you have a way with words. …If you could better hide the animosity you have for me, I might have been impressed."

Elsa took her finger and gently pushed on his forehead, and Subaru's frozen body loosened up. As Subaru gasped and heaved, trying to get his breath back, Elsa put her finger to her lips.

"Well then, I'll be going now. I have a feeling we'll meet again."

"If the next time we meet is in a bright place with lots of people around I'll be able to relax, too," said Subaru cynically, but it was all he could do just to get that out.

Elsa gave a longing smile as if she didn't want to leave Subaru just yet, but turned back around, with her black robe fluttering as she melted back into the darkness.

After Subaru watched Elsa literally vanish from sight, he leaned up against the wall, feeling like he had run a mile.

"I…I definitely didn't expect to run into her again just yet. I guess she was just wandering around the area before she went to the loot cellar…?"

At the unexpected encounter with the final boss, Subaru felt as though his spirit was about to break. In terms of how mentally prepared he was to deal with either, meeting Elsa had much more of an impact on him than meeting Not-Satella. Subaru prayed that this was the last time he was going to have to see Elsa.

"I think that Felt's place is just farther down ahead, but…Elsa couldn't have found Felt and already wreaked havoc, could she…?"

She was a deranged psycho who derived pleasure from cutting open people's stomachs. It was not unthinkable that she would have slaughtered two or three people just to kill time. Plus, with this being the deepest part of the slums, Subaru had a bad feeling about what he might find.

"I-it's probably all right. I didn't see or smell any blood. …I think."

Given the stench of rotten garbage that filled the alley it would be impossible to discern the smell of blood, and it was so dark that Subaru wasn't sure he'd be able to see traces of blood if they were there. But it was probably okay. Surely it was. So Subaru hoped at least.

About five minutes after his encounter with Elsa, Subaru reached a dilapidated shack.

"With the information I was given, I think this is it, but...does this really count as a living space?" said Subaru, confused as he stood in front of the wooden plank that was serving as a door to the shack.

The inside of the shack was about the size of two portable toilets, the kind used at construction sites. It was as though someone took the phrase, "You only need half a tatami mat for standing, and a full one for sleeping," to heart.

"Well, I suppose if it's just a place to sleep, then it fits the description..."

However, the thought that such a small girl was living in a place like this made Subaru feel pity for her. He supposed he could forgive her for being so obsessed with money.

"So she's living out her life here, huddling her already small body into an even smaller space. I guess it's no surprise she'd turn out as twisted as she is. Ah... How pitiable, how pitiable is she."

"Oh come on! It's not that bad. Just who do you think you are, kid, belittling my place?"

Just as Subaru was entering his pitying mode, he heard a voice behind him and turned around.

There in front of him, glaring at him, was the little blond figure of...Felt.

The way she looked was not particularly different from the other times they had met. If anything, she looked a little dirtier than before, but that seemed like the result of her getaway being a quite a bit more rough on her than last time.

"What's with you, looking at me like that with those pitying eyes?! You underestimating me just because I'm a girl and just a little bit filthy?"

"I think you're reading the wrong emotion there, but...I'm just glad I've found you."

While Felt didn't even try to hide how irritated she was, Subaru subconsciously relaxed his shoulders in a sense of relief. Subaru was genuinely happy to meet up with her again. He was worried about what might have happened after his near-miss incident with Elsa, but in the end, things seemed to be looking for the better, rather than the worse.

In response to what Subaru said, Felt replied, "Oh, so you're a customer." She breathed out her nose, pleased with herself.

"The fact that you came here means you've got business with me, right? From the way you look, it's clear that you're not from around here."

"Oh. You're quick to see that I'm not really one of you. You've got good eyes there."

"The people around here would at least take a little bit more care about the way they look. You're trying way too hard. Plus, the way you're trying to fool us with that dirty trick of yours, you look like you're even worse a person than I am."

As always, this girl really knows how to be insulting, doesn't she? Subaru thought, quickly wanting to take back everything he'd said about pitying her.

"So, what do you want? If you want something stolen, I'll need the money first. Depending on who the target is I may ask for more later, though."

"'If I want something stolen,' huh… This is quite a business you're running here. Are you really that proud of your thievery?"

"It's called making a living. If I don't do this, I'd have to sell my body. Anyway, so what's it going to be? Or do you have some other business for me? Depending on your answer…" said Felt, quickly moving her fingers as if showing off her dexterity.

In her hand was a small knife that appeared as suddenly as if it had been summoned by magic. It was clear that she meant to show that she could defend herself.

If Subaru had to fight Felt, given both her dexterity and the fact that she had a knife, he had no chance of winning. But Subaru had no intention of fighting.

He lifted up his pointer finger and shook it left and right while clicking his tongue, as Felt continued to be on guard.

"I only have one item of business to discuss with you. I would like to buy from you that badge you stole."

6

Having come this far, Subaru thought that being indirect or trying to dodge the topic would just worsen Felt's impression of him. There was also the fact that Elsa was still wandering around the area, so Subaru wanted to dive right into negotiations.

However, Felt put her hand over her chest where it was likely she was holding the badge.

"How do you know that I stole a badge? The only person who should know that is the one who hired me, and I only stole it just a little while ago. This is way too quick a response for you to have just heard about it on the street."

"When you put it that way... Yeah? That's a good point. That was too careless, even for me, right?"

"...You really need to do a better job of hiding your intent, kid. A little taunt like that and you're already spilling the beans?"

As Subaru held his head in his hands at his mistake, Felt looked as though she had lost the heart to keep up her hostility.

Felt dropped to her knees so that she was eye level with Subaru.

"So you want to buy this badge off me, huh? What are you trying to do? You can't be on the same side as that woman, right? Is she your rival or something?"

"More like my archenemy, maybe? Like how you'd feel if she killed your parents. Or rather, if she killed you."

"What are you talking about? Well, whatever, I don't really care about that."

As Subaru was trying to figure out how he was going to talk his way out of this one, Felt just laughed. She then took the dragon-adorned badge out from her breast pocket and waved it in front of Subaru.

"I'll sell this to whoever can offer me a higher price. Even if there's a chance that woman'll be angry if I break off our deal."

"Yeah, there's definitely a possibility she'll just snap, but... Anyway, I'm just talking to myself, you can ignore me."

Subaru cleared his throat, and put on a serious face.

"So does this mean you'll hear me out?"

"Only if it looks like there's money in it for me. That's obvious, right?"

"Sounds good to me. ...I've prepared an item that is worth more than twenty blessed gold coins, and I would like to buy your badge with it."

Felt's ears perked up, and her red eyes narrowed like a cat's. It looked as though she was trying not to appear shaken, but if she had a tail it would be twitching back and forth, so Subaru could not help but smile.

"Huh, I see. That's quite a price. It looks like my hard work's finally gonna pay off. ...But unfortunately for you, your rival has already offered me the same amount, you know?"

"Cut the crap! The deal was for ten blessed gold coins, right? You get too greedy and you'll die! No, like, seriously."

In actuality, it was pretty clear that that was why she died the first time. Cause of death: greed.

With Subaru having gotten the price right, Felt must have thought that she couldn't play it off anymore. After staring wide-eyed at him for a few moments, Felt lightly scratched the side of her head.

"What, you know that much, too? ...Yeah, okay? The deal was for ten blessed gold coins. But you know, if I tell the person who hired me that another offer was made, she might counteroffer with more, you know?"

"That one's not a lie, you know?" Felt, the thirteen- or fourteen-year-old, added, curling the edges of her mouth.

"You really are sly, aren't you? I'd like to say just give it up and take the deal, but I don't suppose you'd listen to me, huh?"

"Of course not! Plus, I'm not sure I can trust you. My ears didn't miss a word you said. You didn't say you brought twenty blessed gold coins, but only something worth that much. Isn't this a little unfair, with me knowing nothing about what you've got up your sleeves, but you knowing all about me?"

"I think it's more of a matter of how much you can prepare that really matters in negotiations…but it is true that without showing you this first, we're not going to get anywhere."

Subaru wanted to avoid having Felt sulk too much and wasting time, so he took his key item for the negotiations, his cell phone, out of his breast pocket. Upon seeing the small device, Felt raised her eyebrows a little bit, but that was it.

As always, she didn't respond to anything unless it was clear that it would lead her to money.

"Twenty blessed gold coins for this thing? It only looks like a hand mirror to me…"

"This is one of those immensely popular metia. It can take a slice of time and freeze it, saving it away."

Subaru turned on the continuous shooting mode. A light and mechanical sound went off several times. The bright light flashed through the alley and showered Felt with light.

"Whoah!" she said, in a rare show of girliness as she reacted.

Felt looked as though she was about to complain, but Subaru quickly showed her the cell phone's screen.

"This is the power of this metia. Using it you can leave behind a clear image. Another thing to add is that this is a very rare item. This is the only one like it in the entire world. How about that?"

Subaru had gotten used to explaining the cell phone's function at this point, and when he finished, Felt went, "Hmm…" and looked carefully at the cell phone in Subaru's hands, before nodding in agreement.

"…It doesn't seem like you're lying. But this is me? You said a clear image, but I think I'm quite a bit better looking than this."

"If you weren't in such a terrible environment and eating better, and—while it may contribute to what you might think of as shrewd business sense—if you could rid yourself of that sly, dirty personality of yours, I'd say there's hope for you! It's really just a matter of how you're dressed up."

"If we're talking about choosing the right words to say, you have no talent when it comes to holding a conversation, do you? Geez."

While Subaru might have scored himself a bit of irritation from that last statement, things were going well overall. However, one of the strong points of the people who lived in the slums was that they never easily agreed to anything.

"I'll accept that this thing you have is rare, but I'm still not sure I believe you when you say it's worth twenty blessed gold coins. I'm not such an airhead that I'll just take you at your word."

"Well...that's to be expected. I don't mind personally that you've got a spongy brain, but you're right. We need a third party's opinion."

It would have been great if Subaru could have pushed the negotiations through then and there, but he expected that that wasn't going to work. The problem was who to use as a third party...

"Deep in the slums, there's this place called the loot cellar. It's just as the name suggests, but I think that the quickest way will be to ask the weird old man that's there. He's fair when it comes to appraisals. He's very experienced, so I think he won't have a problem, even with this metia."

"I thought this would happen..."

Subaru had expected Felt to suggest Rom. It was also her meet-up point with Elsa, as well as a place where she'd have a bodyguard if things went south.

Given that an appraising eye was necessary for Subaru's metia card, there really was no other choice. However, Subaru really wanted to have everything settled before they ended up at the loot cellar.

"I have no problem with having the old man look at it, but..."

"Are you really going to call him 'old man' without even having met him yet? You may regret it, you know? He's pretty rough with people who don't know how to show respect."

"Despite that, he seems to be quite doting on a certain foul-mouthed young girl, always giving her milk and all..."

Subaru thought about the bald old man who always looked at Felt with calm eyes. From Rom's perspective, it must be like taking care of a granddaughter. But Subaru had no problem with him; it was the place that was the issue.

"I don't know what you seem to have a problem with, but if you're in such a hurry, we should go ahead and get going to the loot cellar. To be honest, there was something else that I was planning on doing, but..."

"Planning on doing?"

"Well you see, the person I stole this badge from is a lot more persistent than I thought, so I thought I'd try to sabotage her a bit. After all, you give the guys hanging around a little money and they'll do anything for you."

"All right, let's get going, immediately. Right now. Let's go go go!"

Subaru pushed on Felt's back as she started walking and hurried her along toward the loot cellar.

"What's with you?" complained Felt, puffing up her cheeks, but Subaru was proud of himself for being able to avoid as many casualties as he could.

A little cash was way too low a price to offer for anyone to stand in Not-Satella's way when she was in a hurry. If the alternative was getting hit with a block of ice and squirming on the ground, Subara was sure they'd rather clutch their hungry stomachs instead.

"My only condition is that we have the old man take a look, settle the deal quickly, and then get straight out of there."

"Why are you in such a hurry, kid? You're all sweaty, you know. Live strong and take care of yourself."

"Everyone seems to say that, but is that like the slogan of the slums?!"

Subaru had the feeling they should change it from "live strong" to "live rough."

As Subaru put that thought behind him, he made his way with Felt to the loot cellar for the third time in total this fourth time around.

He would leave immediately. He would dash right out of there, even if he had to leave everyone else behind. Having made his decision, Subaru pushed harder on the back of Felt in front of him.

"That hurts!"

"Ow!!" said Subaru as he was kicked.

7

After meeting up with Felt at her shack, Subaru and Felt made their way through the slums toward the loot cellar.

The space between buildings was very narrow, and it was difficult for sunlight to make it through into the winding alleys. This additional darkness from the shade of the buildings only made the slums seem even drearier.

"..."

Subaru could feel a dampness underfoot. There were broken bottles of alcoholic drinks and scraps of paper all over the place, and every now and then there was a strong unpleasant stench that struck the inside of his nose.

Whether it was with Felt or Not-Satella, this was not the kind of place to be walking alone together with a young girl.

"Now this would just be so much better if we were holding hands and in a more beautiful and colorful place."

"Cut it out with that disgusting talk. Don't tell me that you're into little girls."

"I'm more into older women. You don't have to be so cautious, come on over here."

Perhaps because Felt had sensed danger from what Subaru had said, she started to pull away, but Subaru called her back. Reluctantly, Felt edged closer.

"No funny business, okay? You're the one who's going to be more in trouble if this deal goes south. We clear?"

"Why can't you just see that I'm doing my best to get this wary little kitten I'm dealing with here to relax so we can be friends? If you're so against me being friendly, why don't you stop messing around and actually take me to the loot cellar?"

"...How did you...?"

"How did I figure it out? Oh, come on, I'm not that stupid. I mean, I'm not incredibly familiar with this area, but I'm confident in my sense of direction. The way we've been zig-zagging around like this, even I'm going to start to get suspicious," said Subaru, looking down at Felt, who went silent, and shrugging.

With Subaru being right on the mark, Felt couldn't help but look away, but Subaru himself was extremely nervous, his heart racing.

After all, everything Subaru had just said was mostly a bluff. Subaru had been bothered by the fact that Felt's route didn't quite match up with the way he thought was the right way to get to the loot cellar, but what really caused him to question Felt was the fact that he had seen the same graffiti that was written on the wall twice, though at a distance, in a short period of time. However, at this point, his bluff was all he had to rely on.

"I know it's asking too much for you not to doubt me, and from your perspective, what I have to offer probably sounds too good to be true, so I can't blame you for wanting extra time to look me over."

"You've figured all that out, and you're not angry?"

"Well I understand that it makes sense for you to doubt me, and I *am* being unreasonable. However, I will not compromise on time. Please, take me straight to the loot cellar. I'm begging you, please," said Subaru, raising his hands, pleading.

Felt was startled, her eyes opened wide as she hesitated for a moment, not sure how to react, but she then took her hand and roughed up her blond hair.

"Well damn, I just don't get you. I don't get you but…I feel like I've got to pay you back for not getting angry at me just now. Fine, I'll take you straight there. I'll just leave the rest of my doubts in Rom's hands."

"I don't dislike that attitude of feeling totally free to rely on others, but…well…I, uh…nevermind."

Just as Subaru was about to lecture Felt, he realized what he was about to say and muddied his words.

What did Felt really mean when she said she'd leave everything to Rom? Rom treated Felt like she was a cute granddaughter of his, and he felt so strongly about her that he was ready to lay down his life for her. But how did Felt feel about Rom?

Subaru didn't want to think that that bald old man, whom he couldn't bring himself to hate, was just being used by her.

Felt narrowed her eyes as Subaru suddenly trailed off, but she didn't pry. Instead, having changed her attitude toward Subaru, she led Subaru straight to the loot cellar, without taking any detours this time.

As Subaru kept after Felt as she trotted on ahead, he thought again about the course of events that would happen once they got to their destination. It was already Subaru's fourth time doing this. He wanted to go the best route he possibly could.

As Subaru continued to walk, lost in thought, he saw that Felt had stopped, and was glaring at him.

"Stop looking down as you walk! You'll get infected by the gloominess around here, you know?"

"Well, I'd love to keep my head up, but it's not exactly clean and organized down around my feet, so it's dangerous if I don't pay attention. …What do you mean 'infected by the gloominess'?"

"You know exactly what I mean. I'm talking about the attitude of all the losers who live here."

Felt nodded her head to show she was talking about the surrounding area, the slums. The way she spit out her words showed clear animosity and hatred for the place, and Subaru opened his eyes wide.

"Losers…? Don't you think that's a bit harsh?"

"How's it harsh? I'm talking about people who languish in this alleyway life and lose the will to even try to get out of here or better themselves someway. I hate losers like that."

Subaru had spent a good amount of time talking with the people who lived here in the slums. It wasn't as though they had fallen so far that words wouldn't reach them, but like Felt said, he couldn't deny that they seemed to be content with life here, or rather, they seemed to have given up on getting anywhere else.

It would be easy to say that that kind of attitude couldn't be helped, but Felt wouldn't accept that answer. In the dim light of the alley, the light from Felt's crimson eyes would not fade one bit.

"I have no intention of living out my whole life here in these slums.

If a chance comes my way I'll cling to it and make it mine. The same goes for this deal now."

"So that's why, huh…"

The second time around, Felt had done everything she could to find weaknesses in and get more out of Elsa and Subaru. It was easy to explain those actions simply by saying she was greedy, but knowing what he did now, Subaru thought he could understand why Felt was so persistent.

Felt wanted to leave the slums, to break out of the circumstances of her orphaned childhood. At the root of all her actions was a desire for something more.

"So, with twenty blessed gold coins, will that dream of yours come true?"

"…It'll definitely be closer to coming true, and if I were going alone it might just be enough, but I don't know," Felt muttered.

"If you were going alone?"

Subaru's sharp ears wouldn't let that one slip, and he raised his eyebrows in response. Felt realized her mistake, clicked her tongue, and looked away.

"It's nothing. We're not so friendly that I'm going to talk about… Why am I being so talkative today in the first place?" said Felt, clearly regretting the slip of her tongue.

"Maybe you're loosening up a little because your goal's in sight?" replied Subaru, as he felt himself grinning.

Felt said if she were "going alone," she might be able to make it. This meant that she had someone else in the slums she couldn't leave behind. For Felt, who held such a feeling of animosity toward the people of the slums, there could only be one person she could feel that way about.

Thinking about who that was, Subaru couldn't help but grin.

"What's your problem? That smirk of yours is starting to tick me off."

"It's no big deal. I just realized that I was worrying too much about something I didn't need to be worrying about. Of course that's how it is. Of course. I don't know why I was worrying so much," said

Subaru, showing his teeth as he smiled. Everything suddenly made sense to him.

The second time around, Felt and Rom seemed to treat each other like family. Both were killed by Elsa, but even as they were dying they must have been thinking of each other.

Plus, Felt had saved Subaru's life in the nick of time once before as well.

If Subaru felt indebted to Not-Satella, then he should feel indebted to Felt as well.

"Let's hurry up. We've already lost too much time."

"I still don't understand why you're—Hey, wait. I said stop that!"

As Subaru started off and walked past Felt, he put his hand on her head and roughed up her blond hair. Her hair with its thin strands, which had probably never been combed, didn't feel bad flowing through Subaru's fingers. After Felt left the slums one day, and was dressed up a bit, Subaru thought she would probably shine bright.

So, in order to also put Felt on a path to reach her dreams...

"I've really got to make this work, don't I? ...I'm the only one who can do this!"

"Stop saying all these weird things and getting obsessed with yourself! I'm gonna bite you!"

With Subaru's hand still on Felt's head despite her protests, he silently solidified his determination.

He would change the fates of not just Not-Satella, but Felt and Rom as well...all of the people who had moved his heart.

That must be why Subaru kept repeating this day over and over again.

"I said, cut it out!!" Felt said, before biting Subaru.

8

"To the giant rats...?"

"Where might I find me some boric acid–laced dango? Now that's some poison."

"To the great white whale...?"

"You know, the first guy who comes to mind when I think of the word 'captain' is that good ol' Captain Ahab. Bet he has some fishing hooks."

"…To our most honorable great dragon…?"

"Since this is a fantasy world, I bet they really exist, but man, if I ran into one of those I can guarantee you I wouldn't be able to do anything. But you know, they are really cool, so I do kind of want to see one, but what a contradiction, huh? Those mixed-up feelings of mine can burn in hell!"

"Can't you just say the passwords without having to throw in all that nonsense?! Can you be more irritating?!"

The door to the cellar slammed opened so hard it looked as though it was going to come off its hinges, but Subaru, who expected this, had stepped back and was dealt no damage. Growling in frustration, too tall for the entrance, was the bald giant Rom, whom Subaru had grown used to seeing at this point. His face was red, his blood pressure probably high.

"If you get all angry like that, you'll pop a blood vessel. Even if we had modern medicine, I'd say your situation looks pretty bad."

"If you think it's so bad for me, then don't make me angry! Just who are you anyway?! I'm not supposed to let anyone in today, so scram!"

"Uh… Sorry about that. This guy is actually my customer, so could you please let him in?" said Felt, who had been hiding behind Subaru's back and just peeked out from behind him.

Rom slowly relaxed his shoulders. As Felt looked between a disappointed Rom and a whistling Subaru, she let out a sigh.

"You really have a terrible personality, kid. Without being too mean, it's simply the worst. Anyway, we're coming in, Rom."

As Felt slipped past Rom, still looking down, she entered the loot cellar as if it were her own place.

Rom first looked at Felt for further explanation but was ignored, so he turned his annoyed face toward Subaru.

"She really marches to the beat of her own drummer, huh? Us normal guys just get left behind, am I right?" said Subaru.

"I'd like to start back at square one, where I was first teaching her what different words meant... Anyway, get inside," replied Rom, with the tone of a man who had given up and washed his hands of everything, before shrinking his giant body back away into the cellar.

Subaru followed after Rom into the dusty air of the loot cellar. He tossed a few cautious glances this way and that, but fortunately there was no sign that Elsa or Not-Satella were hiding somewhere inside.

Felt was casually sitting at the bar counter, drinking a glass of milk as if it were her own.

"What? This is the only cold one left. I'm not letting you have it," she said.

"I can't believe you're not the least bit bothered by how shameless you're acting... Hey, old man, I'll just have some alcohol, whatever you've got. Thanks," said Subaru.

"You're one to talk! I'm not sharing with you! You're not getting any, you hear?!" shouted Rom as he ran across the room and rushed behind the counter, creaking the floorboards as he went, trying to hide what looked like his stash.

Rom's overreaction was enough to inspire pity, and Subaru just said, "I'm joking," with a chuckle.

"Well then, old man. We've already wasted a lot of time, so before we get sidetracked, I'd like to get straight to the point."

"I get the feeling we've already gone way off track, but...what's up?"

"Basically, I want you to appraise something. I would like you to put a price on this metia I have here, and guarantee its worth to Felt."

When Rom realized that the conversation was turning to business, his gray eyes turned serious. Old Man Rom looked at Felt, who nodded in confirmation, before turning to look back at Subaru.

Realizing that Rom was wordlessly asking to see the item, Subaru took his cell phone out of his pocket and handed it to Rom. It seemed that the metallic look of the phone was what first caught Rom's eye, and while he ran his fingers over it it looked like a tiny toy in his oversized hands.

"So this is a metia. Even for someone like me, this is my first time seeing one of these..."

"I'm pretty sure this is the only one of its kind in the whole world. Also, it's rather delicate so please be careful with it. If you break it I really have to kill myself, and I'm not joking about that...of course, meaning so I can start over."

Rom spent a while carefully looking over its outward appearance, but then slowly opened the folding phone. Rom had his first surprise as the phone started up and let out a sound, and he got his second surprise when he saw the phone's wallpaper.

"This picture..."

"I thought that this would be a good time to use that one. In order to show you the device's abilities, I put a scene from Felt's day as the wallpaper."

The wallpaper was one of the pictures that Subaru had taken of Felt when he met her in the alley. He picked the one he thought looked the cutest, and given the image quality he thought it was quite nice overall.

Rom looked from the image over at Felt, who was sipping her milk, and said, "Well, you've certainly surprised me. I don't think there's anything else out there that could draw such a perfect picture."

"This is a metia that takes out a slice of time and stores it away. It doesn't even compare with a picture someone has drawn, does it? If you'd like I can take one of you as well."

"I'm interested, but it seems kind of dangerous. It doesn't take any of your life away, does it?"

"No matter what age and no matter what world, it looks like that superstition about photographs persists, huh...?"

Subaru gave a weak smile in return to Rom's reaction, something that seemed like it should be out of the Taisho period, or before, and replied, "Even if I take your picture, you'll easily live until you're eighty or so."

Felt's reaction as she was listening to the conversation was also cute, and so after getting his permission, Subaru took a picture of Rom and showed it to him.

"Hmm..." Rom nodded.

"This is certainly something. If I were to take care of it, in terms of blessed gold coins maybe fifteen...no, I could absolutely get more than twenty for this. I believe it's worth that much."

Rom's business sense sparked; his eyes were shining as he made his appraisal.

While Subaru thought he was unsure how proud he could be to get the seal of approval from someone in the business of selling stolen goods, it certainly did put him at ease. His nostrils flaring with confidence, Subaru turned to Felt.

"Well, there you have it. This is the card I have to play. Like I said, it's worth more than twenty blessed gold coins. So now, I'd like to trade you this for that badge you've got."

"I see you seem to make that face a lot, but it really is annoying."

Apparently unimpressed that everything looked as though it was going according to Subaru's plan, Felt made a face. However, that didn't change the fact that this new information made the deal sound even better to her.

"Well, to be honest, I'm happy that I've got a guarantee that I can turn this metia into cash. It looks like I don't have to doubt you anymore about it being worth twenty blessed gold coins, either. I accept the card you have to play."

"Right?! So anyway, it looks like our negotiations have gone well. It'll be your job to sell it, but I wish you the best of luck! Now that's wrapped up, how about we go off somewhere and have a drink to celebrate our success?"

Subaru quickly walked over to Felt and put out his hand to take the badge, but Felt slowly pushed it back.

"Wait a minute. Why are you in such of a hurry?"

"Life has its limits. You've got to treat every second of it as precious, and it's a shame to waste any—"

"Right, right, enough of that," Felt said, narrowing her red eyes, and with a calm attitude stuck at the heart of her doubts.

"Why do you want this badge in the first place?"

9

Subaru paused, holding his breath, and as both Rom and Felt saw that, Subaru realized he had made a mistake. What he should have done was say a bunch of nonsense, just like he had before. However, nothing would come out.

As Subaru kept his silence Felt's mouth loosened up into a smile.

"The older lady who asked me to steal it in the first place didn't want to talk about it either, and it looks like you're the same?"

"…Well, stealing is pretty bad itself, so with theft involved, I'm sure everyone has some ulterior motives they wouldn't like to talk about…"

"But in your case, you stand out more than one usually would. If I slow down and think about it, you're trying to steal this away from whoever wanted me to steal it in the first place."

Felt's attitude was like one of a cat torturing its prey.

"Just what is this badge anyway? It's worth more than it looks, isn't it? That's why everyone wants it. In other words, it's worth more than even this metia."

"Wait, Felt. That line of thought is really dangerous. I pretty much already know what you're planning on saying right now, even if I'm just drawing on my experience from playing games, but…really, you need to stop."

As Subaru watched Felt's miserly gauge rise, he broke out in a sweat as he tried to stop her. If negotiations dragged on any longer than this, the bad end that was just waiting for them was going to be a reality.

"This deal is for more than twenty blessed gold coins! Just take it! Don't be any greedier than that! El—The one who commissioned you can only pay twenty blessed gold coins herself. She won't pay any more than that."

"How do you know that?"

"Well…"

"The more you talk the more you're giving away. You're in league with her, aren't you?"

Subaru wished he could just tell her that he knew because of his Return by Death ability, but of course he couldn't. Even if he did explain it that way, there was no guarantee she would believe it.

As Felt's eyes filled with even more doubt, Subaru knew that whatever he said, she wouldn't believe him anymore. At this point, he might have to wrestle the badge away from her.

But if I did that I'd have to deal with this muscular geezer...

"Well, she's got you dancing in the palm of her hand, doesn't she, kiddo? Must be embarrassing given that she's younger than you."

"It's all your fault for giving her free rein. She's so tough I feel like I'm about to cry."

If Subaru tried to be violent, all that would happen would be his getting beat to the ground by Rom. Even if he was able to grab it away from Felt, he didn't think he could outrun her. Subaru had seen how she could run like the wind. There was no way he could escape.

"Felt, please..."

"Don't think begging is going to get you anywhere. Look, I accept your deal as an option, but it's not fair to make a deal without hearing what my original client has to say about it all. If you would tell me how much this badge is really worth and are able to prepare what it's really worth in payment, then I may reconsider, though."

In Felt's eyes was not even the slightest amount of compassion or mercy. Her two eyes were desperately trying to draw out the truth from Subaru's attitude. However, Subaru's reasons for wanting the badge were not the same as Elsa's. He only wanted to return it to its owner.

But while Felt didn't know Subaru's intentions, he knew hers. Subaru knew why Felt was so desperate to negotiate the best deal possible. He knew who she was trying so desperately for. So after a pause, he told the truth.

"All I want is to return that badge to its rightful owner."

"...What?"

Telling the truth was the most sincere thing he thought he could do. So while Felt's eyes opened wide, Subaru just repeated what he said before.

"I want to return that badge to its rightful owner. That's why I want it. That's all."

Felt's red eyes glinted full of animosity, but Subaru stayed silent. He didn't have it in him to joke around at this point, so he just bowed his head.

"...Felt, I don't think he's lying," said Rom.

"Don't you be tricked by him! This has got to be a joke! Return it to its rightful owner? By paying all of this money to buy it back from the person who stole it? How stupid can you get? If that's what he wanted to do, he should have brought a guard with him to round us up!"

Of course Subaru couldn't do that. Not-Satella didn't want to get the guards involved. That's why Subaru had refused Reinhard's offer. Subaru couldn't go against Not-Satella's wishes.

It was the least that Subaru could do, and it was his answer to the one who had saved his life.

"If you're going to lie, do a better job of it! Even if you act like you're serious, I won't be tricked! If I don't... That's right. I won't be tricked..." Felt said, as if shaking some thoughts from her head, ending in a feeble-sounding voice.

"Felt..." said Rom in a caring tone with a painful expression, probably knowing what was going on inside Felt.

Either way, it didn't look as though Felt was going to change her mind. In other words, negotiations had failed.

"...Who is it?"

Suddenly, Rom's expression changed and he looked toward the entrance. Subaru, still in a state of shock from the negotiations breaking down, was too late to react to Rom's voice.

"It could be my client. It does seem a little early, though."

Felt went over to the door, with her angry expression still on her face, and reached to open it.

Subaru suddenly identified the impatient feelings welling up inside him. The loot cellar, a knock at the door, Felt's client—all of those signals could only lead to one thing.

"Don't open the door! We'll all be killed!!"

It was earlier than Subaru had expected. From the windows he could see the sun still high in the sky. It was too bright to be past sunset.

The first and second times around, despair had come knocking after sunset. Subaru hadn't let his guard down about their limited time, but still, this was way too early.

Subaru still hadn't accomplished anything he needed to do to change this world. Subaru didn't make it in time. Her hand was already on the door, and it was pushed open from the outside, and the reddish light of early sunset swept the dimness of the cellar away. And then...

"What do you mean, 'be killed'? I'd never do anything that violent without warning!" said a silver-haired girl with a sour look on her face as she stepped into the cellar.

CHAPTER 5

STARTING LIFE IN ANOTHER WORLD

1

"I'm so glad you're here... I won't let you get away this time."

Upon seeing the girl, Not-Satella, walk in through the door, Felt wordlessly stepped back.

Felt looked mortified and her mouth twisted in frustration.

"You really are a persistent woman, aren't you... Why couldn't you just give up already?" said Felt, sounding as though she was on the verge of grinding her teeth together.

"Unfortunately, this is not something I can give up on. ...If you'll be a good girl and hand it over I won't hurt you," replied Not-Satella, the tone of her voice incredibly cold.

As Subaru felt the tension of the atmosphere in the cellar rise, he couldn't help but shiver.

Why was Not-Satella here?

The sun had only just begun to set. The first time around he and Not-Satella hadn't even reached the entrance to the slums yet. By the time they had reached the loot cellar, the sun was completely down.

"...Which must mean that without me, she would have found this place a lot faster..."

Even if Not-Satella hadn't run into Subaru in the alley and healed him, she would have found this place all on her own.

Subaru couldn't describe how he felt, with the uselessness of his actions across both space and time so thoroughly proven.

But even as he drowned in his empty feelings, the situation advanced without him.

As Felt continued to step back, she had already crossed from the center of the room to the back, and Not-Satella, while continuing to block the exit, changed her stance and pointed her palm forward.

With the faint sound of shattering air, Satella activated her magic. It seemed that her specialty really was ice magic, and as icicles formed in the air in front of the palm of her hand, the temperature of the room dropped.

"I only have one demand of you: Return my badge. It is very precious to me."

There were six icicles floating in the air. The tips were rounded, so that their power seemed more in their weight rather than their sharpness. However, it was clear that if one hit, it would do far more damage than if a stone were thrown.

Of course, Subaru himself was counted among the possible targets, and so he tried his best not to incite Not-Satella, just wordlessly looking on.

"...Rom," called Felt, a little over a whisper.

"I can't make a move. It's your fault for bringing in such a troublesome thing along with such a troublesome opponent, Felt," replied Rom, his giant body tensed as he shook his head.

Rom had at some point grabbed his club and still held it in his hand, but his arm was slack and he didn't look ready to swing it. He seemed to be gripping and releasing it as though he was still hesitating.

"You're going to give up before the fight's even started?" said Felt, challenging Rom.

"If this were an ordinary magic user I wouldn't be complaining, but...this one's a problem," replied Rom, with a hint of admonishment in his voice, narrowing his eyes as he looked at Not-Satella.

In Rom's stare as he looked down at her was both an extreme sense of caution and an element of awe.

"You're an elf...aren't you, miss?" said Rom, his lips shaking.

Subaru looked up reflexively. Rom guessed that she was an elf, but that would make him only half right. Subaru knew from what Not-Satella had told him about herself the first time around.

Upon hearing Rom's question, Not-Satella closed her eyes for a few moments, and then after a small sigh, she responded.

"Technically, you're mistaken. Only half of what I am is an elf," she said in a tone as if she was making a painful confession, and Subaru furrowed his brow.

However, the other two had a much more exaggerated reaction, especially Felt, and with a shudder she continued to step back and said, "A half-elf...and with silver hair?! You...you can't be..."

"I'm not her! We only look the same! It's... It's a problem for me, too."

Subaru didn't know what was going on, but he could tell that this was a conversation that Not-Satella didn't want to be having.

However, Not-Satella's denial didn't seem to calm Felt down; rather, it put her even more on edge, and she turned her red eyes full of animosity toward Subaru, who was still standing silently on the sidelines.

"You... You set me up, didn't you?"

"What?"

"I thought it was fishy when you said you wanted to return this thing to its owner. The fact that you kept me from hiring people to block her way was also part of the plan, wasn't it? You two are in this together, aren't you?!"

As Felt said those words, gushing full of hatred, Subaru realized a few things. One, that Felt was having another misunderstanding, but secondly, why Not-Satella was able to find this place in such a short time.

Normally, it really would be impossible for her to reach the loot cellar in this short amount of time.

Normally, Felt would have hired people from the slums to get in Not-Satella's way, delaying her arrival.

Because Subaru had rushed Felt and stopped her from doing that, Not-Satella had been able to come straight here.

While Felt's doubts were untrue, they weren't very far off. It was true that the current situation was moving in Subaru's favor. Subaru did want to get the badge and return it to Not-Satella himself so he could receive her praise, but as long as she got it back, he wouldn't complain.

If things kept going at this rate, it would work as a nice backup plan. However...

"Huh...? What do you mean? You two aren't together?"

Not-Satella seemed puzzled as to why Felt was turning on Subaru, but Felt just laughed.

"Ha! Cut the act! I'm the one who's backed in a corner here. So go ahead and take this badge from me and laugh at my stupidity, why don't you?"

"Oh, come on. Just because you're at a slight disadvantage doesn't mean you have to cave so easily," replied Subaru.

"That's all you have to say after bringing this girl here? Damn it, I've been had!" said Felt, roughly scratching at her blond hair and clicking her tongue.

Satella seemed to frown at Felt's far-from-ladylike attitude, and Subaru gulped at the dangerous state of circumstances and misunderstandings, not knowing where to fix his gaze.

As Subaru looked around he realized that there was a red flower decoration pinned to the left breast of Not-Satella's cloak.

"Haa..." Subaru sighed, and then smiled. All of his hesitation up to this point just seemed so stupid now.

Seeing Not-Satella's stern expression and attitude had reminded Subaru of the way she had rejected him in his last loop, and had caused him to be unable to do anything. However, he knew that no matter how many times he looped back, Not-Satella, at her core, wouldn't change.

The fact that she had saved that little lost girl this time as well was proof of that.

"The more we all talk about this, the more confusing it's going to get, so, Felt, why don't you just go ahead and give that badge back.

Now, Ste—I mean, you should take it and get out of here, so you don't get it stolen from you again."

"Why are you acting like you know me all of a sudden? I really don't get what's going on here..." said Not-Satella.

"I don't get what's going on either. Just who do you think you are?" asked Felt, looking at Subaru.

Subaru had tried to get things moving again and change the mood, but Subaru only got turned on by both girls, and failed to get anywhere.

Subaru looked to Rom for help, but...

"It's a magic user we're dealing with. I can't really make any moves. Don't be so hasty," replied Rom, misunderstanding what Subaru was trying to say.

Ugh, this old man's useless, thought Subaru, just barely holding himself back from clicking his tongue in irritation, then trying to figure out how he was going to respond to both girls' stares.

But just then...a black shadow silently seemed to slide in and creep up behind the girl with the silver hair.

"Puck! Block!!"

A sensual smile melted into the shadows and raced forward, and a silver glint seemed to squirm as it lunged toward Not-Satella's white neck.

In that instant with Subaru's eyes opened wide, the girl's head went flying—at least it would have.

There was a loud clash, not the sound of steel cutting through bone but of steel shattering glass. As Not-Satella was thrown slightly forward there was a bluish white magic circle activated behind her head.

The light of the magic circle took the tip of the blade and had just barely kept the silver-haired girl alive.

Not-Satella then leapt forward and turned around, her silver hair waving, and behind that curtain of hair Subaru could see a gray-colored furry animal standing. Puck lifted up its nose, proud of its save before looking toward Subaru.

"That was just in the nick of time there. You saved us."

"Nice going there, Puck. Really, I'm the one who's saved. Thanks," said Subaru, giving the cat a thumbs-up, even as he was still shaken.

It was still before the sun had set—in other words, Not-Satella's very reliable backup partner was still on its working hours.

Subaru's quick response was important, but it was due to Puck's amazing performance that Not-Satella was still safe.

As for the aggressor, her surprise attack blocked...

"A spirit, a spirit, huh? Ah...ha-ha... That's wonderful. I haven't ever opened the stomach of a spirit before."

Lifting her dangerous weapon in front of her face, the woman's expression was one of ecstasy. It was the murderer Subaru had seen so many times before: Elsa.

Both Subaru and Not-Satella were immediately on guard in response to the sudden new arrival, but the first one to react was neither of them.

"Hey! What's the meaning of this?!" Felt yelled, stepping forward with her voice raised in anger.

Felt pointed a finger at Elsa and then took the badge out of her pocket with her other hand.

"All you're supposed to do is buy this badge from me. Turning this place into a bloodbath was not part of our agreement!"

"Buying the stolen badge from you is certainly what I came here to do, but it's hard to hold any negotiations if its owner had already come and taken it away. So, I decided on a change of plans."

Felt's face was red with anger, but upon seeing Elsa's eyes fixed on her, wet with murderous intent, she gulped. Elsa looked on, with an almost loving gaze, at Felt's fear.

"I'll just kill everyone here, and then I'll pick that badge up from the sea of blood afterward," said Elsa, all while holding the expression of an affectionate mother on her face. She then tilted her head and continued on cruelly, "You weren't able to do your job. Do you really expect me not to throw away something that's useless to me?"

"..."

Felt's face twisted as if in pain, but the emotion behind it was not of fear, but something else. Elsa's words must have touched upon something sensitive, deep inside her. Subaru didn't know what that was, but...

"Don't give me that, you bitch!!"

...it was enough for Subaru to shout out in anger at Elsa, and forget about how weak he was compared to her.

Elsa turned and looked at Subaru, surprised, and she wasn't the only one. Felt and Rom turned to Subaru and even Not-Satella was no exception. However, the one most surprised was none of them, it was Subaru.

He couldn't understand himself, just why he was so angry. In part because he could not understand it as this emotion rose up inside him, he spit all of it out.

"Is it really that fun for you to pick on such a little kid, you intestine-obsessed sadist?! Just because things aren't going exactly the way you planned, you're going to wreck everything and throw a tantrum?! What are you, five?! How about you treasure life for once?! Do you know how much it hurts to have your stomach ripped open?! *I* know!!"

"...What are you trying to say?"

"I'm just taking this moment to let the unforeseen sense of justice inside me rant about the injustice of this damn world, and right now, to me, the injustice of this world is you, and this situation, so right now I'm channeling all of my anger about everything on to you!"

As Subaru's shouting continued to make no sense to her, Elsa let out a rare exasperated sigh. But while Subaru was kind of hurt by her nonserious reaction, with spit flying, he shouted one more time.

"All right! That's enough buying for time. Get her, Puck!!"

"That was such an amazingly lame tirade there, I want to write it down and leave it for future generations. ...Guess I'll have to respond to your expectations, huh?"

Compared with Subaru's shouting and stomping, Puck's voice was aloof and detached. Elsa immediately looked up, but all around her, from all sides, were sharpened icicles, more than twenty in all.

"It seems I haven't introduced myself, little lady. My name is Puck.

I'd like it if you at least remembered my name, as you say farewell to this world."

Immediately afterward, the icicles flew at Elsa.

2

"…!"

The crisscrossing icicles whipped up a white mist and Elsa's black coat was lost in the low-temperature storm. The speed of the icicles was far greater than what Subaru had seen in the alley, and he could just barely follow them with his eyes. Subaru thought the sharp-tipped icicles would easily cut through Elsa's body, the tips of the clear bullets stained red with blood. There were twenty of them. If any of them hit their mark it should be a lethal. However…

"Did we get her?!" said Rom.

"Now why did you have go and to say that?!" Subaru yelled back.

Even though Rom had been quiet all this time, he had said the worst possible thing at the worst possible moment.

"It pays to be prepared… I don't like wearing it because it is heavy, but it looks like I was right to wear it this time."

Cutting through the white smoke, Elsa leapt out, with her black hair dancing behind her.

She had her kukri held high in her hand, and in her light steps it appeared she had no injuries. Other than the fact that she had thrown off her black coat and was now only wearing her black skintight outfit, she looked no different from before.

"You're not going to tell me that because that coat is so heavy that just by shedding it you're suddenly a lot faster, are you?!"

"That would be interesting, but the truth is simple. That coat has a formula woven into it that can ward off magic a single time. It looks like it saved my life." Elsa politely answered Subaru's question before kneeling down and striking upward with the tip of her knife. The target was Not-Satella, and the strike was aimed to drive the knife into her chest.

Subaru instinctively started to cry out, but…

"I'd like it if you didn't underestimate spirit mages. We're pretty frightening if you make enemies of us."

Not-Satella clapped her hands together in front of her chest, forming a multilayered ice shield that was easily pierced by Elsa's blade, but it took the knife and stopped her attack. Elsa immediately leapt back to retreat as a few smaller icicles were hurtled her way.

The counterattack was due to Puck, who was standing on Not-Satella's shoulder by her silver hair, sweeping his arms this way and that like a battle commander.

"One manages defense and the other attack... In reality, it's two against one," said Subaru, impressed.

"That's the tricky thing about spirit mages. One'll attack, and the other defends. Depending on the situation, one might use simple magic, buying for time, as the other prepares a special attack... That's why we on the battlefield say, 'When you meet a spirit mage, lay down your weapons and wallet and run,'" muttered Rom, still gripping his club.

Subaru nodded. It didn't look as though the pairing between a spirit mage and their spirit could be easily beat.

"By the way, old man, what is it you're planning on doing?"

"I'm looking for an opening so I can help out that elf girl. Of the two, she seems the one more willing to listen to us."

"Wait! Wait! Wait! Wait! Wait! Wait! Wait! No! You'll only get in their way! If you go out there the only thing that's going to happen is you're going to lose your right arm and have your throat slit. Stay right where you are!"

"Don't say that! The way you put it makes it sound like I've already been cut down!"

As Subaru had seen Rom get cut down twice already, his words had a sense of truth in their tone. As if Rom was feeling what had happened to him in those different dimensions, he put his hands on his arm and neck.

While Subaru was able to talk Rom out of it, the truth was that the fight between Elsa and Not-Satella was so intense, it didn't look like there was anywhere anyone could cut in.

Countless ice shards had been created and were flying all over the room. However, in the midst of all of that, the way Elsa was handling it could only be described as superhuman.

She would spin around, duck down so low it looked as though she were crawling on the ground, and at times she would step on the walls to evade attacks as though she were completely ignoring gravity. If even with all of that she didn't seem able to dodge an attack, she would use her blade to cut through the ice crystals and shatter them. She had paired with what her opponent could do in number with an overwhelming degree of skill.

"She really looks used to fighting, despite her being a woman," muttered Puck, impressed with Elsa's godlike skills and fighting sense.

"Well, it's been a very long time since someone called me a girl."

"From my perspective, most people I deal with are like babies to me. But even so, you're so strong I almost feel like I should pity you."

"To be complimented by a spirit such as yourself, I must say I'm honored."

As Elsa gladly took Puck's praise, she fended off another shard of ice with her knife.

Almost a hundred pieces of ice must have been thrown at her, but other than that very first attack, it didn't seem as though a single one of them had made their mark.

"I think if they keep this up, Elsa will tire out before they do...but I'm still anxious," said Subaru.

"That woman in black's movements really are incredible, but I don't think they can lose if they continue to hold the advantage in numbers...but it's not like that spirit will be able to keep itself here forever. As soon as that spirit's out, the balance of power will shift," replied Rom.

"Damn, you're right. How soon is it to five o'clock?!"

The first time around, Puck went to sleep just a little after sunset. It wasn't as though much time had passed since the start of the battle, but with this much magic use, wouldn't he be using up all of his stored mana or whatever?

"Just when things were starting to get fun... It pains me to see that something else is distracting you from paying attention to me," muttered Elsa as she twisted her body to dodge an icicle attack, confirming Subaru's fears.

"As a popular male, it really is tough on me. I can never put the girls to sleep. However, you know if you stay up too late it's bad for your skin," replied Puck in a light tone, but he didn't deny what she was saying.

Just as Subaru was beginning to worry that Puck had reached his limit, Elsa's movements suddenly stopped. In response, Puck winked his black eyes at her.

"Don't you think it's about time we draw the curtain on this performance? When we keep repeating the same act it begins to get boring."

"My foot..."

As soon as Elsa tried to take a step, she fell forward, catching herself with her hands on the ground. Elsa's right foot had been frozen to the floor.

The fragments of the ice shards Elsa had broken had piled up on the ground, and some had served as a way to bind Elsa's feet.

"You didn't really think I was scattering all of these things around for no reason, did you?"

"...I guess this means you've got me."

"Just blame it on the gap in our ages. You have plenty of reason to congratulate yourself for getting this far. Now, good night."

Throwing its chest out, Puck's body, still standing on Not-Satella's shoulder, started to oscillate at a high frequency. Puck was posed as if he was about to release his ultimate move, with both paws out in front, focusing more magic than ever before, and Subaru watched as that magic was shot off like an arrow. The magic did not take the shape of ice, but was simply a load of destructive energy.

Along the path of the bluish white light everything froze, and in one fell swoop the loot cellar was filled with white. The energy passed through Elsa and broke into the door that formed the entrance to the cellar, blowing it off its hinges, and residual freezing energy from the attack even reached outside.

As the brilliant light from the attack passed, everything was frozen, from the counter to the stolen items, to even the ground they lay on.

Of course, if directly hit, even a human being would quickly turn into an ice statue, but...

"It can't be..." said Puck.

"Of course it can. Ah, that was wonderful. I really thought I was going to die there."

...this was all assuming the attack would hit.

"...With you being a girl, I can't say I approve."

While Puck's attack was dodged, Puck didn't seem any angrier than what his words conveyed. He simply wasn't happy with what Elsa had done.

Subaru saw blood dripping, and a bit of steam was rising from the frozen ground.

The blood was coming from Elsa's right foot. She was standing barefoot just out of the line of fire from Puck's attack, and bleeding profusely from her right foot, and it wasn't hard to see why. After all, she had sliced off the sole of her foot.

"I was afraid I might lop the whole foot off, seeing as how I hurried. That was a close one."

"Even if you only cut that much, it must hurt a lot," said Puck.

"Well yes, you're right. But it's wonderful. It makes me feel alive, and in addition to that..."

In response to Puck's worried sounding words, Elsa nodded with a look of ecstasy in her eyes, and without hesitation pushed her bleeding foot against a piece of ice. A sound that sounded like air shattering came erotically from Elsa's throat, and then immediately afterward she took her knife to the ice around her foot. With that, she had managed to stop the bleeding with the ice.

"It's a little hard to move, but this should be enough," said Elsa with a laugh, clicking her ice shoe against the ground, looking as though she was having fun.

Subaru had no words to say in response to how Elsa's addiction to fighting left her without any hesitation when it came to maiming herself, but right now it was her opponent, Not-Satella, who was in trouble.

"Puck, do you think you can keep going?" whispered Not-Satella.

"I'm sorry, but I'm really tired. I think I really underestimated her. At this rate I'm going to disappear from having run out of mana," Puck replied, for the first time without the confidence that had filled his voice before.

As the cat stood on Not-Satella's shoulder, its figure began to shine, and looked as though it would fade at any moment. They were out of time.

"I'll find a way to handle the rest on my own, so go ahead and rest. Thank you."

"If something happens, I'll obey my contract. If need be, call me out, even if you have to use your od," said Puck with a warning, as his body disappeared in a wisp of mist.

Subaru bit his lip, but he wasn't the one most disappointed by Puck's departure.

"Aw… You're going away? That's terribly unfortunate," said Elsa, the one who had been fighting with Puck with her life on the line. She sounded truly disappointed.

She readied her kukri again and with the high-pitched click of her icy shoe, began to head toward Satella.

A number of icicles materialized around Not-Satella in response, but there were far fewer than when Puck was with her.

Even though Elsa had her movement limited now, the match appeared even.

"It looks like we can't just sit around and watch this anymore, can we?" said Rom, gripping his club and getting ready to move.

"I don't know who's going to win this anymore, so if we just wait around we're going to miss our chance. You understand, right, Felt?" continued Rom.

"I know, I know. Whether we help or run, we're going to have to make a move soon," said Felt, talking for the first time since Elsa threatened her.

Felt moved beside Rom and then turned to Subaru.

"About what you said before… Thanks. It made me feel better."

"Huh?"

"Only a little bit! Plus, don't call me a little kid. I'm fifteen years old. You're not much older than me, right?"

"…Actually, I'll be eighteen this year. I'll be able to get a license to drive a car, and I can get married, too."

"You can't be that old! Your face looks younger than mine! Age a little, why don't you? At least on your face!"

Well, Subaru had lived his years lazily in the peaceful country of Japan, aiming to live every day as ordinarily as possible, so it couldn't be helped.

Subaru felt as though his lack of determination was being mocked, and so he looked down at the ground, feeling useless.

The weakest one here was Subaru, and it was enough that he was completely lacking in the ability to fight, but also…

"My legs just can't stop shaking… I guess this is what happens when you lack resolve."

Forget about being qualified to fight, Subaru was physically unable to. Rom had strength in his arms and Felt strength in her legs and Not-Satella had strength in her magic, and so all of them could manage to fight. However, Elsa's abnormality trumped all of those abilities.

"It looks like she's starting to get pushed back," said Rom, and that was enough to completely describe what was happening.

Not-Satella hadn't stopped shooting projectiles at Elsa, but Elsa just slapped them away with her blade, rendering them useless. In response to Elsa's dance of slicing attacks, Not-Satella would block the attacks with her ice shield, and freeze the ground in front of her feet to slide away, barely dodging Elsa's continuing attacks. After Not-Satella gained some distance, she would continue her barrage, but you could not deny that her position was inferior to Elsa's.

To change the current situation, some kind of support was absolutely necessary.

"All right, I'm going!"

Apparently Rom had thought the same as Subaru, and after letting out a yell, Rom joined the fight.

As Rom swung his club, it brought a gust of air along with it, and as Elsa ducked her hair was caught up a little in the blast.

"Oh, how rude of you to interrupt our dance," said Elsa.

"If you want to dance that much then I'll make you dance a fine dance, so give it your best shot!"

As Rom swung his thorny pointed club at Elsa, he changed his line of attack. He thrust the club toward Elsa's throat, but Rom froze at the result.

"What the hell is this?!"

"I'm only able to do this because you're so strong," said Elsa from above as she stood on the tip of Rom's club.

That kind of technique could only be accomplished with a godlike sense of balance. Before that balance could be broken, Elsa swung her blade horizontally at Rom. The strike was level with Rom's forehead. If it landed, the top of his head would be sent flying.

"You think I'd let you?!"

Shing! went the sound of Elsa's sword as it collided with a knife thrown by Felt. The collision had altered the path of Elsa's sword, but the side of it still collided full force into the side of Rom's head. A dull sound rang out as Rom toppled over to the side.

"What a naughty little girl," said Elsa as she landed lightly back on the ground and turned just her eyes toward Felt.

"..."

Felt's small knife had saved Rom's life. She probably had aimed for Elsa's arm, but in the rush of the moment her aim was a little off. However, without that slight miss, Rom might not have been saved.

"You don't have the determination or power to fight. You should have just cowered in the corner like a good little girl."

The high-pitched click of Elsa's step rang out as she instantly closed the distance between herself and Felt. Rom was unconscious, and Not-Satella, who had been trying to keep her distance, was now too far away. Felt herself had frozen like a frog being stared down by a snake, and...

"Aaaaahhhh!!!"

…so the only one who was able to tackle her to safety was the coward who had been shivering beside her moments before.

3

Subaru dove into Felt at about hip level, and while hugging her light body tumbled across the ground. Just before he hit the ground, he felt something metal scrape across the back of his head, which made all his hair stand on end. But, feeling the weight of the person in his arms, he did his absolute best to ignore it and kept rolling to put as much distance as possible from where they were before.

When at last Subaru looked back, standing on his knees, Elsa was staring back at him in surprise. Feeling as though he had pulled one over on Elsa, Subaru couldn't help but smile back, awkwardly but proudly.

"Are you all right?!" he said to Felt. "I was desperate there, so if I accidentally touched somewhere I shouldn't have, please forgive me, okay?!"

"If you hadn't said that I would have thanked you like normal! … But why?"

"I don't know! My body moved on its own. If I had to give a reason…well, you don't know about this, but with this now we're totally even, okay? Remember that! We're even now!" said Subaru, clenching his fist after he let Felt go.

The second time around, Felt had saved Subaru from Elsa's blade. That memory didn't mean anything in the world this time around, but with this he was able to repay his debt.

Subaru thought that even so, his debts should be returned, so nothing about what he needed to do before had changed.

"Listen here, Felt. Right now I'm going to do the same sort of thing as Rom did before he was knocked out to help stall for time. When that happens I'll be sure to open up a window for you, so I want you to use that opportunity to run out of here as fast as you can. You got it?"

"What?! No! Are you telling me to just turn tail and flee?!" said Felt, glaring up at Subaru with her red eyes. But Subaru just got closer and stared right back at her. As he did so, he was sure not to miss the moment when Felt looked as though she was scared at what Subaru was trying to say.

"Yes. That's what I'm telling you to do. Turn tail and flee. To be honest, that's exactly what I want to do right now. I don't want to stay another second in this violent space," Subaru said, patting Felt roughly on her head.

As Felt started to say, "But..." Subaru interrupted her and continued.

"You're fifteen and I'm seventeen. Out of all of us, you're probably the youngest one here. So it's the right thing to do to give you the highest possibility of getting out of here alive. It's what's only natural."

"D-don't give me that... You were just shaking yourself a minute ago!"

"That was then, this is now! I'm not shaking now, so it's okay! Really, before I remember and start shaking I've got to do this now. Okay? So get ready to run!"

Subaru put his hand on Felt's forehead as she looked as though she was going to object again, and then pulled himself to his feet. Not far away on the ground was Rom's club. It looked really heavy, but Subaru thought he would still be able to swing it.

As Not-Satella continued to shoot barrages of ice at Elsa, there was not a sign of dullness in her movements as she danced to avoid the shots. In the first place, Subaru wasn't really sure if he, faced with a superhuman like Elsa with absolutely no real fighting experience himself, could open up a window for Felt to run. All that he could do was wordlessly spring a surprise attack on her when she wasn't paying attention to him.

So right after Elsa had swung her knife and shattered a large icicle, and Subaru was completely in one of her blind spots, Subaru sprang forward at her, forgetting even to breathe, and swung the club down on her.

Perhaps Subaru's adrenaline had finally kicked in, because the speed of his swing was far faster than he had imagined it would be. It sliced through the air toward the back of her head, and...

"You picked the right moment and angle to target me, but unfortunately I could have sensed your intent to kill a mile away."

"Intent to kill?! I have no idea how I'm supposed to hide that!"

In order to block the swing that came directly behind her, Elsa struck the club with the blunt edge of her blade, changing the course of the swing enough for it to miss its mark. However, at that very instant Subaru opened his mouth wide, with his teeth bared, and yelled.

"Now, Felt! Run!!"

"!!"

Like a spring Felt launched her small body onto the wind and raced forward. She was going so fast that Subaru couldn't keep track of her with his eyes, and the girl, now turned to wind, rushed to the exit.

"Do you really think I'd let you go?"

To stop Felt, Elsa took another knife out of her breast pocket and threw it toward Felt. As if it were a symbol of payback from what Felt did before, the simple undecorated knife flew straight at her back. However...

"Too bad, but I wanna let her go!"

Subaru kicked the round table that was beside him upward, which collided with the knife and sent it off course.

"Man, I'm awesome! That was awesome! Wow, my toe hurts more than I thought it was going to! ...Uwah?!"

Maybe it was Subaru's adrenaline again, or some power that had awakened in him that failed to activate the last three times, but as Elsa's long leg came up and kicked him in the side of the head and sent him flying, his self-congratulations were cut short.

He was hit so hard the world seemed to spin around, and together with the onset of pain and taste of blood in his mouth, Subaru threw up.

"That's the first time in a long time someone's made me actually a little bit angry."

"Well, that's something I'm happy to hear! Ha-ha! Serves you right! I let one of us get away!!"

Subaru stood back up and pretended to be in better shape than he was, doing his best to continue drawing Elsa's attention.

As if Elsa had read Subaru's mind, she smiled at him, and forgot about Felt for the time being.

"Fine, if that's what you want, I'll pay attention to you. Your dancing had better not bore me."

"I'm going to go ahead and warn you, but if you're going to dance with me, you'd better be careful. I haven't learned a thing about dancing so I'll be sure to step all over your feet," said Subaru, spitting out the blood that had risen in his mouth. He readjusted his grip on the club that was still in his hands.

It wasn't as though Subaru was going to have very many chances to land a hit, so he used everything he had to focus on striking Elsa as she rushed toward him.

"You'd better not forget about me!" said Not-Satella, along with a chunk of ice lobbed from behind.

But without even looking back, Elsa swung her blade and broke the ice to pieces. With Elsa's superhuman senses on full display, even Subaru wasn't able to keep taunting her.

"I've started to get tired of this little game... Are you sure you'll be able to keep me entertained?" asked Elsa in a low voice, with her smile the color of blood.

As Subaru gazed at her smile, he felt a shiver run down his spine, and looked over at Not-Satella to make eye contact.

"If you've got some kind of hidden true power available, I think that now would be a great time to use it."

"...I do have another trick up my sleeve, but if I use it, I'll be the only one left alive."

"I would like it if you held back on that, then. No self-destructs, please. ...Okay fine, I get it. Damn. Use it if you have to, but don't be too hasty, all right?"

Subaru intended that to be a joke, in order to help shake off some of his cowardice, but Not-Satella took Subaru's statement seriously.

After seeing him take a deep breath and solidify his determination, Not-Satella's lips relaxed into an almost smile.

"I won't use it. I can't while you're still trying your best. You can do this, so keep on struggling. Relying on the power of one's parents is my absolute final option," replied Not-Satella.

As she said that she really did look as though she was running out of options, and that lit a fire inside Subaru.

In one way, Not-Satella looked as though she was just about ready to give up; at the same time she looked ready to accept the fact that Subaru was weak and wouldn't help much.

To Subaru, Not-Satella was someone who, no matter how tough things got, would never look down and give up. Because that was the way she was, Subaru had worked so hard to see her smile.

Subaru had died several times and come this far in order to save her. He hadn't come this far just to see her give up.

"I didn't see anything right now."

"...What?"

"This conversation we just had, it didn't happen! I just remembered the reason I'm here. Just leave it to me, damn it! I'm going to make sure you never have to use that final option of yours!!"

Subaru pointed at Not-Satella and then at Elsa, and made his declaration. He spit as he did, stomped on the ground, and let all of his emotions howl out from his soul.

"I'm going to blow you away and we're going to have ourselves a happy ending. You don't belong here, so scram!"

"...Well, don't you look overexcited," replied Elsa.

"I'm just ready to give it my all. This time's gonna be the climax. I've got a lot more energy than before!"

As Elsa leaned forward, Subaru swung the club as if he was declaring he was going to hit a home run. Elsa's lips then curled into a smile and she melted away into the darkness.

From such a low height that it looked as though she was crawling on the ground, Elsa slid toward Subaru. As he kept his eyes on the dull glint of her blade, Subaru swung the club with all his might.

Subaru's swing held nothing back; he was prepared to beat Elsa to death. But Elsa just ducked even farther, like it was nothing, and was so low it looked as though she was licking the ground.

"You spider-woman!!"

"Well, I suppose it's correct to say that you're tangled in my web."

As Subaru saw Elsa's sword rising upward, Subaru quickly threw his body back. However, he still couldn't pull out of the striking range of her sword. Fear raced up Subaru's spine, and without thinking he kicked up his knee. Even though he hadn't meant to aim his knee anywhere, as Elsa was right in front of him, it landed straight in her stomach. The path of the blade shifted a little, and then right in that path came a bluish white light, followed by a high-pitched sound.

"An ice shield! Nice cover!"

"I'm not good at making those at a distance. I could have accidentally frozen someone!"

"Her, right?! You mean her, right?!" replied Subaru, with a mix of jest in his thanks.

Not-Satella continued to draw Elsa back with her barrage of ice.

"I've started to grow tired of you little buzzing insect. ...I think it's about time I wrap this up."

"Hey, don't underestimate bugs, okay? It's not my fault if you get stung and break out in hives!"

"Well, don't you sound all high and mighty when you're out of my striking range?" replied Elsa as she focused on dodging Not-Satella's attacks, while Subaru continued to try to draw her attention away.

While Subaru would have loved to try to aim for Elsa's back as she continued to dodge, he didn't want to run the risk of becoming victim to friendly fire, so he really couldn't move. That was probably the reason that Not-Satella's attacks were muted when Subaru made his move before.

It was the kind of problem you have to face when working on an improvised team.

Subaru continued to watch as Elsa deflected Not-Satella's attacks, every now and then diving in with an attack of his own, before retreating again, but he could sense the situation getting worse.

If Elsa really wanted to, it was clear that she could quickly take care of Subaru, like she did Rom. The only reason it appeared that they were on equal footing was because Elsa would not divert her full attention to him. Elsa's caution was instead directed to the possibility that the spirit Puck would appear again. That was enough to keep the current situation holding.

Another reason that Elsa didn't act was because Subaru's cowardice was holding him a step back. He was taking care not to put himself in range of lethal danger. If Subaru had been a brave idiot, she would have cut him down and the balance would have shifted. However, it didn't look as though Subaru's cowardice would serve him much longer.

As Elsa's counterattacks grew more severe, Subaru's retreats weren't making it in time, and he was getting slight cuts all over himself.

Subaru had cuts on his upper arms, on his calves, his underarms, and even a few slight cuts to his neck, and as those injuries increased, Subaru's gray tracksuit began to be stained with blood.

"Damn, it hurts! Argh!! How about this?!"

Even though the pain was enough to bring him to tears, Subaru swung a kick, trying to do something new to catch Elsa off guard.

However...

"I'll just take that," said Elsa.

"...Damn."

Elsa had easily avoided Subaru's kick and to top it all off, she had easily grabbed his leg. Elsa raised her kukri, aiming to lop off the whole leg. With the strength of Elsa's swing, its speed, and the sharpness of the blade, Subaru knew what would happen next. His leg would be cut off at the thigh and he would die from shock as the loss of blood and pain overwhelmed him. Subaru could just see the words BAD END 4 rising up in front of his eyes.

I shouldn't have done that! Subaru's thoughts screamed.

He tried to raise the club to block, but with the handicap he was facing, with one leg held in the air, he wouldn't make it in time.

Not-Satella screamed. The cut would mercilessly reach his leg in moments. As Subaru thought of the pain and spilling of blood it would bring a scream rose in his throat, the blood he would vomit when...

"That's enough."

A flame appeared, burning through the roof from the center of the loot cellar.

The flame was filled with a ghastly malice that swept through the room, and stopped even Elsa in her tracks.

Subaru's leg released, he hopped back before falling down. Right before his eyes, in the middle of a rising pillar of smoke, he saw a red, burning, shining figure.

"That was close. I'm glad I made it in time. Now..."

"Y-you're..."

The flame wavered and stepped forward. Its very existence was enough to make Subaru, Not-Satella, and Elsa all freeze.

Taking in the gazes from everyone present, without being shaken one bit, stood an absolute sense of will. With sky-blue eyes shining with a pure sense of justice, the young man smiled faintly.

"I think it's time to draw the curtain on this performance!" the hero declared, brushing back his red hair.

4

As Felt sped like the wind through the entryway to the loot cellar, she felt as though she had been released from despair.

Behind her, Felt could hear the freezing of the air, and the sound of metal clanging on ice. She also heard the sound of a blunt object swinging through the air, along with "Hii!" and "Wahhh!" and other stupid-sounding utterances from someone dodging attacks.

The battle still raged on behind her.

As Felt's legs started to shake as she ran, she shook her head to try to deny the mess of thoughts running through it.

It was clear that if she had stayed behind, she would have been killed.

Against an opponent who could knock Rom out with a single

blow, Felt didn't have a chance. The same went for that silver-haired half-elf. Without support from her spirit, there was no way that she could win against that woman, either.

Subaru was even worse off. It was clear that he had little experience fighting, and didn't seem used to it at all. His clean hands and fingers were proof that he had never even tried to hold a weapon before, and his clean hair and skin was proof that he had never been wounded before.

In other words, Subaru had lived a sheltered life, one in which it was not necessary to consider fighting. Given that he had such an expensive metia on him, it all made sense.

Felt should just accept that it served him right. Despite not knowing anything about the world, Subaru had let a notion of chivalry get the best of him and try something far beyond his means. Felt should simply laugh at his idiocy. Subaru went and tried to act cool and let her get away, so he would probably be happy to see her keep running. But…still…

"Someone! Anyone!"

Though Felt knew in her mind that she should be winding down alleys, she had run straight toward the main street. Out of breath and with an expression of panic on her face, Felt looked this way and that.

This was strange. Felt reached up and frantically rubbed her teary eyes. Even if she had reason to be sad about Rom, Subaru was someone that she'd just met. Why should she care if he died?

But Subaru had gotten mad at Elsa for Felt's sake, and he had just about thrown his life away so she could get away alive.

Felt didn't understand what she was feeling, but because those feelings were there in her heart, she kept running about. She had felt something in response to Subaru's actions. Because of those feelings, her feverishness did not subside, and while she felt like she wanted to scream, Felt kept running.

Then, finally after running down a few streets…

"Please…help me."

"Understood. I'll help you."

...she found a young man like red fire, and changed the fate of the world.

5

"...Reinhard?"

"That is correct, Subaru. I suppose it hasn't been too long since we've last met. I'm sorry I'm late."

The red-haired young man Reinhard turned to face Subaru, who was still toppled over on the ground, with a slight apologetic smile.

Even as Reinhard wiped the dust from his sleeve, every motion seemed trained and deliberate. The way Reinhard carried himself was different from when Subaru first encountered him in the alley with Dumb, Dumber, and Dumbest, and as Subaru watched him, he thought he was now seeing a glimpse of Reinhard's true self.

Without letting his guard down for a moment, Reinhard looked ahead, and turned his eyes toward the black-clothed beauty who was now focusing her animosity toward him. Reinhard's blue eyes narrowed, as if he were remembering something.

"Black hair and black clothes, and your weapon is the bent blade particular to the northern countries. With all of those character-istics aligned, there's no mistaking it. You are the 'Bowel Hunter,' aren't you?"

"What's with that super-violent-sounding alias...?" muttered Subaru.

"It's an alias given to her based on the way she kills. She's well-known in the capital to be a dangerous individual. However, from what I hear she appears to be more of a mercenary," replied Rein-hard faithfully in response to Subaru's rhetorical question as he trained his clear eyes on Elsa.

"Reinhard. Ah, yes. The knight among knights...and of the 'Mas-ter Swordsman' lineage. Well, that's amazing. I never thought I'd meet such an enjoyable opponent. I'll have to thank my employer now for giving this job, now won't I?"

"There are many things I would like to ask you. I recommend you surrender, however..."

"Would you say to a starving predator as it stands before its wounded prey, a perfect specimen and already dripping blood, to bear its hunger and move on?"

Elsa licked her thin red lips erotically with a look of ecstasy in her case as she stared at Reinhard.

"I see." Reinhard responded, scratching at the side of his cheek as though he wished there was another way.

"Subaru, I'm going to have to ask you to get farther away, and please take that elderly man with you out of harm's way. After that, if you could stay beside that other person there, it would help me a lot."

"Understood. ...That woman's quite the monster, so don't let your guard down, all right?"

"Fortunately, you could say that fighting monsters is my specialty," said Reinhard confidently, and walked forward without any sign that he was preparing himself for battle.

Reinhard did not even reach for the sword at his waist, but continued on empty-handed.

After a sharp intake of breath, the kukri in Elsa's hand flew forward, in a flash, toward Reinhard's neck.

Unlike when Subaru was her opponent, there was no sign that Elsa was holding back as she made her silver strike, and it seemed to kill the very air as it raced toward Reinhard's slender neck.

Yet Reinhard was completely defenseless. Not only did he not make any move to defend himself, he didn't even make a move to dodge the attack.

Subaru could already picture Reinhard's head flying off his body. However...

"I don't really want to be violent against a woman, but..." said Reinhard, starting off in a gentlemanly way, but Subaru thought that the tone of his voice had dropped.

"...you'll have to excuse me."

Reinhard planted one foot down, the pressure behind it fracturing the ground beneath him, and with the other leg launched a kick so strong it created a shock wave as it collided with Elsa and sent her body flying. The back blast was strong enough for Subaru to feel it where he stood. He was speechless.

All it was, was an ordinary forward kick, but the air pressure it caused was enough to create a wind that shook the entire building.

Elsa, who took the hit head-on, was blown away like a leaf. However, she was able to reduce the damage taken by springing off the walls to kill the force of impact with her legs. Still, when she looked up, you could see the look of shock on her face.

"No, no, no, no, no. There's no way. You're kidding me, right? ....Just what the hell was that?"

Subaru had described certain things as being "on a totally different scale" several times before in his life, and it was at this very moment that he realized he had been mistaken. That phrase, "on a totally different scale," existed solely for the purpose to describe this hero who stood in front of him. Before Reinhard's existence, all of the extraordinary phenomena of this new world dulled in comparison.

"It's just as they say...or rather, you're more than what everyone says you are," said Elsa.

"Well, I can only hope I'll live up to your expectations."

"Will you not use that sword of yours? I would like to have a taste of its legendary sharpness."

Elsa pointed at Reinhard's sword. She wanted to face Reinhard at full force, without him holding back. However, Reinhard shook his head.

"This sword is made so that it can only be drawn when it should be drawn. The fact that the blade has not removed itself from its sheath means that now is not the proper time."

"I suppose I've been underestimated."

"Personally, I would have preferred to take you up on your offer. So..."

Reinhard suddenly turned his eyes away from Elsa, and looked about the inside of the loot cellar. Eyes eventually settled on an old-looking two-handed sword propped up against the wall. Reinhard used his foot to kick up on the hilt, sending the unsheathed sword spinning through the air. He easily grabbed it in his hand, and swung it once lightly as if testing it out.

"...I'll use this one to face you. Any complaints?"

"No... This is wonderful, wonderful! You had better show me a good time!"

As Reinhard gripped his blade, Elsa made the first move, darting to the side. As she made her slicing attack she leapt to increase its speed. In response, Reinhard readied a stance to swing his sword from below, straight upward.

In that moment of attack and defense, Subaru was able to get a clear view of what was happening.

Reinhard's strike was sublime, it was magical, it was perfectly trained. In his hands, even a throwaway sword at its end of life, sleeping away in a cellar, shone like some treasured sword passed on by legend across generations. Reinhard's sword technique captured every ounce of performance that could be extracted by the sword and he used it at will.

Reinhard's blade hit its mark, just where the blade of Elsa's kukri met its handle. Despite the fact that it was two pieces of steel striking together, Reinhard's sword showed an unbelievable amount of cutting power and sliced the blade of Elsa's blade right off its base.

Elsa had no words for the fate of the kukri she held in her hand. The blade had become just a handle, and as for the remainder...

"Now that you have lost your weapon, I recommend you surrender."

...as Reinhard turned around, he held the blade of Elsa's kukri in his free hand. With a flick of his wrist he threw it, and with a sharp sound it stuck, lodged in the wall.

Even Subaru could hear Elsa gasp.

"He really is not normal. I can't even find the energy to joke about it." Subaru just barely squeezed out what he thought, and hurried to put distance between himself and the battle taking place.

Along the way, Subaru went over to Rom, and somehow was able to drag his giant body to a spot along the wall.

"Rom. Old Man Rom. Hey. Baldy. You alive?"

"Who…you…callin' baldy…"

"Who else? My only goals in life are to never go bald or get fat. You are, like, the best example for me of who I don't want to end up like."

Even though Rom's response was weak, after giving him a few more slaps on the cheek, Subaru let out a sigh of relief.

Other than the fact that Rom had hit his head pretty hard, everything else looked all right. There was a chance that Rom's memory might take a hit, but considering he was alive, it didn't seem like much of a problem.

"Does it look like that person's going to be all right?" asked Not-Satella as she came running up beside Subaru, her long silver hair trailing behind her. Checking the state of Rom's injuries, she muttered, "He needs treatment," and her hands began to glow with a faint blue light.

"Hey now, I'm just saying, but this old man's in league with the one who stole your badge. You know that?"

"That's precisely why I'm doing it. Once I heal him I can use his gratitude to get information out of him. People don't tend to lie to people who've saved their life. I'm only doing this for my own sake."

It was like she could not justify any of her actions unless she made a case for them being for her own sake.

Subaru gave the ever-roundabout Not-Satella a weak smile, and looked back toward the battlefield.

Elsa was on her knees but Subaru couldn't see her face. All Subaru could think was that Reinhard had taken away her will to fight. With his old sword down by his side, Reinhard approached Elsa with his defenses down.

Surely Reinhard had confidence in the difference in ability between himself and Elsa, but pride always leads to the worst possible outcome. An alarm rang inside Subaru's head.

"Reinhard! She's got another blade!"

As Elsa's second kukri was drawn from her waist, it took a bit of Reinhard's bangs as he leaned back. With her surprise attack evaded, she turned her eyes toward Subaru.

"I'm surprised you knew."

"Well, I've already experienced it once before!" said Subaru, giving her the middle finger in a bragging tone—although it really couldn't be called bragging.

Elsa apparently decided that what Subaru was saying was nonsense and ignored him.

"However, you'd be wrong to think I have only two of these fangs. …Shall we start over?" she said to Reinhard.

"Will you be satisfied if I destroy all of your weapons?"

"If I lose my fangs, I'll fight with my nails. If I lose my nails, I'll fight with my bones. If I lose my bones, I'll fight with my life. That is how I, the Bowel Hunter, do things."

"In that case, I'll just have to have you forsake your ideals."

Elsa drew a third knife from her waist and held both at the ready. Worthy of the "spider-woman" insult that Subaru had lobbed at her before, Elsa seemed to fly about the room as though she were ignoring gravity, using all space on the ground and in the air available to her.

As blade met blade and steel met steel, each violent collision sent sparks flying. Kicking off from the walls and from the ceiling, Elsa continued her fighting style of attack and retreat. Reinhard met her attacks as they came.

As the battle seemed to go back and forth, Subaru gulped as he watched on.

"It can't be possible that even Reinhard lacks the ability to settle this, can it…?"

Elsa's abilities had stepped out of the realm of human possibility and it was hard for Subaru to even track her movements. However, Reinhard's ability was, at its very core, legendary. Their battle was like two gods colliding with each other in the heavens, but Subaru could see that, in terms of pure ability, Reinhard was far ahead of Elsa. But then why was the battle still raging?

"…We're holding him back," muttered Not-Satella in response to Subaru's doubts as she continued to heal Rom.

"Huh?" replied Subaru, and Not-Satella bit her lip, frustrated.

"Because I'm using spirit magic, he can't fight full force. At least not until I finish my healing."

"I have no idea what you're trying to say."

"If Reinhard decides to fight full force, all of the mana in the atmosphere around us will turn away from me. …I'm almost done. When I give the signal, call out to him."

"O-okay."

Subaru still didn't understand her explanation, but while still a little unsure, he agreed.

The blue light continued to heal the bump protruding from Rom's head, and another wound that had been bleeding a little. Subaru looked on amazed as the traces of blood and the opening of the wound gradually disappeared, when Not-Satella took a deep breath and let it out.

"I'm done."

"Leave it to me. Hey, Reinhard! I don't really understand, but get her!!!"

Subaru delivered the message to Reinhard, who had continually been on the defensive, that Rom's treatment was complete.

Reinhard glanced back. When his and Subaru's eyes met, he gave a slight nod.

"…What is it you're going to show me?"

"The House of Astrea's sword," Reinhard replied in short and with dignity as Elsa leaped at him.

Immediately afterward, Subaru felt all of the space in the cellar warp.

6

"What?"

Subaru saw the air in his line of sight twist, and he couldn't be sure, but he thought that the room had lost some of its light. Apart from that, the room's temperature, which had already been falling because of all of the ice magic, dropped even further. Subaru found himself shivering and hugging his shoulders.

"Wait? Huh? Why are you..."

"I'm sorry, it's just... Could you lend me your shoulder?"

As Not-Satella started to lean on him, Subaru, while flustering about, rushed to support her. Her slender body was incredibly hot and Subaru could feel his heart racing from a completely different reason from before. But one look at Not-Satella's face and any ideas Subaru may have gotten were blown away.

Not-Satella was short of breath and looked as though she were in pain. It was as though she was running a high fever.

"What happened? Did you suddenly start to feel...?" asked Subaru.

"No, it's the mana... You know, right?" replied Not-Satella.

Subaru didn't have a clue. He would have liked to fold his arms and declare so, in his usual humorous way, but now didn't seem to be the time for that. It was not the weight on Subaru's shoulders that made him decide to stay silent; it was how the entire room had changed its atmosphere, and what was happening at the source of that change.

In the center of the room, Reinhard held his sword ready with both hands in a low stance. But that wasn't it. That stance itself had been something that Reinhard had been holding since the battle had begun. However, as Subaru looked on, it felt to him that only now, for the very first time, Reinhard was holding his sword at the ready.

"Elsa 'The Bowel Hunter' Gramhilde," said Elsa, licking her lips.

"Reinhard van Astrea from the line of master swordsmen," Reinhard replied majestically with a nod.

The presence of Reinhard's sword overwhelmed the room, and the animosity between Reinhard and Elsa shook the air.

In this place, turned mostly to ruins, a black-clothed murderer and a lightly armored hero faced each other, and what would clash would be the blood-soaked blade of a knife against a rusted old two-handed sword. But despite the faults of one side's weapon, Subaru held his breath. After declaring their names, both were going to try to end the battle at once. Subaru felt that he was witness to a verse from an epic tale of heroism.

Someone screamed out. Subaru couldn't tell if it was Elsa, or Reinhard, or even himself, but a brilliant light blew off the roof of the loot cellar and ripped right through it, cutting the entire space into two halves.

Subaru couldn't help but feel that the entire world had shifted as an immense light filled the room and whited everything out in an instant. As the light cleared, the world was subjected to another sudden shift, as the displaced space tried to return to where it had been before.

Air was distorted as residual waves from the attack swept over the room and caused strong gusts to rush, spiraling back into the center of the room. Along with those gusts, stolen items, furniture, and even materials from the building's structure itself were pulled in.

Subaru desperately tried to protect both Not-Satella and Rom from this storm of collateral damage.

"Just what is... H-hey! Hey!!"

Subaru couldn't really explain how all of this was happening, but he knew who caused it.

The "Master Swordsman" had, at full power, swung his sword. Once. Only once, and this was the result.

Subaru kept yelling, trying to get through the pain and the wind, as finally, the storm lost its strength and the various items tumbling to the ground signaled its end, along with the chorus of dull creaking sounds from the building.

Subaru tossed away the remains of a scroll-like object that had landed on his head and checked that both Rom and Not-Satella were still okay. It looked as though Subaru's cover wasn't completely enough, as Rom looked as though he was covered in milk and other things, but Subaru thought he deserved to be cut a little slack.

"What do you mean, 'Fighting monsters is my specialty'? You're enough of a monster yourself!" shouted Subaru.

"Even I get hurt when you say things like that, Subaru," replied Reinhard, the root cause of all of this destruction, with a weak smile as the gusts of wind blew his fiery red hair.

After all of this, even Reinhard had beads of sweat formed on his cool-looking face, and in his hands...

"I'm sorry for pushing you so hard. Rest well."

...his two-handed sword disintegrated. Something of such a poor making could not last even one of Reinhard's true swings. The strike was enough to make the steel of the sword's blade rot away, so as for Elsa...

"Forget a corpse, I don't even see any trace of her left... This is all just from one swing of your sword?"

In the path of Reinhard's attack, which had seemed to rip through the very fabric of the world, there was absolutely nothing left. In the destruction, the counter next to the cellar's entrance was blown completely away with all of its chairs, and the residual waves of damage extended even into the open space in front of the building. The resulting gusts of wind had wrecked the supports of the building, and it seemed ready to collapse at any moment.

The space where Elsa had been standing was of course within range of Reinhard's attack, and her tall, black-clothed figure was nowhere to be seen.

"But then, that means..." Subaru said, stretching his stiff body and breathing a big sigh of relief.

Still unable to quite believe had happened, Subaru turned to look at the silver-haired girl still leaning against him. Not-Satella's breathing was still shallow, but when she saw Subaru looking at her she turned her violet eyes toward him.

"Is it over...?" she asked weakly.

"Yeah... In the true sense of the word, it looks like it is," Subaru said, helping her stand.

Not-Satella ran her fingers through her own hair, and with still uncertain steps, let go of Subaru, while Subaru stared.

"Why are you staring at me like that? That's very rude of you," she said.

"Your limbs and head are all still attached to your body, right?"

"...Why wouldn't they be? Could you please not say something so ominous?" replied Not-Satella, not understanding what Subaru was trying to say.

As Not-Satella stared back at Subaru with an annoyed look in her eyes, Subaru gave her a thumbs-up and smiled.

"That's right. I mean, that makes perfect sense. I, myself, have all my limbs; I don't have a knife stuck in my back or a huge hole in my stomach!"

"The way you say that, it sounds like you had experienced all of that at one time."

Well...he had.

Because of Subaru's uselessness, Not-Satella had had her life taken, Rom lost his arm and his head, and Felt was cut down, too.

"Now that I think of it, Reinhard, I haven't thanked you yet. You really saved us there. There's also what happened in the alley... Did you hear the screams of my heart or something, my friend?"

"Well, I certainly would be proud of myself if I could do that, friend," replied Reinhard, relaxing his shoulders, looking sorry. With his chin, he motioned toward the entrance of the loot cellar. As Subaru followed with his eyes...

"Oh hey," said Subaru as he saw the person there, feeling his mouth form an unexpected smile.

At the entrance to the loot cellar, which had been at this point pretty much destroyed, was a small blond-haired girl with a canine tooth poking out from her mouth, hiding in the shadow of one of the few pillars left standing.

"That girl over there was running frantically down the street, where she asked me for help. The only reason I was able to come here is because of her. After that, I was just doing my job as a knight."

"Is flattening old buildings part of your job description?"

"Don't you think that's a bit harsh, Subaru?" said Reinhard, wincing and putting his hand over his chest.

Despite having dealt this much destruction, the fact that he was acting just as friendly with Subaru as he had before was frightening in and of itself.

"That's..."

Not-Satella, still trying to regain her footing, had noticed Felt.

Subaru stepped between them, running to Felt's defense.

"Wait a minute. If she hadn't called Reinhard for help, we both probably wouldn't be here right now. So for my sake, overlook her crimes and please don't turn her into an ice statue."

"I wasn't going to do that! And what do you mean, 'for your sake'?" Not-Satella rubbed her fingers up against her brow, looking tired.

Even in that action of hers, Subaru was able to feel happiness in some way.

Since everyone was alive, they could all be joking around.

"I guess now it's all up to my negotiation skills...which are something I'd never want to put my trust in!"

"What is with you, all of a sudden? The way you're flailing about like that is really lame."

In response to Not-Satella's words, Subaru put his hand on his chest and reenacted Reinhard's previous reaction. Of course, it didn't look remotely as cool and dignified as when he did it.

As Reinhard watched Subaru's antics, he smiled. He raised a hand toward Felt, who was looking in on everyone, and started walking toward her.

Subaru watched from behind at Reinhard's gallant figure as he walked over to Felt, and he couldn't even feel envious of him. Subaru could only shrug his shoulders and think that this was the difference between someone who had it and someone who didn't.

Even while Felt was cautious of him, perhaps because she was feeling gratitude that he had come to save everyone, Felt didn't try to run away as Reinhard approached.

Watching the two, Subaru felt like smiling, when...

"Subaru!!"

...Reinhard suddenly turned toward him and yelled, and Subaru realized that they hadn't escaped danger yet.

Scraps of the building had been thrown up, and underneath them was a black shadow. The black shadow, with black hair trailing behind it and blood dripping from it, kicked firmly off against the ground and accelerated. Holding a blade that was bent out of shape, a bloody Elsa wordlessly raced toward Subaru.

"Enough already…!"

After having somehow survived Reinhard's incredible strike, Elsa's murderous eyes were filled with a pitch blackness. The murderous intent that she released was greater than any she had before, and it sent chills racing down Subaru's back.

It would only be a few seconds before she was close enough to strike, and in that short amount of time, Subaru sent his thoughts racing.

One instant and it would all be over. Elsa was counting everything on this one strike. Reinhard wouldn't make it in time. If Subaru could stop Elsa this one time, Reinhard could handle the rest. Not-Satella didn't even have time to turn around.

Where was the target this time? Subaru had experienced this twice before: two deaths, the fear and the pain. He would protect her the third time.

Protect the girl!!

"She's aiming for your stomach!!"

Subaru pushed Not-Satella out of the way, and using the club from before still in his hands, he guarded his own stomach as Elsa's strike collided with him.

The horizontal slice felt less like a cut and more like being struck by a heavy blunt object. The force of the collision swept Subaru off his feet and he felt the world spin 180 degrees as he vomited blood. It wasn't just his vision but his entire body that was spinning.

Unsure of how far he had been thrown, Subaru struck the wall, unable to catch himself.

"There you go, getting in my way aga—" spat Elsa, clicking her tongue as she watched Subaru fly.

"That's enough, Elsa!"

As Reinhard came running up, Elsa understood that there was no longer any meaning in continuing the fight. She threw at Reinhard her knife, which had been completely bent in that last attack that Subaru took. Her aim was off, but the throw succeeded in drawing Reinhard's attention away from her, and that was enough.

"One day, I will open the stomachs of everyone here, so take care of your bowels for me until then!" she cried, using a part of the collapsing building as a foothold to leap up onto the roof.

It didn't look possible to chase her down as she leapt lightly from roof to roof as she made her getaway.

Reinhard, who was not interested in pursuing this fight any further, didn't run after her.

After Reinhard watched Elsa go, he ran over to the silver-haired girl.

"Are you all right?"

"I'm perfectly fine! Can't you see?! Rather than me, you should be worried about..." shouted Not-Satella, before racing over to the wall with her unsteady feet where Subaru was collapsed upside down.

"Are you all right?! What were you thinking?!"

"Ugghh... Oh... It's no big deal... If there was ever a time to act before thinking that was it, don't you think? I'm the only one who could move, and I was able to quickly guess where she was going to attack," said Subaru, raising one hand to Not-Satella as she walked over to him and using the other to carefully touch his tender stomach. He was immensely bruised, and everything under his clothes as he lifted them up was purple.

"Ugh..." said Subaru, disgusted by the way it looked, before turning over and getting back on his feet.

"She's completely gone now, right?"

"I'm sorry, Subaru. This is all my fault for letting my guard down. If you weren't there we would have been in trouble. If that person there had gotten wounded, then..."

"Stop stop stop stop! Don't say it! Don't say it! I forbid you to speak any more than that! You're going to steal my thunder," said Subaru to Reinhard as he tried to apologize, and smiled at him as he went quiet.

After that, Subaru slowly turned around to face the silver-haired girl looking up at him. She fidgeted and then stood up beside him. They were about two steps away from each other. If Subaru reached out with his hand, he could touch her. It had been a long time coming, and Subaru paused to think about everything that had happened for him to get here.

As Subaru closed his eyes in silence, the girl looked as though she wanted to say something, but before she could open her mouth, Subaru pointed a finger up to the heavens.

With his left hand on his hip and his right hand pointed in the air, Subaru disregarded the surprised stares coming from all around him, and declared in a loud voice, "My name is Subaru Natsuki! I know there's a ton of things you want to say and a ton of things you want to ask, but before all of that let me confirm just one thing!"

"W-what…?"

"I totally just saved your life right now from that terrible weapon, didn't I? We okay so far?"

"O…kay?"

"It means everything's fine. So, are we okay?!"

Subaru used his upper body to form an O and a K, and while the silver-haired girl in front of him seemed to twitch a little, she replied.

"O-okay…"

"I'm the person who saved your life! Your rescuer! Now you are the heroine I rescued. Don't you think that I should get some kind of reward? Don't you think so?!"

"…I understand. Only if it's something I'm able to do, though."

"As long as you understand! Now I only have one, just one request of you!" Subaru put his finger out in front of him to emphasize this point.

While the girl looked a bit worried in response, she seemed to find her determination and nodded firmly.

"So my wish is…"

"Go on."

Subaru smiled, showing his teeth, then snapped his fingers and then gave a thumbs-up, striking a pose.

"…I want you to tell me your name."

The girl's eyes opened wide in shock, and a moment of silence fell upon the two. Subaru's gaze would not waver, and he looked the silver-haired girl in front of him straight in the eye.

The girl then put her hand to her mouth and started to giggle, her white cheeks blushing, and her silver hair swaying behind her as she smiled.

That smile of hers was not one of resignation, or a faint fleeting smile. It was not a tragic smile, either. She was simply smiling because she was happy. That was all there was to it.

"…Emilia," she said, laughing.

"…"

Hearing that single response Subaru took in a short breath, and then breathed out.

In response the girl straightened herself, put a finger to her lips, and smiled in a teasing sort of way.

"My name is Emilia. Just Emilia. Thank you, Subaru. Thank you for saving me," Emilia said, holding out her hand.

Looking down at that hand, Subaru hesitantly took it in his. Her fingers and wrist were slender and her palm was small, and her hand was very warm. It was a living hand, with blood running through it.

—Thank you for saving me.

Subaru wanted to say the same to her. She was the one who had saved him first. With this, he had finally repaid her, after dying three times from blade wounds to get here.

After all of that pain and suffering, after all that fighting with everything he had, his reward was her name and a smile.

Ahh…

"Man, that wasn't worth it at all," said Subaru, smiling as he gripped Emilia's hand.

7

That would have been a good place to end the story. However...

"Though really, I have to say I'm surprised to see you're all right," said Reinhard, as though he had been waiting for the right moment to jump in after Subaru and Emilia had finished, breaking the silence he had been forced into before.

Even from the perspective of a man with Reinhard's skill, Elsa's final attack must have seemed overwhelming.

Subaru gently put pressure on his hurt abdomen and pointed to the club lying on the ground. The spiked club was thick and sturdy and had worked well as a shield, even though that was not its true purpose.

"I quickly guarded myself with that thing. If it weren't for that, right now I'd be cut in two," said Subaru.

"You're right. If it weren't for this—" Reinhard started to say, reaching for the fallen club to pick it up.

"—I wouldn't have been able to avoid 'BAD END 4,'" Subaru laughed, finishing his sentence.

"Huh?"

As Reinhard picked up the club, part of it slid across a smooth cut going through it, and fell to the ground with a thud. Cut completely in two, its service was done.

Reinhard slowly looked up at Subaru with an uncomfortable look on his face. Subaru followed Reinhard's gaze nervously and pulled up his tracksuit. Just as before, everything was purple and bruised, but there was a slight change. A red line suddenly ran straight across his abdomen.

"This doesn't look good. Even I can see what's coming next."

Just as Subaru finished his statement a searing pain shot through him, and then his stomach opened along the cut, spilling bright red blood everywhere.

"S-Subaru?!"

Right beside him, Subaru could hear Emilia's panicked voice.

Subaru had finally been able to hear her name and now it looked as though this was going to be the end, again.

But even if that was the case, Subaru was sure he would return to this place again.

Subaru's vision shifted sideways, and he thought that he must have fallen over. He could see that Reinhard was panicked as well, and as Emilia looked straight at him, close to his face, he could see that she was very distressed.

She looks cute even when she's panicking... What a place this fantasy world is, Subaru thought, feeling he had thought something similar before, before the pain and shock swept his consciousness away like a storm at sea.

EPILoGUE
THE MOON IS WATCHING

Reinhard looked on from a distance at the faint blue light, its wavelengths those of water, the element of healing, and let out a soft sigh that no one around him could hear.

Signs of grief showed on his handsome profile as well as traces of tension left over from the battle. If you were to take the image of his figure as he stood in front of the ruins behind him, it would surely be a masterpiece of art. Such was the way he stood.

However, Reinhard had a deep sense of regret in him, the weight of which could not be lessened by words.

"…All right. That should do it," came a voice like silver bells to Reinhard's ears, as he had continued to blame himself, his eyes closed.

Emilia brushed her hand across Subaru's forehead, as if wiping it, and brushed away his hair as he lay propped up against the wall. She made sure that there was still a look of redness, of life in his face. Emilia then stood up and nodded.

"I'm done treating him. He's probably made it past the worst of it."

"That's good to hear. Now that that's taken care of, Lady Emilia…" Reinhard said as he walked swiftly over to Emilia, knelt down on one knee, and bowed his head. Reinhard's every motion was executed without any fault, and perfectly adhered to proper etiquette.

"Due to my shortcomings, I have caused you a great deal of stress.

I am prepared to take whatever punishment you deem necessary in response to my failure."

Reinhard placed his sword in front of him as he knelt and apologized for his failings.

As a knight, this was the most sincere way he could apologize. No matter what might befall him, Reinhard was prepared to take any punishment without complaint.

Emilia, however, stuck out her finger and waved it back and forth, looking annoyed.

"I never understand why you all are like that."

"Meaning...?"

"You saved us all from grave danger, and everyone made it out alive. Yet here you are, trying to take responsibility for our pain and all of the trouble we went through."

Emilia pointed her finger toward Subaru, who was now sleeping soundly.

"That one over there is a lot more honest. He saved me and then demanded a reward, even if he didn't really ask for much."

Reinhard saw Subaru strike his pose and ask for Emilia's name. As Emilia smiled, remembering that moment, Reinhard couldn't help but smile as well.

"So, thank you for saving us. That is all I have to say to you. I don't see any fault of yours to punish you for. If that's not enough for you, then work harder next time you save someone."

"Understood. Thank you for your kind words," said Reinhard, bowing further to show his respect before standing up again.

When the two stood facing together, it was clear that Reinhard was much taller than Emilia, and so when he looked at her, he had to look down at her. Where was that grandness that he sensed from her just moments before?

It must be a difference in the capacity of our characters, mused Reinhard, taking heed of his own narrow-mindedness.

Surely Emilia was simply one of those "chosen ones," he reaffirmed within himself.

"I just remembered, talking about how you saved us, but…how and why did you come here?" Emilia asked suddenly.

"Today is my day off, and I was wandering aimlessly about the capital. If I had been patrolling off duty, my squadron leader would have gotten upset at me, so I really was just walking around, but then…I met him," said Reinhard, pointing to Subaru as he answered her question.

It all began after Reinhard had met Subaru in that alley. As they talked Subaru had given a description that matched Emilia's and had mentioned some place called the "loot cellar." With the mixture of this prior and newfound knowledge, Reinhard had also made his way to the slums to investigate. As he was looking around…

"Then I ran into that girl over there, and the rest you know."

"Yes, that girl…"

Now that Felt had come up in conversation once more, Emilia turned her eyes to a corner of the open area in front of the loot cellar, where Felt was taking care of Rom, who had yet to wake up.

The blond-haired girl turned around as she felt Emilia's stare and looked down awkwardly.

"Lady Emilia, who is that girl…?"

"Reinhard, I appreciate all of your help, and thank you for saving us. However, please…I must ask you to refrain from interfering from here on out," said Emilia in a strong tone, and that was enough to keep Reinhard from pressing any further.

Emilia closed her eyes, trying to figure out how she would approach Felt. As Reinhard looked at Emilia's beautiful face, he sighed.

"I won't ask what's going on, but your safety is very important. I would ask that you take care of yourself. I will send knights to take you home, so please go along with them."

"Normally I would have to refuse, but after all of this I suppose there's no helping it. All right, I'll take you up on your offer," Emilia replied.

"Understood," replied Reinhard.

Emilia giggled and when he followed her stare, it landed on Subaru's peacefully resting face.

"What relation do you have to him...to Subaru?"

"I just met him," Emilia replied immediately, and Reinhard paused, giving her a doubtful and confused look.

Perhaps because she found Reinhard's reaction amusing, Emilia smiled.

"It's the truth! There's no other way to put it. I don't have any memory of meeting Subaru before. The first time I had ever seen him was when I walked into this place not long ago..."

"But earlier, he said that he was looking for you. He said he had something he wanted to give you. Then there is the fact that he was present here for all of this, and..."

...the fact that he put his life on the line to protect you, Reinhard was about to say, but stopped. He thought that if he said it, he would be belittling the brave act that Subaru had performed.

"That's why it's so strange," said Emilia. "I'm beginning to think that weirdo is somehow involved in all of this."

"Please refrain from speaking that way about Provincial Lord Roswaal. He is a very upstanding citizen. I will admit that he does have some peculiarities, but..."

"The fact that you linked the word 'weirdo' to him makes it clear what you really think."

"...My apologies. Please keep this a secret from Lord Roswaal," said Reinhard with a wink.

"Of course, of course," Emilia replied.

Reinhard then turned the subject back toward Subaru.

"What shall we do with him? If you would like, I could have someone from my family take him in as a guest..."

"...No, I'll take him with me. I'll be able to find out more about him that way, and even if he isn't connected to that weirdo, it does not change the fact that he saved my life," said Emilia.

"But thank you for offering," she added, to which Reinhard replied with a slight nod.

With that, Reinhard and Emilia had just about finished all they had to talk about. Afterward, Reinhard would go and send a few knights to escort Emilia back to her residence, and then he would have to start working on cleaning up the aftermath of the battle.

As Reinhard looked at the loot cellar that he had destroyed, he closed his eyes before the extent of the damage. As always, he was frustrated that he could not properly control himself. All of this damage was the result of a slight miscalculation of power on his part. If he had been even more careless he could have leveled an entire block. He needed to be more careful.

"What is it that you plan on doing next to deal with the area?" asked Emilia.

"We'll have to declare the area off limits for a while, and pass out wanted posters for the Bowel Hunter. She is already a person who has a lot of rumors floating around about her, so I'm not sure it will help, but..."

"What about the girl, and the old man?"

"...It's hard for me to grasp all that has happened, but given my occupation, I do not think that what they were doing is something that I can just ignore. However..." Reinhard paused, and then shrugged his shoulders.

"...today happens to be my day off. If I might add another thing: If there's no victim filing a complaint, then the lack of evidence makes it hard to convict. But above all else, it's really hard for me to grasp what happened."

"Ha-ha-ha... You really are a terrible knight."

"Well, that is the truth, despite everyone calling me the knight among knights," said Reinhard jokingly, and Emilia put her hand to her mouth and giggled.

Finally, after all the laughing had subsided, Emilia's thoughts were in order. She walked toward the blond-haired girl who was still hugging the old man beside her. When she noticed Emilia coming, she looked up, prepared to face her.

"Is this old man your family?" asked Emilia, squatting down so that she was on the same level as Felt. Felt looked shocked. Of all the things she had expected to hear, that was not one of them. Even

Reinhard, who didn't know what had happened between the two, could tell that they were not on particularly good terms.

Felt scratched her cheek and tried to regain her composure, and then, as if trying to hide her embarrassment, she slapped Rom a few times.

"I-it's kinda like that. To me, Old Man Rom is like my only…uh… grandfather figure sort of thing."

"I see. I only have one family member as well. He's always sleeping when it counts, and when he's awake I don't think I could ever say that to him."

"Well…I can't say these sort of things when Rom's awake, either."

Reinhard couldn't be sure, but it looked as though the intensity of Felt's slaps was increasing. She probably wasn't paying attention. The frequency was also increasing, and the old man's white bald head was turning red.

Felt then looked up at Emilia, with a weak light in her red eyes.

"I was sure you were going to be angry at me."

"Well, that might have happened if things were as they were before, but I don't feel like I have it in me anymore. So while only a little bit, I'll forgive you for his sake," said Emilia with a weak smile and a shrug, before pointing back over to Subaru, who was still sleeping.

Felt looked at Emilia, then at Subaru, and then looked down before quietly saying, "I'm sorry. He saved my life, too. I can't be so ungrateful as to ignore that. I'll return what I stole."

"Good. That makes things easier on me. I really, really would feel bad if I had to sic this guy over here on you," said Emilia with a wink, pointing back at Reinhard.

After hearing those words and looking at that young man with the red hair and blue eyes, Felt grimaced.

"The knight among knights… I would have to be crazy to try to run away with someone like that on my tail. It's the first time I've ever seen anyone faster than me. It really surprised me."

Upon hearing those words, Reinhard just smiled back at Felt, wordlessly.

With a slight click of her tongue, Felt stood up and walked over to Emilia, who stood up as well.

"All right, I'll give it back," said Felt, digging around in her breast pocket. "If it's that important to you, make sure you hide it better so it doesn't get stolen again."

"That warning feels a little strange coming from you. …If possible I would like it if you stopped your thievery altogether."

"That's something I cannot do," said Felt in a flat refusal. "Just so you know, I'm only returning this to you this time because I owe my life to you all. I don't think I did anything wrong, and I have no plans to stop."

Felt put on a strong-willed smile.

Considering Felt's age, it was almost painful to watch. As Felt declared her intentions, Reinhard looked on in silence.

Given his occupation, Reinhard knew that this was not something he should overlook, but what other way of life did she have? What right did he have to talk of justice without offering her any alternatives?

Reinhard had seen enough of the capital to not be so naive as to ignore that fact. Emilia seemed to realize this as well, and after lowering her eyes for a few moments, she stuck out her hand without another word.

"Understood. …I was asking for too much."

"If I was able to eat without having to work for it, I might quit, but that's not happening. Anyway, here you go."

Felt reached out to put the thing she had taken out of her pocket into Emilia's hand, to give back what she had stolen.

For an instant, Reinhard saw a flash of red cross in front of his eyes. That bright light was something he had seen before, and as he narrowed his eyes Reinhard searched through the sea of his memories for it.

Then after he had found what he was looking for…

"Huh?"

"Reinhard…?"

...he reached out and grabbed Felt's hand, still holding on to the badge.

Both girls looked up in surprise at Reinhard, but when they saw his serious expression, both fumbled for words.

"Th-that hurts... Let go..." said Felt, shaking her head and trying to resist.

However, Reinhard did not loosen his grip. The strength in his hand was such that, if he wanted to, he could bend steel. Even if he wasn't using his full strength, it was not something that a slender girl like Felt could shake away from.

"I don't believe it..." muttered Reinhard, his voice shaking.

Upon hearing those words, Emilia responded, her eyes trembling.

"Wait, Reinhard. I understand that it is hard to let her off without a word, but she didn't realize how much this badge is worth. Plus, I do not find fault with her. It was my fault that I let it get stolen in the first place."

"You're mistaken, Lady Emilia. That's not what I have a problem with," said Reinhard in a forceful tone. Confused, Emilia went silent.

Reinhard stared intently at Felt, so much that he had already forgotten how rude he just was to Emilia.

As Felt looked back at the young man with hair as red as her eyes, those red eyes of hers wavered with anxiety.

"...What is your name?"

"It's F-Felt..."

"What is your surname? How old are you?"

"I-I'm an orphan, all right? I don't have a surname and I...I think I'm about fifteen years old. I don't know my own birthday. But enough about that. Let me go!"

As Felt spoke, she seemed to regain a bit of her composure and tried to wrestle herself away from him.

Reinhard kept his firm hold on Felt and then turned to look at Emilia.

"Lady Emilia, I am no longer able to fulfill your request. I'm taking this girl with me."

"...May I ask why? If the reason has anything to do with this badge..."

"That is certainly not a crime I would like to ignore, but considering the far greater crime it would be to watch this moment before me unfold without any action, it is a trivial matter."

Emilia furrowed her brow, in both hesitation and confusion.

But Reinhard accepted Emilia's confusion. He felt that there was no helping it. After all, this was something she was used to. It would be cruel to tell her to realize what was happening.

"You're coming with me. I'm sorry, but I can't let you refuse."

"What are you, crazy?! Just because you saved me doesn't mean you can just... Huh?"

Just as Felt was about to continue yelling at Reinhard, her body went limp. As the power drained from her body Felt glared at Reinhard, until the very end, finally saying, "Burn in hell... Damn it..." before her head drooped and she fell unconscious.

"That's again not a very knightly thing for you to do... If you do it that roughly, it's going to leave lasting effects on the gate."

"Fortunately, this is something I've had to live with all my life, so I understand how to keep everything in moderation. ...Lady Emilia, I believe you'll hear again from me soon. Please understand."

Reinhard gently took Emilia's badge out of Felt's limp hand and gave it to her. The dragon on the badge was, in fact, the state symbol of the Dragonfriend Kingdom of Lugunica. In Reinhard's hand the red jewel shone with a dull light, but when it was returned to Emilia's hands it shone bright, as if delighted to be back in the hands of its owner.

"I ask that you take good care of Subaru," said Reinhard with a bow, after Emilia silently took her badge from Reinhard and continued to look at him.

Feeling Felt's light weight in his arms, Reinhard brushed her blond hair away from her forehead. When she was unconscious like this and didn't have to be so on guard, her white face looked both innocent and charming. If she were given a change of clothes and a bath, surely she would shine.

A strong wind blew and Reinhard's bangs danced in front of his face. Through those bangs Reinhard looked up at the sky and saw floating in the twilight above the capital, the moon.

It was a full moon that shone with a bluish white light, and its beauty was both alluring and bewitching.

"This may be the last time I can look up at the moon and feel at ease…" muttered Reinhard, his words only reaching the moon that looked down upon them.

AFTERWORD

To all of you who are just picking up this story for the first time with this print version, it's nice to meet you, I'm Tappei Nagatsuki.

For those of you have been following the story in its web version for some time, Hello, it's *Nezumi-iro Neko* ("Mouse-Colored Cat").

Whichever of those groups you may fall under, first of all I would like to thank you very much for deciding to pick up this book.

For those of you who may be confused, I'll go ahead and explain. This work, *Re:ZERO -Starting Life in Another World-*, was first serialized on a website called Let's Become Novelists! and has been edited for its publication in print.

Fundamentally, the print version follows the web version, but it has been made easier to read, with more events added, and the heroine has been made cuter, and the protagonist has been bullied a bit more.

I imagine that those from both the web version, as well as those new to the series, have looked at the cover illustration and beautiful insert illustrations with a chorus of "oohs" and "aahs," but I will tell you right now that the one making the most "oohs" and the most "aahs" is none other than me, the author himself. Silver-haired heroines are the best.

The one who drew our bullied protagonist and our cute heroine is the artist Shinichirou Otsuka. When Mr. Otsuka used his overflowing design powers to illustrate characters that I did not have a clear image of in my mind, it was then that those characters truly came to life.

In other words, I am the mother and Mr. Otsuka is the father. The characters are a collaborative work.

I ask for your cooperation so that this first collaborative work of mine can continue.

By the way, if you happen to be just standing and reading this at the bookstore, please buy it, and the next volume in the series as well. (Ha-ha…)

Anyway, with that clear sales promotion out of the way, I'd like to go over some of the aspects of the plot.

This is a work of otherworld fantasy fiction. One of those so-called "otherworld trip" types, which is a large genre that has given rise to several hit works.

I think that a fantasy world of swords and magic is one that everyone, if you're a boy, or at least some percentage of the population if you're a girl, has dreamed about. This work's protagonist is an ordinary Japanese boy who too has shared that dream.

He can't use a sword. He can't use magic. He does not have the wit or the physical strength to win in a fight. So this is a story about someone who, when pressed on all sides, uses only his inability to give up as a weapon. So it is a story about not giving up.

If he were going to use his inability to give up as a weapon, then how would you depict that? Here is one answer.

You have that protagonist struggle and struggle and not give up. Now by doing all of that, what does he gain in the end? For that answer I invite everyone to follow along and see for yourselves. I would also invite everyone to yell, "Silver-haired heroines are awesome!" at the top of your lungs as well.

As it looks like I'm starting to let my personal preferences slip out all over this afterword, I'll go ahead and get to the part where I thank everyone.

First of all I would like to thank my supervisor, Mr. Ikemoto, for inviting me to bring this story from the World Wide Web to print, with a "Why don't we give this a shot and show everyone what you're made of." Really, I can't thank Mr. Ikemoto enough.

Despite us both being adults, we would go into a fried pork joint and while pouring each other sauce over our cabbage argue over points such as whether to add "-tan" to the heroine's name and other, at the time, meaningless seeming talk, but it was because all of that that my story became a book, and in the joy of that result I can now look back on those times as good memories. Thank you very much.

I also need to thank Mr. Otsuka who, despite having such a busy schedule, was able to complete illustrations for the book at an incredibly fast pace. After each and every illustration was completed I would squirm with such excitement that I would give myself charley horses as my legs cramped up.

As the number of characters will be increasing from here on out, I absolutely cannot wait to see more. Thank you very much.

I would also like to thank everyone in the editing department, my proofreaders, people in the industry, and everyone who contributed to this work.

This work appearing in print form was the result of the efforts of very many people. I couldn't have done it without you.

I intend to work hard so that we may continue working together for a long time.

Now, finally, I would like to thank everyone that picked up this book, and everyone who continued to support this work on Let's Become Novelists!

May we meet again, in the next volume, *Re:ZERO -Starting Life in Another World-*, Vol. 2!

February 2013
Tappei Nagatsuki

IN COMMEMORATION OF
RE:ZERO'S SALES DATE
A ~~REGRET~~ REVEAL
OF MY INITIAL DESIGNS!

S·M·O

(SUBARU, TOTALLY AN
OLD MAN)

YEAH...

THAT IS TOTALLY
NOT THE FACE OF A
BOY IN HIS TEENS.

HE LOOKS LIKE A
THUG, AND HE
LOOKS TOO STRONG.

IF SUBARU LOOKED
LIKE THIS, HE'D
PROBABLY BE ABLE
TO FIGHT JUST
FINE EVEN IN A
DIFFERENT WORLD.

CONBINI/
CONVENIENCE
STORE
こビニ

E·M·J

(EMILIA, TOTALLY
A PLAIN GIRL)

HER CLOTHES
ARE PLAIN.

SHE'S JUST
SUPER PLAIN.

I'M REALLY
HAPPY THAT
WE DIDN'T
GO WITH
THIS DESIGN.

NEXT VOLUME,
I'M PLANNING ON
RELEASING INITIAL
DESIGNS OF
BOTH OO AND XX.

WELL THEN,
SEE YOU LATER!

SHINICHIROU OTSUKA

ラム

Ram

FLAT

"Big Sis, Big Sis, We have a grave matter on our hands. We have been called to do the preview of the next volume of Re:Zero!"

"That's right. Finally it will be the second volume…and there's reason to celebrate, as the main heroine of this series will finally be introduced."

"Yes, I am sure that all of the readers will be very happy to see you, Big Sis, the star actor, make your appearance. The brilliant decision of the editing department to release the first three volumes in only three months' time means that we can introduce you to everyone very soon, and that makes me, Rem, very happy."

"I hear that the release date for the next volume is on February 25th, but why don't they just release all three volumes at once?"

"Big Sis, from what I heard, there's going to also be a special running in Monthly Comic Alive as well."

"Oh, I hadn't heard. But what does that have to do with the three-month consecutive publication…?"

"Well, Monthly Comic Alive's March issue, which will be on sale starting on January 27th, will also for three consecutive monthly issues run specials on Re:Zero, complete with an extra appendix, and they will include double-sided illustrations from Mr. Shinichirou Otsuka—an extraordinary addition. These issues will be put on sale alongside volumes of Re:Zero."

"I see. So I suppose there really is some meaning in the three-month consecutive publication. What will the appendix contain?"

Rem

レム

The appendix will be called "Re:Zero Visual Complete" and have character illustrations from Mr. Shinichirou Otsuka as well as a short story written by the author. Apparently the story will be about Lady Emilia, Big Sis, and me."

"There doesn't seem to be any mention of the protagonist. Oh well, I suppose no one would enjoy the story of any man other than Lord Roswaal, so that too is an excellent decision by the editing department. They sure know what they're doing."

"Yes, I am sure that the editing department would be very happy to hear those words from you."

"Despite trying to act cool, the protagonist showed very shameful behavior upon the next stage set in a noble-man's mansion. The only thing Subaru is good for is showing how disgracefully he can struggle."

"For what reason will he be chased? For what reason will his life be targeted? Given how thoughtlessly and brazenly Subaru lives his life, there are many reasons that I can guess, and I'm sure he will struggle quite a bit in the next volume."

"-Starting Life in Another World- Volume 2 will be out on November 1st. Be sure to hurry along to your bookstores."

"I love that about you, Big Sis, how you never forget the job you're supposed to be doing, to the very end."

Re:ZERO

~Starting Life in Another World~